THE WRITERS' RETREAT

SAMANTHA VÉRANT

Storm
PUBLISHING

Ebook ISBN: 978-1-83700-020-3
Paperback ISBN: 978-1-83700-021-0

Cover design: Blacksheep
Cover images: Shutterstock

Published by Storm Publishing.
For further information, visit:
www.stormpublishing.co

ALSO BY SAMANTHA VÉRANT

The Lucky Widow

The Private Chef

The Writers' Retreat

The Perfect Catch

This one goes out to Jessica—my sister, best friend, and partner in crime. You can always borrow my shoes and vice versa.

PROLOGUE

People always tell aspiring authors to write what they know. To kill their darlings. To trim the fat and get to the meat of the story. Yada. Yada. Yada. I'll get to the point.

I have better life advice. Cut out the people who hurt you, the ones who have made your life a living hell. The kind of people who are intense and dazzling at first and make you feel like the most intriguing person alive. Until they withdraw their attention from you. Then it's like being plunged into complete darkness.

But it's in the darkness that you can finally see the light.

The blade is in my hand. The scene is a mess. What can I say? This was a crime of passion and I'm a very, very passionate person.

I'm also careful.

I wipe off any traces of my existence—the countertops, the doorknobs, everything. No leaving my DNA behind. The murder weapon? The police will find it eventually, exactly when I want them to.

I'm the one controlling this narrative. And I've also taken one piece of writing advice to heart. I've cut another darling out of my story. Now, it's time to break out the red pen, making a couple more edits as I turn the page.

ACT ONE

ONE

(NOW)

Revenge is best served in twelve-point Times New Roman. Or so I tell myself as I tap my pen on my chin, feeling a mix of satisfaction and unease. But there are sharper and crueler weapons in the world, and these days I wonder if the pen truly is mightier than the sword.

I care about these things because I want to be a writer. A published author. And, I know, I know, honey, don't quit your day job, but I have to believe in myself, because if I don't, who will?

The small café tucked in the corner of the bookstore where I work bustles with activity. Patrons sit at wooden tables, the soft murmur of bookish conversations mixing with the clinking of cups and saucers. I make my way behind the counter, a lump in my chest.

New York is a state of mind and mine is absolutely spent.

Don't get me wrong. I love my job as a bookseller at Brooklyn Bound, a hip and trendy bookstore in the borough of Williamsburg. However, surrounding me on all sides, the shiny covers of bestsellers with their book-club stickers seem to mock me.

Worthlessness is a familiar feeling—one I'd like to shake off.

All I've ever wanted is a sense of belonging, to forge a deep connection with somebody, to be liked. I want a family, a sister. For now, all I can do is create imaginary relationships within the pages of my journal.

A customer seated at one of the tables looks up from her book. "You look really familiar." Her gaze narrows and she gives me a head to toe once-over, eyes glistening with recognition. "Aren't you friends with Kat Sterling? The socialite? Heiress to the Sterling Spirits fortune?"

I wince as she mentions my former roommate, the woman who upended my life. My mouth feels dry and metallic. She Who Won't Be Named—it's like speaking a curse. And, surprise, she's just been named when I'm least expecting it.

I'm not really a fan of surprises. In fact, I absolutely hate them. In my experience, unexpected events come packaged with mind-numbing and life-altering glitches. My parents splitting up after sixteen years of what I'd thought was a solid relationship. My mom moving to Italy to find herself. I'd soon learn that "finding herself" meant meeting Gianni, starting a new family, and abandoning me. Surprise!

But the biggest shock of my life came two years ago when I'd walked in on my best friend in bed with my fiancé, Steven, after a cocktail-infused party to celebrate our engagement. And not only my fiancé and one of my best friends— another woman, too. The setup of my worst nightmares, all in one horrifying montage, complete with discarded wine glasses and tangled sheets. It was like a bad soap opera; I could practically hear the audience in my mind gasp in shock.

Kat had always been possessive of me, wanting to be included in every aspect of my life. After I found her in bed with Steven, I foolishly thought I could move away and escape her. But as I stand in the bookshop, staring out the window, I realize just how wrong I am.

"I think you must have me confused with someone else," I finally say.

The woman frowns and shakes her head. "No, no, I'm certain I know you from somewhere."

She scrolls on her phone, walks over to me, and then holds up a photo from Instagram. It's of me and Kat, her green eyes blazing into the camera. Kat tow ers over me in her designer heels. Louboutin. Jimmy Choo. YSL. Who knows? And there is no mistaking me, wearing her hand-me-downs, standing in *her* shoes.

The woman's lips pinch together, a know-it-all look. "You're Liv Montgomery? Aren't you? You're friends with Kat Sterling."

I clear my throat. I've encountered her type before—always stirring the pot. "We're not friends anymore." Period. End of this story. For now. "If there's anything else I can help you with?" I eye the coffee stain on the book she's been reading and tilt my head to the side, my smile tight. "Should I ring you up?"

She juts out her chin, handing over her credit card.

Once the woman completes her purchase and strides out of the store in a huff, I take a deep breath. I carefully extract the well-worn printout of the query I sent to my dream agent just one week ago. The paper is creased from being folded and unfolded countless times. My heart beats faster as I read the words I've scrawled heavily at the top of the page: *She will represent you. Your book will be a bestseller.*

I look down as the Great Catsby—a twenty-pound Russian Blue—snakes around my ankles. His emerald eyes glint and his motorcycle-like purring offers comfort. Maybe I'm just a booktrovert—the kind of person who has fictional and animal friends instead of real people because real people know how to hurt you, know exactly where to stick the knife into your heart.

"Do you think I'll be published one day?" I ask, scooting down to stroke Catsby under his chin.

He blinks but doesn't respond. I'm glad because I would be questioning my sanity if he did. Before the white coats come and take the crazy cat lady away, I refill Catsby's bowl with kibble.

Although I'm technically not supposed to check my personal accounts at work, I pull out my phone anyway. I've been working on my book—a creative memoir of sorts—for three years, the story going through substantial changes as it evolved. A couple of weeks ago, I finally pressed send to about two dozen agents. Since then, in addition to reading everything under the sun, refreshing my email has become my latest addiction. My jaw unhinges as I stare at the screen. There's a response. I close my eyes and pray to the literary gods.

Please don't be a rejection.

I've worked so hard on this book—hours staying up until three in the morning or getting up at five to work on the manuscript. This could be my big break, my ticket out of a soul-crushing cycle of self-doubt. My hand shakes as I click the email open, my heart racing. I hold my breath and I read.

TO: olivia.montgomery.thrillerauthor@xmail.com
FROM: victoria.foster.assistant@fosterliteraryNYC.com
SENT: Monday, September 18th, at 9:25 am
SUBJECT: RE: Form Submission—New Form—IN HER SHOES
(85k psychological thriller)

Dear Olivia,

Thank you very much for thinking of Foster Literary Management for representation. We were quite taken with the voice and concept in your query. I realize this is very short notice, but there is one spot left on our upcoming writers' retreat—and it would be a great opportunity to discuss the concept of your book further. Should you be interested in attending, details can be found here. It would also be nice to catch up. A reunion! 😊

Best regards,

Miriam Richards on behalf of:
Victoria Foster—Managing Director/Literary Agent
Foster Literary: Where We Foster the Talent of Our Literary Stars

I shake my head to clear it and pull up Miriam's photo on the agency website. She's about my age, but her features are more severe, more angular, and she has seriously intense hazel eyes.

Catch up? She looks vaguely familiar, but, for the life of me, I can't place her. Maybe I'd met her at one of the five-minute pitch sessions I'd been frequenting, trying to get the proverbial pen into the door. Speed dating for desperate writers and bored agents. What a waste of time that had been.

A writing retreat is exactly what I need to get my head together, to formulate a plan. I click on the link. The screen loads a movie of a place called Nyx Sanctuary. My eyes take in every detail as a soft voice and the sounds of nature soothe my ears.

"Nestled on the tranquil edge of a sparkling pond and surrounded by lush forests with sweeping views of the majestic Catskill Mountains, lies a hidden gem. The Nyx Sanctuary... a Resort and Spa which offers unparalleled beauty and seclusion in a glacial valley. A haven, our guests come here to unplug and reset in nature..."

For a moment, I find myself zoning out. Be still my beating heart. *Yes. Yes. Yes.* This is exactly what I need. But my heart lurches when I survey the departure date and price. Leaving tomorrow until Sunday for five thousand dollars. How can I swing this? The pros and cons volley in my head. I mean, I would be investing in my life, the career I want, right? Plus, my student loans are paid off and, considering that I live in a tiny studio above the bookstore, my rent is a steal—the manager's bonus.

My eyes light up when I click the details for the retreat. Oh my gosh—the mentors! Rebecca Stiles from SilverGate Publishing; Anna Hale, the romance author compared to E. L. James; Victoria Foster, dream agent extraordinaire; and Miriam Richards, her assistant and associate literary agent.

The schedule is sheer perfection. In addition to writing sessions and meetings with the mentors, they offer yoga, paper- and perfume-making workshops, guided hikes, sunrise bird watching, and canoeing. Aside from the bird watching (not my idea of a good time), this place sounds like a dream. All meals are farm to table, served with local wines and spirits. Plus, spa treatments are offered throughout the day as optional add-ons. I could really use a backrub—get out all those knots of tension from what Kat did.

I tap my nails on the counter, deep in thought, and then bang my fist on the front desk. "Yes! I'm doing this."

I secure my place for the retreat, quickly covering my shifts—another bonus of being the manager. I let out the breath I've been holding, feeling a sense of satisfaction knowing that Kat will finally get what she deserves. At least fictionally. And, if everything goes as planned, in real life, too.

TWO

(NOW)

I have no clue as to what I'm supposed to wear at a writing retreat, so I've hastily packed options for every occasion. Will it even matter? I'm going to be judged on my prose, not my appearance. Before slamming the suitcase shut, I tuck my journal in the bottom compartment. Like an American Express card, I don't go anywhere without it.

It's early in the morning when I drag myself and my heavy bag onto the sidewalk. I feel like I've walked into a sauna, the city seeming to exhale along with me as I catch my breath. We're in the midst of an Indian summer, and everything feels heightened. New York City, particularly Williamsburg, Brooklyn with its edgy energy—seems in tune with my nervousness. That's why I love living here: no space for softness, no forgiveness in the crowd.

And it's funny because I've been trying hard to work on forgiveness. But I'm finding it impossible to forgive *her*. I pull my phone out of my purse, and snap in my ear buds, a song coming to mind. I click on Spotify. Soon, Timbaland's "Apologize" featuring One Republic resounds in my ears.

People brush past me without a second glance, every person a moving part in the city's endless machine. Mechanics. I love envisioning how everything works, the reason I'm drawn to writing. I watch. I observe. I take everything in.

Across the street, a deli owner pushes his sidewalk sign onto the street, and a couple hustle down the block with impatient strides, laughing, oblivious to the heat. Somewhere down the street, a car horn blares. A couple of teens swagger by, blaring Eminem's "Houdini." I love the madness and the magic that makes up New York City. I feel like I'm a part of it even when I'm standing on the sidelines. I can blend in, remain anonymous, just another face in the crowd. Invisible.

As I walk down the street, I hold my chin up high, feeling like I'm leaving behind the Olivia who lets rejection define her. The Olivia who's been drowning in self-doubt. It's time for Liv to take back her life.

After hailing a taxi to take me to Penn Station, I sit quietly in the backseat. The taxi driver is chatty, asking about my destination and making small talk about the wildly weird weather. It's hot outside? Isn't it? It is. I'm sweating bullets, but it's not only because of the suffocating heat. As we get closer to the drop-off point, his chatter tapers off and we ride in silence. I welcome the quiet, sinking deeper into my thoughts, my plans.

Finally, we arrive. I pay the taxi driver and step out onto the curb, taking a deep breath before pushing my legs forward. Inside, the sight of Penn Station always astounds me. People scramble in front of me, going somewhere, possibly searching for the next corner of life like me, their faces illuminated by the bright neon lights of signs and screens displaying departure information.

The scent of coffee and fast food lingers in the air. The

ground vibrates under my feet as trains rumble through the station. The air is humid, heavy, and my clothes stick to my skin.

I find myself taking in another deep breath. Keep calm and keep moving on.

After grabbing a cup of coffee and a banana, I skirt through throngs of people, finding the signs to lead me to Moynihan Trail Hall, the Amtrak station. A couple of wrong turns later, I make my way to the platform, find the wagon, and take my seat. Five minutes later, the train jolts along the tracks, my heart racing right along with it. The promises of fresh air and blank pages begging to be inked pull me forward like an invisible thread.

As I settle in for my journey, coffee spilling, I take out my phone to text Mark, canceling our plans for this weekend. Before I do, I pull up a snapshot I'd recently taken of him—asleep, curled up, long eyelashes.

When I first met Mark, I thought he was the most beautiful disaster I'd ever laid eyes on. His skin was tanned golden by the sun, made even more glorious and highlighted by the wrinkled white linen shirt he wore, the khaki shorts bringing attention to his muscular legs. I couldn't keep my eyes off him. Athletic build. Tousled black hair and a piercing gaze that could probably melt glaciers.

Only problem? He's Kat's ex. And he's Sienna's brother, another former friend of mine. For obvious reasons, Mark and I are keeping our relationship a secret until we know where it's headed.

ME:

Headed off to a writers' retreat. Back Sunday.

MK:

???

ME:

Long story. Finally queried my book.

THREE DOTS.
MK:

Have u seen the news this morning?

ME:

No.

MK:

Steven Shepherd is dead. Can u talk?

A gasp of shock escapes my throat. The woman seated in the aisle across from me shoots me a concerned look. I blink and stand up, heading into the space in between train wagons to take the call when my phone rings.

"What do you mean, he's dead?" I wheeze. "Is this a joke?"

"I wish it was a joke." He gulps. "They're saying he was murdered. Stabbed. Maid found him yesterday morning."

I stare blankly out the window, everything rushing by in shades of gray, my mind turning black. In my silence, my mind projects its own cruel movie. I see her face, then his. I see them in bed together, laughing, unashamed. I suppose I should be more upset that Steven is dead, but I'm still not over his betrayal. Her betrayal. How can grief even find a place in my heart when it's so crowded with anger and hurt?

"Liv, are you OK? You're not saying anything."

I don't know what I am. I've seriously got to get my act— and my head—together.

"I think I'm in shock."

"Yeah, yeah, me too." He groans. "Everybody is. His

parents will be planning the funeral once his body is released." Mark issues a slow, steady breath. "Look, I hate to drop this news on you like this. But I wanted you to hear it from me first... Steven's will..."

My heart sinks even further. Mark is Steven's family's attorney. "What about it?"

"He left everything to you," Mark says with a sigh.

I shake my head in disbelief, let out a stunned breath. "No, that can't be right."

"His parents called me. He listed you as the sole beneficiary of his estate."

I blink and hunch over, placing my hand on the wall to steady myself, feeling the rumble of the train, my heart. "I can't believe it. Why would he do this?" I ask. "We were done. We were over. Life goes on..."

"I don't know, maybe he wanted to make amends or maybe he just couldn't let go of you completely. His parents will contact you."

I nod, unable to find my voice, and let out a soft groan. "I... I can't think..."

"Let's change the subject to something not as morose."

What's up with this blasé response? I'd expect something more from him, some sign of emotion. "Aren't you upset about Steven's death?"

"Of course I am. We used to be friends," he says with a groan. "Emphasis on used to. Tell me about this writers' retreat. Where is it?"

I swallow, wondering how he could just change the subject so dismissively. But that's Mark. All business. "The Catskills."

"Where exactly in the Catskills?" he growls.

I bite down on my bottom lip. "The Nyx Sanctuary."

He goes silent for a moment and then he sighs. "Jesus, Liv, do you really think this is a good idea? Now?"

"I do. It's the best idea I've ever had." I pause. "I told you Victoria Foster was my dream agent and this is her retreat."

A long pause.

"I suppose Sienna will be there, too. Victoria is Sienna's agent. Just sold her book." He pauses and then exhales. "I know the subject of her is taboo, but she also represents Kat."

I can't let Mark know that I queried Victoria exactly for these reasons, that I overheard him on the phone one night. I roll my shoulders, trying to think of a response. "Your sister doesn't write. She can't even spell."

He lets out a short laugh. "She's been working on a life-style book. Wants to be the next Gwyneth Paltrow."

"Unbelievable."

"I know," he says. "Look, I'll drive Sienna up to the retreat after she's finished with the police..." He pauses. "They've been questioning her all morning." A beep inter-rupts the call. "Shit. I've got to take this. It's Sienna. Sending you a link. I'll see you later."

Nerves are setting in. My hands are moist and my heart is beating furiously. With time to think alone, I can't stop the tears from welling up as I meander back to my seat, staring out the window lost in thought. Finally, I click on the link Mark's sent and I read.

Hedge Fund Titan Steven Shepherd Found Dead in Luxury Apartment—Foul Play Suspected

Steven Shepherd, a controversial hedge fund manager known for his high-stakes investments and powerful connec-tions, was discovered dead in his Tribeca loft yesterday morning by his housekeeper. Authorities have not ruled out foul play as investigators comb through his financial dealings and personal life for potential motives.

With a gulp, I'm trying to keep my composure, wondering why the police are questioning Sienna. Have they questioned Kat? Am I next? Steven's death has brought up more questions than answers. If he's dead and he left me everything, I'm definitely going to be a suspect in his murder, especially if anyone reads the ending of my book. And now, not only do I have to deal with his loss but also the guilt and confusion surrounding my relationship with Mark. I feel sick to my stomach.

I last saw Steven a week ago and I can't shake off his warning or stop picturing the sheer panic in his eyes. Damn it, universe, you've really got to stop messing with my head.

THREE

(ONE WEEK BEFORE)

Working at a boutique bookstore came with advantages, especially when you were the manager and the owner was eighty-two and barely around due to her bad knees and hips. Per my usual habits during the slow hours, I set down the book I had been reading, wanting to savor it, and pulled out my phone. My cell buzzed with alerts. Steven had been texting and calling me non-stop. Shaking my head with disbelief, I read through his latest messages.

> Liv, we need to talk.

> Please call me back. It's important.

> Damn it, Liv. Call me back.

> I'm serious. Call. Or at least text.

We hadn't spoken in two years and for a very good reason. Now, he wanted to talk. That ship had sailed when I caught him in bed with *her*. Lies. They always caught up to you. Cheaters. They got caught—eventually. Before a fresh wave of anger pulled me into a tailspin, I tucked my phone into my purse, saying goodbye to the past, and rang up the store's last customer.

The woman, Mrs. Cohen, one of our regulars, let out a long, happy sigh. "I'm taking a leap into women's fiction, but I do love a good steamy romance, especially ones that end with a wedding, don't you?"

"Yes," I lied, my lips curving into a tight smile. "So much to look forward to."

Not so long ago, I'd been planning my own wedding—the cake, the flowers, the dress, and even checking out wedding venues online. Steven had been so kind and attentive, supportive of my writing career. He'd told me that if I believed in myself, I could do anything. Now I couldn't stop hearing his excuses.

I was drunk.

I don't know how it happened.

I lost control.

I also kept seeing her twisted smile. The tangled sheets. The other woman. Steven in the middle. Even though two years had passed, I still felt the aftershocks of that atomic bomb. People had a way of surprising you when you least expected it.

Take Mrs. Cohen, for example. You wouldn't suspect that a woman who looked and dressed so conservatively in gray suits usually gravitated toward erotic fiction. She'd often surprised the staff with her book choices, and we'd learned not to judge a book by its cover when it came to her or any of our customers.

She hugged her book to her chest and then handed it over so I could ring her up. "This one is about a successful novelist who loses her memory. The words are supposed to rip your heart apart and put it back together again."

I wondered if my heart could ever be put back together.

"Are you still writing, Liv?" she continued.

"I'm trying to," I said.

"Just take it one word at a time," she replied and I nodded.

Mrs. Cohen left the store with a smile and I was headed to the front to lock up when somebody burst in the door, panting heavily, their face contorted in fear and desperation. My heart rate skyrocketed. I thought I was about to be robbed and was preparing to use the keys jangling in my hand as a weapon until I realized the person was Steven. It took me a moment to figure out who he was. This was not the usual put-together man I'd known —his sandy-blond hair was tousled, his expensive suit rumpled and wrinkled, and his usually sharp eyes were bloodshot.

His eyes, once filled with love and excitement for our future together, now appeared deranged. Eyes that used to meet mine when we talked over our future plans. How many kids we wanted to have. Where we wanted to live. The places we'd dreamed of traveling together, arranging them alphabetically—the Amalfi Coast, Amsterdam, Australia. We were on M when the shit hit the fan: Machu Picchu, the Maldives, Madagascar.

He was my first everything—first love, first relationship. I'd wanted somebody to see the real me, to love and accept me, all of my flaws and awkward past included. I'd thought that man was Steven; I was wrong.

"What the hell are you doing here? Stop calling. Stop texting. Just stop. I don't have time for this. I don't have time for you."

"Damn it, Liv, just give me a minute," he pleaded, raising a finger. "One."

I rolled my eyes, crossing my arms over my chest. "Are you forgetting about the restraining order?"

His shoulders slumped and he let out a heavy sigh. "I'm sorry about that. I am," he said, his words slightly slurred. "I really need to talk to you."

My guard went up at the mention of talking. He'd always been good with words, manipulating them to get what he wanted, the reason he was a successful hedge fund manager. I looked at my watch. "You have sixty seconds."

He rocked back and forth on his feet, his body swaying.

"Have you been drinking?" I asked, raising an eyebrow.

He shook his head "no" solemnly, but I could smell the alcohol on his breath.

"Look, Liv, I made a mistake. A huge one," he pleaded, as he ran a hand through his hair. "Our relationship didn't end in the best of ways..."

"Understatement of the year," I said, my tone dripping with sarcasm. "Why are you here?"

"I've kept in touch with her. About a month ago, I told her I wanted you back, that I wasn't over..." His voice trailed off. I met his gaze, his eyes wide, pleading.

I tried to close the door when he stopped me, latching onto my wrist.

"Just hear me out."

Nausea churned in my stomach at the realization that he was still in contact with *her*. I held up my hands in the stop position. "Pull yourself together. This conversation is over," I said with force. "And so are we."

I glared at him and he pulled his hand away, shoving it into the pocket of his pants. He blinked and then nodded, head down. "I know. I know. I just told her that so she'd back off, leave me alone." He gulped. "Liv, she's not right in the head. She went even more ballistic than you did..."

The woman he referred to didn't express her emotions, save for raising her nose and making you feel like shit. She got off on being a prima donna. Maybe she'd changed? Maybe somehow, some way, she'd discovered a beating heart inside her empty chest.

"Whoa! Whoa! Whoa!" I took a step back. "I didn't mean to cut your hand. I gave you that letter opener. Even had your initials carved into it. And I didn't want you to have it after what you did—"

"I can't believe things got so out of control." He clasped my wrist again. "I'm sorry."

"Apology accepted," I said, pointing to his waiting town car and the increasingly impatient driver sat inside it. "And I'm sorry I went—what did you say—ballistic?"

"You had every right to be angry. About the restraining order, she's the one who told me to file it..."

I forced a tight smile, my heart beating faster with each passing second. "Good," I managed to say through clenched teeth. "Now that the air is cleared, can you go away? Now?"

Steven's face contorted in worry, his hands jumping to his hair and pulling at the roots. "Liv, I only came here to warn you. It's getting out of control." His voice trembled. "She was crazy in high school. She's even crazier now. She's been following me, stalking me. And it's gotten so bad over the past month that I'm moving to a new place in a couple of weeks... with a doorman, security..." He gulped, his eyes wide. "She tried to run me over in her car..."

My stomach turned. "And? Your problem. Not mine. What does any of this have to do with me?" I demanded.

His eyelids flickered to a close, his jaw tense. "I think she's going to come after you. You should move..."

"Jesus, Steven," I muttered, "I have to go. Take care of yourself, OK?"

His last words echoed in my mind as I slammed the door shut and locked it, my heart still racing. "You don't know what she's really like..."

FOUR

(NOW)

Oh, I know exactly what kind of a person Kat is. Part of me is terrified to potentially come face to face with her, but the other part of me is confident because I know how she operates. Like a surgeon. Dissecting everything around her.

The rhythmic chugging and rumbling of the train is not a comforting backdrop to my paranoid thoughts, nor is the darkening sky outside, the clouds rolling in ominously. Even the air feels electric, my mind pulsing and throbbing in currents.

I glance out the window into the darkening sky. It's a strange, hazy color that I can't quite place. Colors swirling. Greens. Grays. Blacks. Colors coming together like I've never seen before. And it's making my heart race with a mix of fear and exhilaration.

The calm before the storm.

Steven's warning is running in a constant loop in my mind. Like a song you can't get out of your head. His words have hit a nerve, unraveling a string of memories that I've buried.

And now, hurtling toward my destination, I can't shake off an unsettling feeling. Like the weather, Kat has always been unpredictable. Does she know about Steven's death? If so, is she going to come after me?

My thoughts are interrupted as the train stops at a platform. Every passenger coming onto the train seems to be a potential threat, and now I'm glancing over my shoulder every few seconds.

Whatever happens on this retreat, I know one thing for certain—I'm totally over being a supporting character in my own story. It's time to change the narrative.

Soon, the never-ending landscape of cold concrete buildings slowly fades away, revealing the stunning beauty of the Hudson River, the valleys, the mountains spread out beside me like nature's candy.

It takes two hours for the train to reach the quaint town of Hudson. After grabbing my belongings, the feeling of being watched only intensifies as I reach the exit and step out into the open street. With a shudder, I pull out my phone to check for the pre-booked and outrageously expensive Uber to take me to Nyx. My eyes scan the crowded parking area, searching for the driver's red Honda Civic. After a moment, I spot the matching license plates and begin to make my way toward the car.

Glancing at my watch, I note that it's 9:25 am on the dot. Perfect timing. I give a small wave and notice an elderly man with warm, kind blue eyes peeking at me from behind the steering wheel. "You must be Olivia," he says.

"I... I am..."

"Are you sure?"

I laugh. "Sorry, I'm a little bit out of it."

"Hank." He gets out of the car and pops open the trunk, placing my bag in it. "Hop on in. Get comfortable."

"Thanks," I say and do as I'm told.

A minute or two later, Hank starts up the engine. "So, the Nyx Sanctuary? Should take us about an hour twenty to get there."

"Great," I say, as we pull out of the parking lot. "Have you ever been there?"

He shakes his head no and then pops his lips. "Nope, but I do know a couple of people who work there... and I know what it used to be," he says, his voice trailing off. He clucks his tongue. "That place has quite the history."

My heart stutters. "And what did it used to be?"

His eyes meet mine in the rearview mirror. "Do you know who Tobias Rane is?"

Everybody does. Years ago, his arrest had been all over the news and there's the more recent documentary, but I haven't watched it yet. A local, I'm wondering what he knows. "I don't."

"He was the leader of that cult, Nexus; his followers were called the Rane Makers. About ten or so years back, maybe more, he was arrested and convicted of racketeering, human trafficking, sex trafficking, extortion, fraud and..." He pauses dramatically. "There are also rumors about a connection to a murder."

I blurt out a cough, my eyes so wide they hurt.

Hank laughs, low and warm. "Don't worry. It's changed. Around six years ago somebody purchased his land from the government. Nice price they got, too. Really undervalued, especially with the view they have." He clears his throat. "What I hear from folks is that they're doing great things—

really helping out the local economy by giving people jobs. Great products. My wife buys their perfume..."

"So, it isn't a resort?"

He nods his head. "Oh, it is, but they're doing other things, too."

"What kind of things?"

"Making all sorts of products—candles, soaps, perfumes, paper." He lets out a chuckle. "Even some high-grain alcohol called eau de vie. It's awfully strong."

"Interesting," I reply, nodding my head.

I didn't know about the products. I pull out my phone.

Hank's eyes meet mine in the rearview mirror. "Until we get closer to any of the big resorts, you won't have reception."

I look at my screen. It's true. I have zero bars.

He grins. "You like music?"

"I do."

"Me too. Always puts me in a good mood." He clicks the radio on, the song playing a remake of Tears for Fears' "Mad World." Hank hums along, oblivious to the war I'm fighting in my head. "I like the oldies. Grew up with this song," he says. "I prefer the original, but this one isn't so bad."

A deep frown pulls at my face, the lyrics haunting.

"Mind if I open the window?" I ask.

Hank briefly looks over his shoulder and grins. "Not at all."

The window slides down with a smooth mechanical hum. My nose tingles with all of the scents, mostly pine. The air is pure on my tongue, void of pollutants. It's a refreshing break from the city. Everything is beautiful, cleansing.

But I know better than to trust outer appearances. Forget about my senses, I now rely on gut instinct.

FIVE

(NOW)

The car climbs steadily up a long, steep driveway, tires crunching over the gravel, while my brain wrestles with a mix of dread and anticipation. Towering pine trees flank the sides of the road and the rough scent of damp earth mixes with the crisp aroma of pine.

Nature has a way of making you feel small, insignificant.

Shivers scurry down my spine when a massive black bird glides past the front window and then into the forest. I'd all but forgotten the untamed inhabitants of nature, and my aversion to feathered creatures momentarily resurfaces. This could be a bad omen and my hand involuntarily shoots to the scar on my cheek.

Before I have a panic attack, my gaze fixes on the winding path ahead as the car gradually rolls to a stop before an imposing pair of tall iron gates, the bold bronze Nyx logo gleaming like a beacon on them. Fog curls low across the road, slinking into the trees like something alive. The engine hums softly and Hank glances over his shoulder. "I guess this place really values their privacy—or perhaps they want to keep people in... or out."

Hank lowers his window and reaches out to press the call button. I swear I see a flash, like a photo being taken. My imagination might be playing tricks on me again, but the light is even more electric here, the air at least fifteen degrees cooler. The sky, a dull, hazy gray, is slowly bruising at the edges. A storm is coming, I see it whirling in the wind that's picking up in bursts, whipping the bushes like whips, feel it in my gut.

Ready or not, here I come. I'm over hiding from her. I may not be as calculating as she is, but writing is the way I've been dealing with what's happened in the past, taking creative liberties with the story, with her character. I've got to get my head together. I've got to think like her, act like her.

Kat hates confrontation. She's the type of person who lets things simmer just below the surface, picking apart every exchanged word in a conversation, until it warps into some-thing worse. And then—boom, she explodes. It's not loud—but sharp and precise. At least we have something in common. I can't wait for her to get wind of my book.

A moment or two later, a female voice crackles over the intercom, "Welcome to Nyx. Guest name?"

"Olivia Montgomery," I reply, taking in a deep, steadying breath.

The gates slowly creak open to reveal a long driveway bordered by meticulously manicured bushes and vibrant flowerbeds that lead up to a grandiose building. Kat's perfec-tion—not one leaf, not one flower out of place, every blade of grass and every petal perfectly arranged. Like nothing bad could happen here. The leaves on the trees are already turn-ing, bursting in reds and oranges, the change from late summer to fall. This only makes me think of how people can turn on you in the blink of an eye, how one minute you could be living in the lap of luxury, and the next minute out on the street, trying to stay alive.

The lump of dread settling in the pit of my stomach evaporates as we near the resort—just like the photos on the website, but even more breathtaking in person. Glass and cement, the Nyx building itself commands attention; yet, with its clean lines, becomes one with its surroundings. An enormous terrace juts out of the side of the building as if it's suspended in air and offers a panoramic view of the Catskill Mountains, their rough and steep slopes cloaked in a surreal, ethereal light.

In the distance, a sparkling pond shimmers, drawing my eye to the flurry of movement upon its surface. I watch as geese—by my count at least twenty, perhaps fifty—paddle noisily about, their honks echoing off the water. This is not the welcoming committee I'd expected.

Hank breaks my stunned silence by opening the door. "Man, this place is beautiful," he remarks with an appreciative whistle.

I point at the geese, my mouth wide with horror, and Hank's blue eyes crinkle in amusement. "You afraid?" he teases.

I nod, my shoulders sagging. "Very. I'm terrified of anything with feathers. It's a long story."

Nodding his head with understanding, Hank exhales and then pops his lips. "Sure, sometimes a goose might hiss or even chase you, but if you respect their boundaries, you'll be fine."

I remain immobile, sinking deeper into the seat, every muscle tensed. If I don't move, they can't come after me.

"Do you want me to walk you up?" he offers.

"T-t-to the geese? No, thank you," I stammer.

"No," he clarifies with a low chuckle. "I mean, to the resort."

Taking another measured breath, I remind myself of the reason I'm here—to reclaim my life. Even with that purpose burning inside me, I still ache for some reassuring support. "Yes, please," I finally say. "That's very kind of you."

As I step out of the car, the temperature has dropped enough to make me shiver. Hank scoops up my suitcase and links his arm with mine in a comforting grip. Slowly, we begin the walk toward the resort's main building, each of my steps measured and hesitant. Midway, a plump goose with iridescent white feathers struts boldly in front of us, and I freeze, rooted to the spot. I watch the creature—like a character from my darkest nightmares—sashay past with an unfathomable nonchalance.

Hank, ever observant, shoots me a knowing side-glance. "You know what I've heard about geese?" he asks.

My heart races. "What?"

"If you're scared," he continues in a conspiratorial tone, "just imagine them wearing underpants. Tighty whities."

Despite my rising anxiety, I cannot help but burst into a nervous, shaky laugh as my feet find the first step of the front porch. "Thanks, Hank," I manage to say.

"It was nice chatting with you, Olivia. You'll be just fine," he assures with a warm wink. "Have a nice time."

I watch him stroll back toward his car, a whistle escaping his lips. Reaching for my phone, I want to leave Hank a generous tip, but my heart sinks as I note the absence of signal bars. The realization of how cut off I am from everything hits me hard. Perhaps that is the point: to strip away all external clamor and force me to confront my own thoughts head-on. Yet the silence is far louder than I'd anticipated, especially given the deeper reasons as to why I'm on this retreat—reasons far beyond my aspirations to write. I've already lived through my story, and I've survived. And, if I have my way, the ending is going to change.

Because I'm not the only one with a past.

SIX

(THEN)

KAT

Summer had come to a swift end, and I was looking forward to the start of a new school year hanging out with my tribe. I guess I was the leader of our motley crew. Our families were connected and we basically had the same story to tell. Rich girls shipped off to an elite boarding school on the Hudson River, about an hour from the city. Close, but far enough away.

Despite all the broken promises that piled up like unpaid bills, we led lives of luxury, each moment fed to us on silver spoons. The promises were small things—vacations that never happened, birthday gifts that were always "on the way," and family time together that was perpetually postponed. Yet, even as these letdowns accumulated, we never had to worry about where our next meal was coming from because our lives were cushioned in comfort that made the sting of each broken word just a little more bearable.

"Here, darling, it's a Rolex. Isn't it beautiful? We'll see you at Christmas. Kiss. Kiss."

Woodford Hall was a small school filled with four hundred and seventy-five students, and teachers that resented us. Like our parents, the faculty didn't care what we did with our free time. As long as we got good grades, they turned a blind eye when we snuck cigarettes, went into town bribing the local vendors for alcohol, and, basically, got up to no good, while our parents attended charity functions or cruised around Europe on their yachts.

Reflecting on those years, I wonder if we had too much freedom for our own good. We roamed without boundaries, believing we were invincible and that nothing could ever harm us. If I had a daughter like me, I'd put her on a very tight leash, especially knowing what I know now. The world seemed safer then, but maybe it was just an illusion we chose to believe.

I can see now how naïve we were, how foolishly we rushed into situations without considering the consequences. That kind of unrestrained freedom made us reckless. We thought we were living life to the fullest. But were we just setting ourselves up for the kind of disillusionment that comes with growing up?

Other girls had attempted to join our group, but they never quite fit in, mostly because they tried too hard or wanted something from us.

But I digress.

In those days, I don't know why, maybe I was PMSing, maybe I was bored, maybe, in my heart, I was truly one of those mean girls, but the bullet of insults spraying from my mouth couldn't be stopped.

Did you go dumpster diving today? Nice outfit.

Where did you get your hair done? A pet shop?

Instead of sucking up to us, go suck on one of the teachers.

Maybe I was angry at the world. Maybe I was angry with my parents for shipping me off. Maybe I was angry at everything.

But one day, after a particularly cruel take-down, a girl walked up and pointed a sturdy finger at me. "Why would you treat somebody like that?" she scoffed. "You're nothing but a spoiled brat."

Livid, my head snapped up and I met this girl's intense death glare. Her eyes were the coldest and clearest of ice blues. Her hair, a frizzy strawberry-blond mop on her head, her nose slightly crooked, her teeth with blinged-out braces. She wasn't a beauty in the classic sense, no, but there was something about her that worked. "Who do you think you are, talking to me like that? Don't you know who I am?"

She laughed in my face. I would have, too.

"Oh, I know exactly who and what you are, Kat Sterling."

I swallowed. "And you are?"

"Morgan Rane." She looked me up and down, blue eyes like crystal lasers. "I'd say it was nice meeting you. But no. I'd be lying."

"Wait," I said. "Can we start over? Join us."

Morgan turned around, her hypnotizing eyes locking onto mine. "Why do you say those things?"

"It's a defense mechanism."

"Why?"

I blinked. "Because people always want something from me. And after they get it, I'm always disappointed." I didn't know how this girl had me confessing all of this at first meeting. I didn't know why I wasn't standing my ground. "What do you want from me?"

"Tell me, aside that you're a raving bitch, what do I need to know about life around here?"

I didn't know what to say. Heck, she'd thrown me under a bus. My gaze leapt from hers to Mouse's, landing on Sienna's. They both sat with their jaws agape.

After Morgan sauntered away, shooting a sly wink over her shoulder, Mouse whispered, "Something is off with her. Way off."

Mouse had always been wary of outsiders. Sienna and I were enough for her, gave her plenty to focus on.

"I think she's super cool," said Sienna.

"Let's see what happens with this girl," I said. "At least she'll be entertaining."

The following day, Morgan sauntered over to our table. She placed her tray of food down and plopped right down next to us. "Thank God, they have vegetarian options." She pointed to our chicken cutlets. "But I take it that you're not into eating clean."

"You don't eat meat?" I asked.

"I don't eat anything with a face," she replied.

Sienna directed a finger toward Morgan's plate. "Eggs," she said, pointing out Morgan's hypocrisy.

"Last time I checked, eggs don't have faces." Morgan snorted, her eyes shooting to the table of jocks. "Speaking of eggheads, tell me about them"—she surreptitiously eyed one of the boys—"specifically him."

Sienna's eyes bugged out and she let out a low growl. Morgan had indicated Steven, who we all knew Sienna had a secret crush on. Nobody said anything for a moment, so I jumped in. "The short, squat guy is available…"

"Good Lord, no," said Morgan, cringing. "I wasn't talking about him. I was talking about the cute guy with the sandy-blond hair. Good body."

Mouse piped in. "His name is Steven Shepherd. And he's off-limits."

"Why? Is he your boyfriend?"

"No. Sienna's kind of claimed him."

"Claimed him? What? Like, marked her territory? I get it. I get it. I do." Her posture straightened and she leaned forward, meeting Sienna's angry glare. "But let's get one thing straight. You're not dating him?"

"I'm not," she said.

"Which means he's up for grabs." Morgan shrugged and held up her hand like a gun, index finger pointed out, thumb up. "Bang! It's open season."

Sienna pushed her tray forward, spilling her water every-where. I grabbed her wrist before she bolted. "Look, Morgan, that's not the way things work around here. You'd be breaking girl code." I pointed to the loser table. "There's room for you. Over there."

"Whoa!" she exclaimed, her hands held up in mock surrender. "I was only kidding."

"No, you weren't," hissed Sienna.

"But I was," she said. "Look, if you want to land him, you have to be unattainable. You have to be a goddess. And I can help you."

"Help me what?"

"Tap into your true nature, your goddess nature."

"And what is it that you teach?" I asked.

"Mindfulness, unlocking your full potential... and, well, like I said, tapping into your powers as a goddess."

Mouse snorted. "Bullshit."

"Don't believe me? Come to Nexus and meet the master —my teacher—himself."

Sienna, who'd remained silent, finally spoke up, her voice low. "Nexus. What does that even mean?"

Morgan's smile widened. "It means finding yourself and your true essence. Your goddess self." She paused. "Who has a big car we can all fit into?"

"Why?" I responded, already sensing where this was heading.

Morgan beamed. "Because I don't have a drivers' license. It's Friday, and if you're up to it, we can spend the weekend there."

"I'm sorry, where?" asked Sienna.

"Nexus." Morgan's eyes sparkled. "You'll be able to experience everything firsthand for yourselves."

The three of us exchanged nervous glances.

"I don't know about this," said Mouse, her fingers tapping frantically on her phone. "We're supposed to see our parents on the weekends—"

Sienna cut her off. "One weekend won't hurt. And our parents are never home. We should at least see what it's all about."

Mouse sighed, and I could see her resistance crumbling.

"We'll take my car," I said, making the decision for all of us.

"Great!" said Morgan. "Pack light. You'll mostly need comfortable clothes for the workshops and some swimwear for the pond."

The bell rang, signaling the end of our lunch hour.

. . .

A few minutes before four, we met in the parking lot.

Mouse muttered, "I think this is a bad idea. I bet something like this is expensive."

"You'll be my guests this weekend. I have an in with the founder," said Morgan with a laugh. She leaned forward, her gaze intense. "No more excuses. This will be good for you. For all of you. And you'll find you'll have a home away from home—with people that care about you, believe in you."

"Nope," said Mouse. "I don't do ponds. And I don't do well in group settings. Not my cup of tea."

Stunned, we watched Mouse walk off. "Bye, have fun," she said, looking over her shoulder and waving. "Unlike you derelicts, I'm seeing my parents this weekend. They're sending a car to pick me up."

"She's really missing out," said Morgan, shaking her head, a rogue strawberry-blond curl falling over her right eye. "This is going to be the start of something great. Can you feel it?"

I did. A shiver ran up my spine.

"Welcome to my inner circle." Her eyes met mine, unwavering. "Where you'll learn to harness your true goddess powers."

Her words hung in the air, heavy with mystery. Maybe it was because I was so young and still impressionable, still trying to find my place in the world and understand the people around me. Perhaps it was her unshakeable confidence that made her seem larger than life. Perhaps it was because she dared to put me in my place.

Whatever the reasons, I was completely under her spell.

SEVEN

(THEN)

KAT

Soon the Escalade bumped along a gravel road, flanked by towering pine trees. I stopped the car in front of formidable iron gates, the Nexus logo emblazoned in gold. Morgan jumped out of the passenger seat, rang a buzzer. The gates opened with a loud groan and she jumped back in. "Just pull up in front of the main building."

I did as instructed and the three of us got out of the car, instantly hit with the fresh scents of nature—pine and, if my senses were on point, sage, rosemary, and thyme. A pond sparkled in the distance, a group of people doing yoga in front of it—everybody dressed the same in loose orange clothing, geese honking and waddling around them as if joining in. And then he walked out of the main lodge. He placed his hands in prayer position, bowed, and said, "*Namaste.* Welcome to Nexus."

Morgan raced toward him. He pecked her cheek with a

soft kiss. "Tobias, these are my new friends," she said, waving her hand to indicate us. "The ones I told you about."

One by one she introduced us and then she winked. "Girls, I'd like for you to meet my teacher of life, my dad."

My gaze shifted between them.

"Just call me Tobias," he said with a cheery smile. "Shall we get you settled into your rooms, yes? You can change and then Morgan and I will take you on a tour of the property, tell you a little about what we're doing here."

Sienna nodded, blue eyes wide.

"Change into what?" I asked, eyeing my outfit. I wasn't wearing my school uniform, but casual weekend clothes.

"We're all the same here." He let out a soft laugh. "Time for your first lesson. Material possessions—the designer jeans, the jewelry—are prohibited during your stay. Here our focus is on nature—and human nature, finding out who we are without the constraints of modern society. No competition. No wishing for more. No make-up, hiding your flaws. You can leave your bags in your car. We have everything you'll need. Understand?"

I nodded, thinking this was wildly messed up.

"Good," he said. "Morgan will show you to your room and we'll meet back here in, say"—he looked at his watch, which I noticed was a very expensive gold Patek Philippe—"in twenty minutes." He paused, holding out a clipboard. "First, I just need your signatures on a little paperwork. It's a standard check-in noting that your first weekend here is being comped."

His watch and the words "first weekend" were two details that should have been the first warning signs that things were off. Unfortunately for us, they weren't. And Sienna and I signed on the dotted line.

"OK." Morgan grinned. "You and Sienna are bunking up together. Follow me into the main lodge."

I cringed.

Lodge it was—the structure looking like a grown-up version of a massive house a kid put together with Lincoln Logs™. Reluctantly, I followed, Sienna by my side. Inside, the place smelled earthy, like wet wood, the air sticky and humid.

Morgan stopped, pointing. "The communal dining room is there." She laughed. "Here, we eat anything... that doesn't have a face. So, no meats, no fish. Also, if you need Wi-Fi, this is the only area to get it."

And this situation was getting worse by the second.

We followed Morgan up steps that creaked, precariously. She led us to a room with a bunk bed. As I saw what was missing, a sense of dread slowly crept into my system. "Why isn't there a door?"

"Because doors block energy." Morgan looked at me like I was nuts and then pointed. "Your clothes are on the bed. Settle in, change, and I'll meet you out front in twenty."

Before she left, I exchanged a concerned look with Sienna, but she was grinning. "This is so much fun! We're on a camping adventure!"

My idea of camping would be to hole down in the Ritz.

Glamping with champagne, caviar, and 1,200-thread-count sheets.

I turned around to find Sienna changing into loose orange pants with a horrendous matching top. She looked like a nurse wearing scrubs... or maybe a prisoner. Orange was a very pretty color, but it definitely wasn't the new black.

"What?" she asked.

"Seriously, you're not finding any of this strange? At all?" I eyed the room. "And, well, kind of dirty?"

"No. I like it. I really do. I like the whole concept of connecting to nature and to myself." She grinned. "I'm glad we came."

"I, uh, I..."

"Just go with the flow," she said with a tsk. "And don't forget this was your idea."

Twenty minutes later, dressed in orange scrubs and wearing white Crocs, we met Tobias outside and I wondered aloud where Morgan was, but he instructed us not to talk, brushing the question off. He led us up a path, explaining how the trees have roots, how they communicate underground like a secret network. He glanced over his shoulder. "It's the ultimate Wi-Fi, but better." And then he stopped walking in front of a hedge. "We're all connected."

We followed him through the bushes, leaves sticking into our hair, branches pricking into our skin, finally ending up in a clearing, a large statue in the middle.

"This is Nyx, a statue of the goddess. The flowers surrounding her—the yellow, orange, and purple ones—are nemesia, representing her daughter, the goddess Nemesis. Don't let her name fool you. Yes, the word now means rival or enemy, but Nemesis's role in Greek mythology was about creating balance, the reason one of her symbols is the scale, and"—he chuckled—"nemesia—in Greek *nemesion*—means friendship."

Oh, gods and goddesses, I wanted out of there—away from him.

"Please have a seat. Let the wind blow in your hair, feel the earth," he instructed and so we did. His eyes flashed onto ours. "Nyx was the goddess of the night, the goddess of the stars. Her statue is here to represent our dreams, our deepest desires. Because, sometimes, what do we do when we wish for something?"

Sienna mumbled, "We wish on a star."

"Exactly. And in the darkness, we hope for light," said Tobias. "I'm the light. I'm here to listen to your wishes, to help you come up with the answers to achieve your dreams. That's our purpose here. So, Sienna, what is it in life that is blocking you?"

To my surprise, Sienna answered. "I don't know. I feel stuck. Sometimes I feel like I don't know who I am. Like I don't have a real identity of my own."

"Lemming syndrome?"

"Yeah, I guess."

"Who do you want to be?"

"Me."

"Guess what? You are already you." He winked. "I see a wonderful woman in front of me. A smart woman." He paused. "When you look in the mirror, what do you see?"

"A follower."

"Well, it's time for you to become a leader. And, good thing, we don't have mirrors here. Take the time to reflect... without the reflection."

I twiddled a blade of grass between my fingers. I was so not expecting a therapy session. Been there, done that. Did it work? No, it did not.

Tobias noted my discomfort. "Kat?"

My eyes met his. "Yes?"

"I bet I can guess what you want right now."

"I bet you can't," I said.

"But I can." His blue eyes lit up. "You want to bolt right out of here."

I swallowed. Boy, did he have me pegged. "That obvious, huh?"

"Yes. I know you're the skeptic amongst us." He let out a soft laugh. "But humor me. Aside from thinking about escaping this excruciatingly painful first session amongst your friends, surrounded by the beauty of nature, I'd like to know what you really want out of life."

"I-I—"

He held up a finger, shaking it solemnly. His lips pursed together. "No, I'd like for you to think, really think, before responding."

After a couple of charged moments, me staring at the statue of Nyx, Tobias focused his attention back on me.

"Kat, have you thought about my question?"

My heart sank. "I did."

"And?"

"I'd like to know that my friends are truly my friends." I gulped. "And I'd like for my parents to acknowledge that I exist."

And then I started bawling. I hunched over, feeling hands rubbing my back.

Tobias's voice rang loud and clear. "In order for you to get in touch with your inner goddess, nobody else but me is to touch you. No relationships outside of Nexus. Nothing. Understand?"

We nodded. Of course, telling teenage girls with raging hormones not to have relationships would never work. But what he didn't know wouldn't kill him.

Tobias stood up, raising his arms in the air. Then he made the sign of the cross, tapping his forehead, his left shoulder, and then the right one. "In the name of the mother, the daughter, and the earthly goddess." His eyes met ours one by one. "Say it with me, and feel the power within your-selves—tap into your inner goddesses."

My eyes focused on the statue of Nyx and then I surveyed the land, this place. I was a goner. I wanted everything.

EIGHT

(NOW)

I think back to the stories Kat shared with me about her experiences at Nexus, but they're just that—stories, things she'd probably thought would make her look more human and relatable in my eyes. Kat always thought she was a goddess. Untouchable. Bending the world to do her will. But even the gods and goddesses have histories they can't escape from. I steel myself for the situation I've put myself in and walk toward the doors, which automatically open upon sensing my arrival, and close smoothly behind me.

Once inside, I survey my surroundings, scanning the details from the travertine marble floor to the crystal chandeliers hanging over my head to the gas fireplace roaring in the far corner, everything sparkling in hues of gold. Nyx is definitely not the rustic lodge nestled in the woods Kat had once described, but a luxurious haven. A sanctuary. Part of me can't help feel impressed—even though I know something dirty lingers beneath the surface.

I blink and inhale a calming breath, the aroma of

lavender wafting up to my nostrils. I remind myself of the reason I'm here.

With my head held high, I walk toward the reception area, immediately recognizing Miriam from the photo on the Foster Literary website. She's sitting on a modern, linen settee in front of a picture window overlooking the mountains, a sign on an easel at her side: Welcome to the Foster Literary Writers' Retreat. No longer afraid of being attacked by geese, I stride across the travertine floor straight up to her. She tilts her head to the side, shooting me a tight grin. But it's her eyes that really get me—dark brown, piercing, and utterly unnerving, as if she can see right through my façade of false confidence. I have to pull this off.

"Miriam?" I say, plastering on my best 'I'm totally not intimidated by you' or 'I'm not flipping out' smile. She's so polished and put together I'm suddenly hyperaware of my windblown hair and the coffee stain on my silk blouse. So much for making a good first impression.

"I'm Olivia. Olivia Montgomery. Just arrived for the writers' retreat."

Her gaze locks onto mine, and I swear I can feel her cataloging every twitch and tell as she stands up. Impostor syndrome. Does she know I have it? She raises a brow and laughs. "Liv, I was hoping for more of a greeting. Like an 'OMG! It's been so long!'"

My eyebrows pinch together with dumb confusion.

"You really don't recognize me?" she continues.

"You might have to refresh my memory," I say, hoping I'm not being rude.

She grins, pulls me into a hug, and then takes a step back, placing her hands on my shoulders. "It's me. Mimi! We met in Greece six years ago and a couple of times after..."

I study her face, the past slamming my brain. She sort of looks like the woman I'd met so many years ago, but different, alarmingly so. Maybe she'd had work done? "Mouse?"

"Nobody ever calls me Mouse. Nobody but Kat," she guffaws with a snort. "It was her inside joke, one I've never found funny." She holds out her hand, waggling her ring finger with an enormous diamond on it. "But I'm married and my last name is Richards now."

"Uh-huh," I say. "Congratulations."

She gives me a slight smile. "I remember hearing about your engagement to..." She pauses, blinking. "What was his name? Oh, yes, I remember. Steven Shepherd. He went to Woodford. Sienna had quite the crush on him..."

Apparently, Miriam hasn't heard the news about Steven, because that's the first thing I would have expected her to mention. I let out a shaky breath and lower my head. "The marriage never happened."

Her hand squeezes my shoulder. "Sorry. I've been so busy with work, I'm really out of touch."

"It's OK," I say, internally blowing out a sigh of relief. "Do you keep in touch with Kat?"

"Oh, I do, but only when I have to. Same social circles. Business stuff." She rolls her eyes. "On that, I really don't want to talk about Kat. I'm just glad you're here—even though you didn't recognize me. But I won't hold that against you." She taps her nose. "Nose job." She twirls a lock of hair and bats her eyelashes. "Extensions."

"You look phenomenal," I say, thankful for the change of subject. And it's not a lie: she looks fabulous, like a completely different person.

"You do, too," she says. "I almost didn't recognize you either."

"A lot has changed."

"It sure has," she says, changing the subject with a wave of her hand. "Back to the topic. I remember you telling me you wanted to be a writer when we were in Greece. I was so excited to see your query and then your name on the list for the retreat." She beams at me, her enthusiasm almost overwhelming. "I'm even happier that you're here." Mimi raises a finger, as if she's just remembered something crucial. She tilts her head to the side. "Do you still keep in touch with Sienna?"

"We kind of drifted apart after I moved in with Kat." I swallow. "And we drifted even further apart when I started dating Steven."

I'm expecting her to say something more on Steven. She must know. It's been all over the news this morning. And then I remember—no cell service. We're unplugged.

"Got it. She'd claimed you, just like she'd claimed Steven in high school." She throws her hands in the air and blows out a breath, her eyes wide. "I'm sorry. I have serious foot-in-mouth syndrome sometimes. Did I just completely overstep?"

"No," I say, gulping and straightening my posture. "It's fine."

Miriam's eyes widen with understanding.

"Funny how everything always circles back to Kat." She pauses when she sees my expression—the frown twisting my lips. "Let me guess: she played her Kat games, batted you around, and then got bored when you didn't amuse her anymore?"

I meet Miriam's intense gaze. "Something like that."

"Well, good news is—Sienna will be here, too. I'm working on a lifestyle book with her. Maybe you can get your friendship back on track? I remember how close the two of you were." Her phone buzzes. "Give me a minute. I don't mean to be rude, but I have to take this."

Instead of that cosmic joke of hiding from the past that seeks me out when I least expect it, here I am facing it in real life instead of on the page. As Miriam takes her call, I stare out the window at the pond, my mind swirling back to Kat and all the games she'd played.

NINE

(THEN)

Sienna was my roommate at Syracuse University. Before meeting her in person, I'd talked to her a few times on the phone. She did most of the talking. I was still in my awkward phase. I didn't really know how to communicate with others, which was ironic because I was going to major in communications.

My eyes took in the enormous campus, a small city in itself. A person dressed as a giant orange greeted me by waving a blue flag, and I lugged my things—I didn't have much—up to my dorm room in Haven Hall.

A tall blonde was unpacking her luggage. Unsure of what to do, I cleared my throat. Sienna turned and smiled. "Olivia! It's so nice to finally meet you!" She pointed. "I hope you don't mind, but I took the right side. I know I probably should have waited, but I really, like, wanted to settle in."

"The left is good for me."

She eyed my stuff. "Is that all you brought? Is there more? I can help you carry it up."

"That's it," I said. "Sheets, towels, clothes, shoes, toiletries..."

"Well, if you need anything, you can always borrow something from me." Sienna flopped down on her bed. "I'll help you unpack and then we'll go to the freshman orientation. We are going to have. So. Much. Fun!" She tilted her head to the side, surveying me. "You know what? It's weird. I feel like I know you already. We're going to be like sisters."

I grinned back, excited for the days to come—if I didn't screw things up.

Over the next four years, when I wasn't working at the library, we did our homework together or walked through the campus, seeing all the girls in their sorority sweatshirts laughing with boys or chatting in groups. People always envied Sienna, as did I. "Don't you want to join a sorority?" I asked her one day.

The expression on her face darkened, the light sparking her eyes gone. "No, I'm not a fan of organized groups. I only need one friend here. Sad to say, but you're it."

I didn't ask for details, just accepted her reasoning. I wasn't expecting our friendship to blossom the way it had, but Sienna had grown on me. We became attached at the hip, only parting for classes we didn't share. On holiday breaks, Sienna always invited me to come back home to the city with her.

"I can't," I'd say. "My grandfather and mom would kill me."

"It's only a four-hour ride," she'd reply. "You're always at that library. You even work on summer breaks, saying no to trips to Europe with my family."

"Unlike you, I have to work," I said. "Student loans."

"I'm sure the library will let you have one weekend off. Come on," she pleaded. "It wouldn't hurt to ask."

And so I did. What was one weekend of lost wages? Nothing really, considering the amount I'd eventually need to pay off. I needed a break, to see the world, to live in the moment.

I'd always known Sienna came from money, but little did I know how wealthy she was. Her parents were the epitome of old money: reserved, to say the least. Their Park Avenue home, overlooking Central Park, was like a museum—halls filled with sparkling chandeliers and adorned with priceless paintings. Every surface seemed to glitter. I felt like an intruder.

Sienna moved through this lifestyle with the ease of someone who had never known anything else, but she never flaunted it. Still, the question gnawed at me: what did she see in our friendship? I was a socially awkward nobody, scraping by on a scholarship, while she was practically New York royalty.

I only realized who her dad really was when we went to the restaurant and the maître d' greeted us with a respectful "Senator Knight," while leading us to a prime table in the center of the room. That night, over a lavish lobster dinner, I barely spoke a word. Back from a European vacation, Mark was also in attendance that evening.

Sienna nudged me and whispered, "Liv, stop drooling. A) he's my brother. And B) Mark does and always will belong to my friend, Kat. I'm sure you'll meet her one day."

She shot me a sly wink. "When you move to the city and live with me."

In addition to developing a huge crush on a man who would never be mine, I came back from that weekend with a sack of hand-me-downs from Sienna and her mother. I didn't think anything of it at the time, save for another person's trash was another person's treasure. As I unpacked the haul, I looked toward Sienna. "Do you feel sorry for me or something? Am I a charity case?"

"No," she said. "You're my best friend."

I gulped. "I feel like I'm taking advantage of you."

"You're not," she insisted, latching onto my hand. "You're like my sister and sisters share things."

"What am I sharing with you?"

She nudged my side. "Your heart—way more valuable than money."

After graduating, my plans to move to New York and live with Sienna were put on temporary hiatus thanks to my grandfather having a stroke and my mom taking off for Italy. She sent me a card, a cell phone, and three hundred dollars:

Liv,

Congratulations on graduating from Syracuse... with honors no less. I'm so proud of you! I wish I could have been there, but I can't travel out of the country right now. I married Gianni and we're working hard on getting the visa situation taken care of. I can't wait for you to meet him. Take care of your grandfather. He's done so much for you. Without him, we'd have nothing. I'll call you soon.

Love you to the moon, stars, and back again,

Mom

And that was that. I'd found a decent job in Chicago, working an entry-level position at a big advertising agency. In my spare time, I took over my mom's duties, cooking and cleaning for my grandpa, taking care of him, while Mom made constant excuses as to why she couldn't come back to Chicago.

My grandfather passed away from another stroke two years later, when I was at work. I came home to find him on the floor, eyes open. After calling the paramedics, I called Sienna, sobbing hysterically. She booked the next flight out.

"Move to New York. I'm your family," she said at the funeral.

"You're engaged to Nick."

"Nick will become your family, too," she said. "No excuses. No worries. Just come to New York."

A few days later, Mom called. "I'm sorry I couldn't make it to the funeral. But there's a very good reason. You have to come to Positano when your baby brother is born."

I hung up on her, seething. It dawned on me. I didn't have a family, not anymore. My father was unreachable, and my mother had abandoned me.

Meanwhile, Sienna called me every day, selling the move to New York. I could live in the garden apartment of Nick's brownstone in Park Slope, Brooklyn for free. How could I refuse? Before I took the big leap, I had to settle a few affairs, like finding a job, and selling Grandpa's apartment—selling everything.

I was starting a new life.

And so was Sienna. She was getting married in a couple of months in Greece. She sent me a ticket to accompany her on her pre-wedding planning trip, because, unfortunately, Nick couldn't make it. As her bridesmaid and best friend, I couldn't say no. Who was I kidding? I jumped at the opportunity. Nick, who I'd only met on FaceTime, treated both of us.

All I could think was, let the adventure begin.

For a week, Sienna and I stayed with Nick's father's family in Chania, Crete, scoping out the venue for her upcoming marriage with her wedding planner. We stuffed ourselves to the gills with fresh seafood, flaming saganaki, succulent lamb, drinking wine and ouzo—lots of ouzo—with his family. There was a lot of dancing and singing, not that I was good at either, but it didn't matter.

Then, after leaving Chania, Sienna and I took off for a couple of days in Santorini. The moment we stepped off the ferry, the atmosphere hit me like the shots of ouzo we'd shared with Nick's family. Absolutely breathtaking.

"Race you to the beach?" Sienna challenged, already changed into a flowy sundress that made her look like some sort of Grecian goddess.

"You're on." I laughed, throwing on my swimsuit and a breezy, cotton summer dress.

Sienna's enthusiasm was infectious, but it was also exhausting. She and I were cut from different cloths—mine was way cheaper. Regardless of our differences, I couldn't shake the feeling that this trip was the beginning of something big. With the warm Greek sun on my face, anything seemed possible.

"Thanks for bringing me along with you," I said to her, as my feet sank into the sand, and she clasped my hand.

In the distance, an enormous mega-yacht floated in the sea, towering over the smaller boats like a polished silver skyscraper. I gasped. "That thing has to be over one hundred feet." Transfixed, I watched as a smaller boat was lowered into the water. As the small boat got close to the shore, Sienna let go of my hand. "OMG. I know them."

"What? How?" I began, but Sienna was off, racing toward the shore. Hesitantly, I followed.

"I can't believe it!" she yelled. "What the hell are you doing in Santorini?"

One of the two young women on the boat looked like a supermodel with long, perfectly coiffed hair. "Surprise! We're here to throw you an impromptu bachelorette party!" She shot me a look. Her green eyes seemed to pierce right through me, even from a distance. My heart did a weird little flip. "Who is she?"

The deckhand pulled the boat closer to the shore. I made my approach, knee deep in water. "Hi," I said with a slight wave. "I'm Liv. Sienna's maid of honor."

Sienna quickly explained how the two women on the boat had attended Woodford Hall with her. "Liv, this is Kat." Sienna smiled and then rolled her eyes toward the other woman. "And this is Mouse."

"Sienna, my name is Mimi."

"No, it isn't. It's Mouse." Kat shot me a wink. "It's my pet name for her." She gave me the once-over, scanning each and every detail. "Nick told us you were here. Sienna's bachelorette party is tonight. On my yacht. Sound good?"

"Sounds amazing," said Sienna. "We're in."

Kat grinned. "Bring your bags. You're staying with me on the yacht."

Sienna squealed. "Yes!"

I gulped.

The boat took off back toward the yacht, as Kat waved and blew us kisses. Sienna pretended to catch them. I turned toward her. "Did you know about this?"

She shook her head. "Nope. Surprise!"

"Is this really a good idea?"

"Where's your sense of adventure, Liv?" she replied. "How many times do I have to tell you to live in the moment?"

TEN

(THEN)

We sat on the upper deck of Kat's yacht and sipped on champagne while a couple of deckhands carried our bags to our cabin. Sienna leaned over and whispered, "Kat's the heiress to the Sterling Spirits fortune."

"Where are her parents?"

Sienna shot me a stone-cold look. "Whatever you do, do *not* ask her about her parents. Ever. They died when she was twenty. Horrific accident. She doesn't like to talk about it."

I shot her a sideways glance. "What was boarding school like, anyway? And why do you never talk about it?"

"What's there to talk about? Our parents shipped us off because they didn't want us around," she said with a very un-Sienna-like frown. Then she raised her glass, clinking it against mine, a smile spreading across her cheeks. "You know me. I like to live in the present."

Point taken. My eyes shot to the iced-seafood bar—filled with shrimp, crab, and lobster. I'd never been in surroundings like this—decadence overload. So this was how the other half lived.

"See? I told you we'd have an amazing time!" Sienna gushed, tzatziki dribbling down her chin.

Kat and Mimi stepped onto the deck, dressed to the nines in chic silk dresses that looked like they had been ripped straight from the pages of *Vogue* magazine. Sienna leaned against the railing, lighting a cigarette, her movements slow and deliberate.

"I love your dress," Kat said to me, breaking the silence between us. "It's very... unique."

I shifted in my seat, feeling out of my element.

Kat snapped her fingers. "More champagne, please."

A server instantly appeared, like magic.

Not one to be ignored for long, Sienna perked up when Mouse walked over to talk with her. They started taking selfies with their phones, making exaggerated kissy faces with duck lips and laughing loudly.

Kat leaned in closer to me, her perfume a subtle mix of jasmine, something spicy, and a dash of citrus. "You know," she said, "both of them mean well, but they can be a lot sometimes. I'm glad you're here. You'll balance us out."

I was unsure what to make of her sudden interest in me. This whole scene was surreal—like a bad reality TV show, where I was the unwilling guest star.

"So, Liv," Kat purred, "I can't believe we're meeting in Greece of all places." Her lashes fluttered. "I want to hear all about you. I'm wondering why Sienna's been keeping you from us."

I was wondering the same thing.

I found myself spilling everything—my dreams of becoming a writer, my secret fears of never measuring up in the big city. I even told her about how I'd grown up, being home schooled and then ostracized because of it. Kat nodded along, her eyes never leaving mine. It was like I was hypnotized.

"Good thing you didn't go to boarding school," she said. "Oh, the stories I could tell, the hazing. The cliques." She gave out a soft laugh. "I'm jealous of your upbringing, way more normal than mine."

My life was not normal. "You can't be serious."

"I am."

Just like that, the ice was broken.

"You know," she said, reaching out to touch my hand, "there's something special about you. I can see it. It's your aura."

She must have been talking about somebody else. An aura? I tried to keep my cool, but inside, my stomach did cartwheels.

I swallowed back a sip of champagne. "So, what do you do for a living?"

"I dabble in a lot of things. Including Sienna's brother, Mark." She shrugged like it was no big deal. Her intense eyes met mine. "Have you ever been in love?"

"I barely date," I said.

"But you must love something?"

"Writing. I love writing." I shrugged. "I really don't want to work in PR. I've been an avid reader all my life. Books are my escape." It was time to close this conversation down before I babbled on, boring her.

Mimi sauntered over, taking the seat next to Kat's. Kat squared her shoulders toward me. "A writer? Talk to Mouse. Her family works in publishing."

Mimi leaned forward, glaring at Kat. "Would you please, for the sake of my sanity, stop calling me Mouse?"

"It's our thing."

"It's not funny," said Mimi with an irritated huff. "Anyway, what genre do you want to write?"

"I'm not sure."

"So, where are you going to live when you move to the city?" asked Kat, changing the subject with a wave of her hand.

"Nick has a brownstone in Park Slope. The garden apartment."

"You're going to live right underneath your best friend when she and her husband-to-be are starting out their lives together?" Kat blurted out a caustic laugh. "It's like having your mother-in-law living with you."

I frowned. "It's my only option for now."

Kat's mouth twisted into a Cheshire Cat grin. "You always have other options."

"Actually, I don't," I said with a sigh. "I haven't started my new job yet, money is tight, and—"

"I know of a place on the Upper East Side. Beautiful. A historic brownstone overlooking Central Park. Four bedrooms." She chuckled when I recoiled. "I'm suggesting you move in with me. Eight thousand square feet of luxury— so big it will be like having your own place—"

Mimi stood up and slammed her fists into her thighs. "I thought you didn't want a roommate."

Kat laughed. "No, I just didn't want to live with a mouse."

"You know what," said Mimi. "Liv, word of advice? Don't let Kat get her claws in you and don't believe everything she says. Her life isn't all champagne and caviar."

"Oh, Mouse," Kat purred, voice dripping with honey-coated venom, "always the rain cloud at the garden party. Remind me why I invited you on this trip?"

Mimi snorted, a sound that seemed to physically pain Kat. "Your guess is as good as mine."

And then Mimi stormed off to the seafood bar, shaking her head.

"Don't mind her," said Kat. "Did I mention my offer comes rent free?"

"W-why?" I stuttered.

"Because I've decided I like you." She shrugged. "Honestly, I've been looking to make some changes in my life, and I think you have, too. And, truth be told, it's kind of lonely living on my own."

I ran the pros and cons in my head.

Pro: Financial breathing room.

Con: Possible loss of kidney to organ harvesters.

Pro: Networking opportunities.

Con: Pissing off Sienna.

Pro: Getting closer to my goals much quicker.

I knew I was going to do it. I was going to accept Kat's offer. I was throwing all my chips on the table. When I finally agreed, she popped open a bottle of champagne. "We're celebrating!"

Sienna walked over to me. "Celebrating what?"

"Your upcoming marriage and..." My lips pinched to the side. "And, apparently, when I move to New York, I'm moving in with Kat."

Her eyes darkened and she shook her head. "Not a good idea, Liv."

"Why?"

"You're *my* friend, not hers. You've only just met."

"Sienna, you're getting married. I can't live under you and Nick..."

Her lips pursed together. "Welcome to the inner circle,

Liv." Then she whispered in my ear, "Just be careful. Because there will always be somebody standing on the sidelines to push you out of it." Her eyes met mine, her lips twisting into a wicked grin. "Just kidding."

She wasn't.

Kat tilted her head back and howled, "We are all goddesses of the night," and then she turned up the music. "Let's get this party started. Winner takes all." She paused, unlatching the diamond tennis bracelet on her wrist. "Sienna, put that engagement ring of yours in the pot."

"You've got to be joking."

"I am." Kat cackled. She undid her necklace, a white gold choker with sapphires and diamonds. "I have another one just like it." She looked toward Mimi. "Mouse, we need matching earrings."

Mimi grumbled. "Fine. You gave them to me anyway."

All eyes were upon me and my gaze fell to the simple white gold ring adorning my finger, to the delicate pave diamonds catching the light and sparkling like the stars in the sky. It was a gift from my father before he'd taken off. Maybe it was time to just let the memory of him go.

Sienna's voice snapped me out of my thoughts. "Liv, don't hate the player, hate the game. Life's a gamble. And who knows, you might win the pot."

I whipped the ring off. "Game on."

Thankfully, I've got great hand–eye coordination, and I did win, throwing ring after plastic ring around a champagne bottle. I let out a sigh of a relief.

Kat placed the jewelry in my hands. "Congrats!"

"I'm only keeping my ring."

"No, you're keeping everything. It's how we do things.

Don't worry, I'll probably demand a rematch at a later date," she replied with a wink.

The next few days blurred together like one long, hazy dream. Ouzo flowed like water, seafood piled high on our plates. Champagne corks popped with alarming frequency. Each day was a copy of the last, filled with the same excess. We drank champagne for breakfast, switching to ouzo by lunch, circling back to champagne well before dinner.

The only real trouble came on our last day when Kat had the chef make us tiropitas to soak up all the alcohol sloshing around in our systems. We were lounging on the deck, the sun dipping lazily toward the horizon, when the platter arrived. The smell of warm, cheesy pastry was almost enough to sober me up.

I was taking my time with mine, savoring each bite, when a seagull came out of nowhere. Instinctively, I'd tried to protect my face with my hands—one of which still clutched a tiropita. My screams mingled with the bird's squawks as it snatched the pastry from my hand, its beak grazing my cheek with a razor's edge. The bird soared away, my snack held triumphantly in its beak.

I touched my cheek, feeling the sting and then the warmth of blood. Drops trickled down my face like tears. Kat and Sienna stared, momentarily stunned.

"That was intense," Sienna said, and I could hear the smirk in her voice. She didn't move from her lounger, just stretched out, slathering more sunscreen on her legs.

Kat dabbed at my cheek with a soft linen napkin. "Don't mind her," she said, but I did mind. I minded a lot.

"Hope it doesn't scar," said Sienna, getting up and walking away.

The cut on my cheek throbbed in time with my pulse.

I might have made a huge mistake by agreeing to live with Kat, but what else could I have done? I was a moth attracted to her flame.

ELEVEN

(NOW)

Miriam taps me on the shoulder, bringing me back from my trip down memory lane.

"Liv, sorry about that. I'm negotiating an author's advance and, well, publishing never sleeps." She tucks her phone into her purse. "You look lost in your thoughts."

I snap back to attention. "Just thinking about our Greek adventure, when I first met you."

She sighs. "If only we could transport ourselves back in time."

If I had a time machine, I'd change everything. All the bad decisions I've made over the years. But I'm stuck in the present. If I'd never met Kat in Santorini, any of them, would I be in a better place now? I think about that all the time.

"We'll catch up more later, I promise." Miriam winks. "Now to the task at hand. I've assigned Rebecca Stiles to be your mentor. I sent her your pages last night. And..." Her eyes dart to the left. "Hold that thought—you're about to meet your critique partner, Trinity Powers."

A tall, elegant woman with straight jet-black hair and

striking red lips glides up to us, her movements as fluid as a dancer's. She's dressed in a chic, minimalist outfit that screams high fashion. Miriam excuses herself to check on the other attendees, leaving me momentarily unbalanced.

"It's Olivia, right?" says Trinity, as she air-kisses my cheeks like a European.

"Um, yes," I manage to say, still reeling from her sheer presence.

Trinity studies me with an intensity that makes me want to shrink away. "I read the synopsis for your book. Very intriguing."

"Thanks." I'm unsure if she means it as a compliment. "I appreciate that."

She tilts her head, examining me. "Do you draw from personal experience?"

I hesitate. How much should I reveal to this stranger? Everything I write is from personal experience, but this story is different. "Not really. It's all imagined."

"I always find that the most compelling stories come from a place of personal pain."

"Exactly," I reply.

I glance around the room, searching for a lifeline. I'm way out of my comfort zone. Other attendees are mingling, laughing, sipping wine. They all seem so at ease.

"Well," Trinity says, breaking the awkward silence. "It's always fascinating to see how a new writer handles the intricacies of plot and character."

"I'm looking forward to your feedback," I say, my stomach twisting into a tight knot. Why did I think I could do this? These people are professionals. I'm just playing at being a writer.

I have to say something, instead of just staring at her. "Any insider tips on surviving this literary gauntlet?"

Her eyes meet mine, glinting with something I can't quite place... amusement? A warning? "Just remember, Liv," she says, leaning in slightly, "everyone here has a story to tell. The trick is figuring out which ones are true." Trinity checks her phone, then looks back at me. "I have to run, but we'll talk more during our workshops. See you at lunch," she whispers, adding a conspiratorial wink. "In the meantime, be wary of the wildlife."

Trinity walks away, her heels clicking on the polished travertine floor, and I'm left standing alone. I blink, processing Trinity's cryptic words as she meanders down the hall.

A finger taps my shoulder and I startle. *What now?* "Sorry to sneak up on you," a soft voice says, and I turn to find myself face-to-face with a woman sporting purple-streaked hair and a navy-blue Nyx long-sleeved t-shirt.

"I'm Jenn, the general manager of Nyx," she continues. "I'm assuming you must be Olivia Montgomery—the last-minute addition for the retreat."

"That's me," I say. "Nice to meet you."

"I'll show you to your room," she continues. "One thing you need to know—only the business center and that area"—she points to the nook area Miriam had sat in—"gets cell and Wi-Fi reception. We like for people to get unplugged here, get in touch with nature. Cool?"

I so need to unplug.

"Cool."

Jenn escorts me up a flight of stairs and down a long hallway with travertine floors. The room is stunning—a beautiful space with muted earth tones and soft textures, all rustic charm and modern comfort with a view of the mountains and the pond.

"We don't have room keys, but the doors lock from the inside," Jenn continues.

I'm wondering if I've heard her correctly. I shake my head. "What about burglars?"

"This isn't the city." She rolls her eyes and laughs. "If you brought any valuables with you, give them to the receptionist. We have a safe. While we're on the subject, we have some rules here at Nyx."

"Rules?" I parrot.

"You're free to roam most of the grounds, but the staff quarters are off limits to guests. Otherwise, feel free to corner us with any of your needs. Your welcome gift is right there." She shoots me a toothy grin and points to a basket set on a carved wooden desk. "Lunch will be served in about forty-five minutes on the terrace. It's a bit nippy out, so bring a sweater. I'll leave you to settle in."

"Thanks."

She grins. "No problem."

After the door closes behind her, I peruse the welcome gift. The basket is overflowing with goods—honey, perfumes, shampoos, soaps and a couple of small bottles of eau de vie—all made on the property, apparently. The blue t-shirt with the Nyx logo, just like Jenn's, is cool and soft (made from bamboo), but the pièce de résistance is the navy-blue "vegan" leather-bound journal.

Amazing as everything is, I can't help but wonder what I've gotten myself into. A secluded retreat, a mysterious critique partner, a woman from my past, and a flock of homicidal geese?

As I arrange my toiletries in the bathroom, toothbrush in

the porcelain holder, I take my necklace off, hiding it underneath a washcloth on the vanity. I continue unpacking, a nagging sense of unease in my gut.

The trees outside seem to lean in closer to the window, their branches stretching out like crooked fingers. My mind is blending a whirlwind of faces—the writers, the staff—even the geese by the pond. My imagination is bleeding into reality like ink on wet paper. I take a deep breath and gaze at the beautiful surroundings, trying to ground myself, but instead I just feel more lost. I thought this retreat would be a way to reclaim my life, but now I'm wondering if the only person I'm deceiving is myself.

TWELVE

(NOW)

After changing my clothes into yoga-inspired casual, I make my way to the terrace for lunch, passing by other retreat members. Some give me the once-over with quiet hellos or curt nods acknowledging my existence. Trinity waves me over to a table and I wander over, taking a seat across from her.

"Apparently," she says with annoyance, "we're not supposed to connect with the others until we connect."

"Kind of strange," I say.

"A blessing," she replies. "I met them all in the van on the way here." Her head tilts to the side. "Hey, wait a sec, why weren't you on it? Picked us up in front of the Foster Literary headquarters at 6:45 am. Part of the price of the package. Didn't you get the email?"

I look over my shoulder and my gaze lands on Miriam's for a brief second. She shoots me a slight smile and then continues her conversation. Something feels off about Miriam. It's not her complete makeover. It's her "so good to see you, we have a lot to catch up" attitude. Although I used to like her, Miriam and I never really connected. My radar is on high alert. I place my focus back on Trinity.

"Last minute booking. I took the train to Hudson and then an Uber."

She whistles in between her teeth. "Damn. You made of money?"

"Definitely not," I huff. During an awkward pause, she stares out at the mountains. "Enjoying the view?" I ask.

"This place is certainly... idyllic." Trinity waves a hand haphazardly to the workers maintaining the grounds. "Almost suspiciously so, don't you think?"

My eyes shoot toward the horizon, to the ground below. My mind goes straight to the cult leader, Tobias Rane. "What, do you think there's a mass grave under all these pretty flowers?"

"You never know." She lifts an eyebrow. "I've just never seen people so damn happy. Maybe I'm a pessimist because I'm from the big bad city and I've seen too much in my line of work." She shrugs and leans forward. "But enough about me. So, Liv, I want to know. What brings you to this little literary haven?"

As a server places a colorful dish in front of us, I toy with a loose thread on my sleeve. "Oh, you know, the usual. Chasing that elusive dream, hoping to become the next best-seller." God, do I sound lame. "You?"

Trinity's gaze finally shifts from the landscape to me. "I'm exploring new avenues. I'm an investigative journalist by profession. It can only take you so far before you start seeing conspiracies in your quinoa." She eyes her plate. "Are these flowers edible?"

"I think so. I don't graze on flowers all that much," I say

with a soft laugh. I lean back in my chair. "So, are you here as a journalist, or aspiring novelist?"

A shadow passes over Trinity's face. "Let's just say there's always that one story where you know you have more to uncover."

I raise a brow. "And?"

"Not telling you any more than that for now."

"Cryptic," I muse. "Very on-brand for this whole retreat vibe."

"How about you? You got any demons you're hoping to exorcise through your writing?"

I think of Kat, but I don't want a stranger to know about the hell she'd put me through, and I end up blurting out the first words that come to mind. "To connect, maybe, with myself? And use it for my writing?"

"Good answer," she says, clinking my glass with hers.

As we delve further into the conversation, I can't help but notice there's something in Trinity's eyes. A hint of pain.

My gaze catches Miriam's again. She's staring at our table with an unreadable expression. She whispers something to Rebecca Stiles. Rebecca nods and then her eyebrows pinch together. OK. I'm not being totally paranoid. If I placed a bet, I'd wager that they're talking about me.

"How do you know Miriam?" I ask.

"I don't," Trinity replies, "but something tells me that you do. Did she reject your manuscript?"

"Not yet. She's a blast from my past."

"A good one?"

I shake my head, my gaze sweeping the surroundings— the trees, the mountains, the pond in the distance, finally landing on those damn geese. "Not sure." I blink, needing to take the focus off me. "What do I need to know about the others on the retreat?"

She cackles. "To stay away from them..."

"Are you serious?"

"Dead."

That word sends shivers up my spine. "W-w-why?"

"Some of them are a bunch of spoiled women who don't take anything seriously, and the others are way too serious." She waves a surreptitious hand toward the table behind us—a group of loud women who have been talking incessantly. "Those ladies are the Bees. Bethany, Brittany, Bianca, and Blake."

"You've got to be joking."

Her chin tucks into her collarbone and she cringes. "I'm not." Trinity scratches her cheek and points to another table of six women. "Those women aren't as bad as the Bees. They're all into historical or literary women's fiction— emphasis on literary. On the drive from Manhattan, I'd never heard Proust, Hemingway, or Austen quoted so many times. I cringed every time they tried to one-up one another."

My eyes land on the two young women leaning toward each other and whispering. "And those two?"

She nods with approval. "Yeah, them? They seem alright. Mid-twenties. Writing a vampire series that sounds kind of cool."

Trinity falls silent as the silver fox that is Victoria Foster stands up and clinks her glass with a fork. "Hello, everyone!" She grins. "Welcome to the third annual Foster Literary retreat, where our aim is to foster your creativity. I met most of you while checking in and I can't wait to get to know you and your words better." She pauses and waggles a finger in my direction. "But I don't believe I've met you."

I find myself shrinking in my seat as all gazes shoot to me.

Miriam stands up and whispers something in Victoria's ear. Victoria tilts her head to the side and continues, "Oh, Olivia Montgomery, our last-minute addition. Welcome! Did you want to stand up and introduce yourself to the group? Tell us what genre you write in?"

Talk about being put on the spot. I shoot a shy wave and don't stand up. "I'm currently focusing on writing a thriller." I pause. "And please call me Liv."

Victoria grins and claps her hands together like a seal. "Let's all welcome Liv!"

"Welcome, Liv!"

"Miriam tells me your query was outstanding. Care to share it with the group?"

I'm really being put in the hot seat. My teeth clench together. "Sure?"

"Wonderful!" She nods and shoots me a beaming smile, all teeth. "Please stand."

I keep my internal sigh to myself and pull my wallet out of my purse, fetching my query letter, unfolding it. Before starting, my gaze focuses on the mountains, strong and steady. A former communications major and a marketing manager, I can do this. I stand and clear my throat:

"Dear Ms. Foster: I know you're a fan of thrillers and I believe—"

"Could you please speak louder?" says Victoria. "They can't hear you in the back."

I blink and continue, raising my voice. When I finish, I force a smile and take my seat. "Well, that's it."

An uncomfortable applause later, the spotlight is turned back on Victoria, save for Trinity who is staring me down with a bemused expression on her face.

"I hope everybody is enjoying their first lunch and connecting with their critique partner, or in some cases"—Victoria nods toward the Bees—"critique partners." She swallows. "As you all know, we have some very powerful mentors here, including one of my favorite editors, Rebecca Stiles"—she nods toward Rebecca—"and one of my favorite clients, Anna Hale."

"Hale the queen," the Bees scream from their table.

Anna jazz hand waves, her eyes wide.

Applause.

"In other news, I have a stellar surprise!" She drumrolls her hands on her thighs. "Two clients I've recently signed will be joining us. They're held up in the city, but will be arriving shortly. They'll be available to answer those publishing questions you may have from an author's perspective." Victoria clears her throat. "For now, I'm passing the floor to Jenn, whom you've all met. Jenn? Take it away!"

Jenn walks onto the terrace, her purple highlights glowing. She waves. "Hi, everybody. As you enjoy your lunch, I wanted to tell you more about the concept here. OK?"

Trinity leans toward me. "I'm very much looking forward to this."

"Nyx Sanctuary was named after the goddess of the same name. Nyx—the goddess of the night. And, tonight, for all those who want to, we can gaze into the starry night, thinking about our place in the world, thinking about our creativity."

Mumbles of agreement.

"At any rate," Jenn continues, "what we're doing at Nyx is more than your average luxury resort. We're creating a lifestyle, using the gifts nature has bestowed upon us." She pauses. "Nemesis, our line of perfumes, is named after the daughter of Nyx. In myth, Nemesis was concerned with matters of love and balance, her symbol the scales, her animal the goose, which is why we have so many on the property. Later, we're going to show you how to make and bottle your very own scent!"

The Bees clap, oohing and aahing.

"Anyhoo, that's my spiel. Should any of you want to represent our products—"

"I am so interested," says one of the Bees.

"Me too," others agree.

Victoria stands up. "Jenn, we are here for a writers' retreat... not to be recruited into a marketing scheme."

"If anybody is interested, come find me."

Victoria's eyes shoot daggers at Jenn. "We'll talk about this later."

Trinity taps her fingernails on the table. "This is getting weird," she whispers.

I shiver. The temperature must have dropped five more degrees, and the once bright-blue sky is now an ominous gray. Thick clouds loom overhead, suffocating the sunlight. A musty and earthy scent surrounds us. The air crackles with electricity.

"Now onto the bad news," says Jenn, looking up. "A storm is forecast to start tomorrow. The good news is that we can take advantage of the outdoor activities today and tomorrow morning..."

The Bees groan.

Victoria stands, focusing on something in the distance. "Ah! Forget about doom and gloom, one of my rays of sunshine is here."

My attention is drawn toward whatever has captured Victoria's attention. It's Sienna Knight and I groan.

Trinity raises an eyebrow. "Another blast from the past? And I take it you had a bad experience with her?"

"Definitely bad." I purse my lips.

The urge to spill everything about my history bubbles in my throat. But I can't trust Trinity. I don't trust anybody. I force my face into a look of casual indifference. "I knew her in a previous life."

Trinity nods slowly, still observing me closely. "Let's continue this conversation during our nature walk after lunch," she suggests. "And maybe you can tell me why you're really here."

"I'm here to write," I say, taken aback.

Trinity clucks her tongue disapprovingly. "No," she disagrees, leaning forward. "I think you're here for something else."

She's freaking me out. This woman is way too intuitive. I pick at my cuticles, shaking my head. "You don't know anything about me."

"You'd be surprised what I know," she says, leaning back in her chair.

I meet her eyes, wondering how Trinity fits into my story... or if it was never mine to begin with.

THIRTEEN

(NOW)

I try to focus on the plate a server has just placed in front of me, resisting the urge to steal a quick glance at Sienna. I go silent as her figure glides past us. Dressed in a flowing skirt and boots, paired with a fitted t-shirt, jean jacket, and dark sunglasses, Sienna exudes effortless coolness.

The Bees' high-pitched shrieks command attention. "Sienna Knight is here!" one of them screeches. "I can't believe it!"

Amidst the buzz of the Bees, Victoria taps her fork on her glass. The women quiet down and turn their heads toward her. "Ladies, I am delighted to introduce you to one of our newest and esteemed clients, Sienna Knight." Her voice rings out, clear and confident. "The reigning it-girl of New York will be publishing her lifestyle non-fiction with Silver-Gate. Please feel free to ask her any questions about the publishing process."

Sienna steps forward and addresses the group. "That's right, my lovelies. Ask me anything you'd like to know, save for who I'm dating." She raises her sunglasses to the top of her head and winks playfully. "That answer would be nobody. I'm happily married."

The way the light hits her face makes her seem almost ethereal. But I know she's far from an angel.

The Bees begin to pepper her with questions. As Sienna answers, her head cocks to the side like a curious bird. I can practically see the wheels of recognition churning like gears in her head. And then she makes a beeline right toward my table, walking quickly.

Sienna's eyes lock onto mine. "Olivia? What an... unexpected surprise."

"Life is full of surprises, isn't it?" I find myself forcing an awkward laugh. "And, funny, I was thinking the same thing. I didn't realize you were into"—I gesture at our surroundings—"all this."

She shoots me a tight grin. "Oh, you'd be surprised at what I'm into these days," she replies. "Life has a way of evolving us... doesn't it?" She flips a lock of hair over her shoulder. "I'm writing a lifestyle book, *Be the Bomb*. It was actually Miriam's idea."

"Oh," I say.

"And you? I take it you're here still trying to become a big, famous author. Seeking inspiration for your next masterpiece?"

The way she emphasizes "next masterpiece" makes my skin crawl. She's mocking me. "Something like that."

"Well, enjoy your time here, Olivia," she says, enunciating my name like it tastes bad. "I have a feeling it's going to be... transformative." She laughs. "If you need a friendly ear, I'm always available. After all, what are old friends for?"

Before I can formulate anything resembling a response, Sienna glides away, her shoes clicking on the terrace. I watch her disappear into the crowd, the Bees surrounding and fawning all over her. She moves through the women with effortless grace, like a shark slicing through water. And then, as if pulled by some invisible thread, our eyes lock again.

I look away, meeting Trinity's stunned expression. "Well, that was hella awkward."

I realize I've just been sitting there frozen, staring at Sienna like some kind of stalker. "It was," I say, gulping.

"Are you OK?"

I glance over at Trinity, appreciating her concern. "It's really nothing," I reply, trying to reassure her. "I just don't like surprises."

"Neither do I," she says. "So, not to surprise you, I'll tell you why I came on the retreat." Her eyes scan the vast property. "Did you know that this used to be the property of a notorious cult leader?"

"Yeah, Tobias Rane." My heart skips a beat. "The Rane Makers. Nexus."

Trinity's reaction is sudden—she jerks back, studying me with suspicion. "Wait. How the hell do you know that?"

I hesitate before answering, because the look in her eyes is beyond intense. "My Uber driver told me on the ride over."

"Right," she says, clucking her tongue. "And you probably live under a rock and didn't watch the news when the police arrested him."

I need to find out what this woman is up to.

Deep in thought, my gaze shoots to the mountains. I'm wondering about connections when a pair of hands suddenly covers my eyes. My heart jumps and for a moment I can't breathe. "Surprise!" a deep voice growls and my spine goes rigid.

Trinity raises her eyebrows and clucks her tongue. I see her mouth, "And so the plot soup thickens."

The shock of her words leaves me speechless as I turn to face Mark. "What are you doing here?" I manage to blurt out.

He grins, his dimples deepening. He nuzzles into my neck, kissing my cheek. "I told you I was giving Sienna a ride and with everything going on, I'm kind of worried about you." His gaze flicks over to Trinity. He cocks his head to the side. "And who might you be?"

"Trinity Powers," she replies, her posture straightening. "Liv's critique partner."

"Mark Knight," he replies, his eyes lingering on Trinity with curiosity. "Liv's boyfriend—and I really need to steal her away from you for a minute."

An awkward silence hangs in the air until Trinity clears her throat. "We're here to work together."

He squeezes my hand. "It's about Steven..."

Trinity blinks. "Steven Shepherd?"

Mark straightens his posture. "Do you know him?"

"I don't. But his face was plastered all over the news this morning. Usually happens when somebody is murdered in cold blood..." She angles toward him, narrowing her eyes. "I'm an investigative journalist..."

"Mark, don't get me wrong," I interject, my voice trailing off as I struggle to find the right words and not come off sounding accusatory. "I'm grateful that you're here, but—"

"Don't worry," he says, "I'll stay out of your way. I just need a couple minutes of your time."

Trinity stands up, shooting me an indiscernible look. She brushes her hands on her pants and stoops down to pick up her bag. "Liv, I'll meet you back here in a half hour to continue brainstorming."

I go silent as Mark sits down, watching Trinity walk away. My eyes flash to the group of writers surrounding Sienna. Her lips curve into a tight grin and she lifts up her chin. Mark's gaze follows mine. "She knows about us," he says, blowing out the air between his lips. "And she's not happy about it."

I'd picked up on that with her frosty vibe. "How long has she known?"

"A couple of months." He lifts his shoulder into a shrug. "She saw us leaving my place—the day we had your birthday brunch. Remember? I was running late? And, considering she lives in my building, I'm surprised you didn't cross paths before." He grins and clasps my hand within his. His hands are smooth, not one callus. Strong. "Look, I'm just glad we don't have to hide behind closed doors anymore. Sneaking around was exhausting."

I'd been his dirty secret. And he'd been mine.

My brain sifts back to the day he'd walked into Brooklyn Bound. I'd recently procured a first edition hardcover of Aldous Huxley's *Brave New World*, complete with a signed letter from Huxley himself, and Mark wanted to purchase it for his collection. A mere twenty thousand dollars. Physically, I'd always been attracted to Mark, but the mental connection came when I'd learned he was a bibliophile. Our relationship started off slow, just chatting over coffee about our favorite authors, and it moved on from there, but with rules. Until we figured out where our relationship was headed, we weren't going to tell anybody about us.

My lips pinch into a frown and my forehead creases. "Does Kat know?"

"She will," he says, shrugging. "And I don't care."

My gaze shoots to the mountains. "She owns this place."

He swallows. "I know."

Oh, yes, the plot soup is thick and sludge-like. My head whips in his direction. "And you didn't tell me?"

"Attorney-client privilege."

"You've seen her?"

"Not since I brokered the deal for the land." He sighs. "But we do communicate." He runs a hand through his hair. "About Steven... the police questioned Sienna for two hours this morning. They're questioning Kat now." He shakes his head solemnly. "And they want to question you tomorrow afternoon."

"Me? Why?"

"Because he'd texted you." Mark leans forward. "I guess we've both been keeping secrets. Do you want to tell me what's going on? I mean, I've read a draft of your book and the male character, I assumed to be Steven, is murdered..."

I glower at him. "That sounds like an accusation."

He raises his hands. "It is what it is. And I think there's something you're not telling me."

I lower my head as he drums his fingers on the table. "Spill."

"I saw him last week, but it wasn't by choice."

He rubs his eyes, shaking his head. "And you didn't think to tell me?"

I throw my hands into the air in resignation. "I'm telling you now."

"Go on," he says, ushering with his hand for me to continue.

As I recount what happened, thoughts prick at my brain. Miriam and Sienna are part of Kat's inner circle, as is Mark, and I've never truly been one of them. Now, Mark's asking questions, circling in closer to the history I share with Kat. Steven's murder has changed everything and I'm wishing I'd never laid eyes on any of them.

FOURTEEN

(THEN)

We were all back in Chania on the island of Crete for Nick and Sienna's wedding—me, the doting bridesmaid. Sienna's parents—Eleanor and Richard—welcomed us into the villa they'd rented, with me bunking up in Sienna's suite.

To my surprise, Mark brought along a date—that date wasn't Kat. When I asked her about it, Kat said, "We go through phases. Like the moon. Now is not our time. We always end up back together."

"Aren't you upset?"

She cracked up. "No. Not at all. I'm looking forward to next month."

"What's happening then?"

"You're hilarious, Liv." She snorted. "You're moving to New York." She wrapped her arms around me. "And we are going to have the time of our lives."

"I can't wait," I said.

"But we won't be having any fun, if you dress like that. You'd think Sienna would have better taste." She eyed me up and down, cringing. "Then again, no bride wants their maid of honor to outshine them on their wedding day."

"Wait. What's wrong with this dress?"

Kat's eyes volleyed from the ruffled top to the puffy skirt. "Everything."

"It's silk."

"It's dreadful."

Sienna's eyes bored into mine. She flashed me a fake grin, still pissed off that I was going to be moving in with Kat no matter how hard she'd tried talking me out of it.

Later that evening, after the speeches and the cake cutting and the Greek dancing, I was trying to catch my breath and standing at the bar when Steven made his approach. "You know, it's customary for the best man and the maid of honor to do a shot or two of ouzo."

I lifted a brow. "I've never heard of that tradition before."

"It's true." He shrugged and waved the bartender over, ordering two shots. Then he turned to face me, shot in hand. "Down the hatch."

"Wait! What are we toasting to? The bride and groom?"

"I think we're off-duty now." He shook his head and grinned, looking over his shoulder. I'd already helped Sienna change into her second wedding dress, because, apparently, every bride needs two. He raised his glass. "Cheers to meeting you, Liv." He grinned. "It's serendipity. Your speech blew mine away."

We clinked glasses, his eyes meeting mine. I couldn't help but smile and my heart did a little flip. "All lies, I'm sure," I quipped, hoping he couldn't see my pulse racing, those little veins throbbing in my neck or forehead.

"Another tradition we must abide to." He extended his hand, pulling me toward the dance floor. "Dance with me."

"I don't dance," I protested.

"Everyone dances," he said with a laugh. "Some just need the right partner."

As we swayed together, him twirling me around a few times, me stumbling, I felt that little spark of connection between us ignite. I didn't want to be that cliché, though. The desperate bridesmaid hooking up with the best man. So, I took a step back, smiled. "I had fun tonight, but I'm exhausted. I'll see you tomorrow at the brunch."

He nodded, pondering my statement. "Cinderella is leaving the ball?"

I let out a short laugh. "She is."

"Well, if you're up to it, we can continue our conversation in New York." He grinned. "Heard you're moving in with Kat. It's all she's been talking about. 'Wait until you meet my roommate, the brilliant Olivia...'"

"She's being too kind."

"You didn't answer my question."

"I didn't realize you'd asked one."

His eyes went wide. "I was asking you out on a date."

"Oh," I said, blinking.

"Is that a no?" he asked.

"Sorry," I said, and his lips twisted. "I mean, I'd love to go out with you"—I paused, not wanting to appear overly exuberant—"once I settle in."

He pulled out his phone from the pocket of his tux. "Then, we should probably exchange information now. I'm not staying for brunch, taking off with Mark for Mykonos." He rolled his eyes. "After meeting you, he's the last person I want to spend time with..."

"I get it," I said. "And I'd love to meet up again."

As Steven punched my number into his phone, I looked

over his shoulder to find Sienna sending daggers in my direction. She turned on her heel, gliding away, her figure disappearing into the olive gardens lit by the full moon. Regardless of her erratic behavior, I soon found myself truly excited for this next chapter in my life.

New York City, here I come!

ACT TWO

FIFTEEN

(NOW)

Miriam saunters up to the table and envelops Mark in a warm hug. "It's so wonderful to see you." She pauses. "But I didn't know you and Liv were connected."

Mark grins and clasps my hand. "We've been seeing each other for a while now."

Miriam grimaces. "Does Kat know?"

"She will. The secret's out."

"OK, then," she says, not masking her surprise. "Good luck with that." She turns to me and pats my shoulder. "Liv, you're up for your meeting with Rebecca. She's very keen on meeting you."

My heart races. "Where do I go?"

"The gazebo by the pond," Miriam informs, pointing. "It's right over there. You have five minutes to get there and fifteen minutes with her. Make those minutes count."

"OK," I reply, meeting Miriam's unwavering gaze.

A nagging thought tugs at my mind as I watch Miriam stride away. I'm trying to maintain a calm composure despite the unease brewing inside of me. Everybody is here. Now, I'm just waiting for Kat to arrive.

Mark kisses me on the cheek and whispers, "Good luck. I'm rooting for you. I'm going to hit the trails before the storm hits."

"Right," I say. "See you later."

"Knock her dead," says Mark as I walk away.

"Bad choice of words," I mumble.

With a bitter taste in my mouth, I make my way toward the gazebo. My footsteps falter as I head over to the pond, the geese honking mockingly. It's like they know I'm going to have to wing it. With a deep breath, I do my best to focus on my feet. I'm definitely not on my A-game for this very important rendezvous.

My stomach churns with each step I take toward Rebecca, her silhouette backlit by a slash of light the rolling clouds haven't snuffed out yet. She must have heard the sound of my heavy breathing, because she looks over her shoulder and smiles. She's older, probably in her mid-fifties or early sixties with short-cropped gray hair.

"Olivia, there you are," she says, lowering her glasses to the bridge of her nose.

"Here I am," I say with a modest shrug, trying to find my breath.

"Come join me." She pats the seat beside her. "The view here is spectacular."

The view, once you look past the obnoxious geese strutting in front of the gazebo like they own the place, is truly breathtaking. The rolling hills and dense forests create a picturesque backdrop, and the pond shimmers with the harsh light of the impending storm. The surface of the pond catches my eye, and for a moment, it's like looking into a funhouse mirror, my mouth open in exaggerated fear.

I take in a deep breath. Nothing about this scenario is helping to calm my nerves. Even the clouds rolling in the sky mimic the turmoil roiling around in my gut.

"Don't mind the birds," says Rebecca. She throws some bread to the other side of the gazebo. "I've been bribing them. They'll be on their best behavior."

I force a smile, making a mental note to bring bread with me everywhere I go.

Rebecca's voice drips with false sweetness. "I must say, I was quite captivated by the pages you sent over when you signed up. Have a seat," she instructs, and I do as I'm told.

"Thanks, I—"

"I read your manuscript on the ride over." Her smile turns from sweet to predatory. "Care to explain how you managed to plagiarize a book that hasn't even been published yet?"

My blood runs cold. "What are you talking about?"

Rebecca taps her nails on the iPad set on the table in front of her. "*In Her Skin* by Lila Aiken. It's the book I just procured from Foster Literary. Ring any bells?"

I blink, my jaw dropping open. Bells? Oh, I'm hearing them. I can't say a word.

"Are you Lila Aiken? Are you trying to pull one over on me?" Rebecca continues, her tone becoming menacingly neutral. "If you are, I can assure you that I don't find this game of yours funny." She scoffs. "What did you think, we wouldn't notice? Did you think you could sell your book to another publisher and receive two advances? Believe me, after I'm done with you... you won't. You'll never write again."

Her threat snaps me to attention. I've had it with threats and warnings. I meet her eyes, mine fierce. "Rebecca, I swear I've never heard of Lila Aiken. *In Her Shoes*—the story you've read—is based on my own life experiences, but fictionalized." I pause and breathe deeply. "Wait a second. Why are you asking me if I'm Lila Aiken? You don't know who she is?"

She doesn't answer me for a moment, just lets out a long sigh.

"Nobody does, not even Victoria. Believe me, we've been trying to find out," she says with a frown. "She signed the contract. Victoria is waiting for bank details so we can send the first payment out." Her eyes meet mine. "Should we just cut to the chase and send the payment to you?"

I know a little bit about how traditional publishing works. One quarter of a book advance is paid upon the signing of the contract, one quarter is paid upon approval of a manuscript, one quarter when the book is published, and the rest six months after publication. But one thing doesn't add up. Laws don't protect pen names and there could be potential legal repercussions. "What about the copyright?"

"They're using the name Lila Aiken. And, like I said, I think that person is you."

"I'm *not* Lila Aiken."

She leans forward, eyes narrowing. "Then how do you explain the uncanny similarities? The eerily identical passages? The exact same plot."

My hands clench into fists. This can't be happening. How could someone else have written this story? My heartbeat accelerates. "Somebody must have gotten their hands on the manuscript. I've been working on it for three years..."

Rebecca's gaze softens slightly, but skepticism still lingers. "Olivia, if you're in some kind of trouble..."

I'm in so much trouble. Kat Sterling has made her next play. She's trying to kill my career. What's next? I shudder.

"I don't know what's going on," I say, my voice trembling. "But *In Her Shoes* is my book."

As Rebecca hesitates with her response, a flock of geese take flight from the pond, their shadows passing over us like an omen.

"When did you query Victoria?" she asks.

"A few weeks ago," I reply, my voice screechy. "When did you receive this Lila's manuscript?"

"Two months ago. Made an offer the day it came in," she says, the light in her eyes darkening. "Did you share your work with anyone?"

I nod, head down, thinking. I've only shared the manuscript with two people... and one of them is dead. Steven had only seen an early draft; the entire manuscript changed after the incident. Mark wouldn't betray me like this, would he? No, he's been utterly supportive of my writing. I'm shaking. I want to mention Kat, but something in my gut is telling me not to.

"I'm part of an online critique group," I whisper, rubbing my mouth. At least this is true. "We call ourselves The Fab Five Scribes."

"Do you have their names? Email addresses? I'd like to look into them. We have a system at SilverGate." She clucks her tongue. "This is bad. Really bad."

My lower lip quivers. If only she could see the position I've been put in. This is supposed to be a moment of triumph, not an inquisition. This is supposed to be the way I reclaim my life, not destroy it. "I know."

"Do you have any proof that you wrote this book?"

My head bobs yes up and down like a madwoman. My words come out in a breathless whoosh. "I always email myself copies of the manuscript as I write. You know, in case my computer goes haywire, or I mess up a draft and have to get it back. And I also stored everything on the cloud. Aside from that, I also have the whole story written down in one of my journals. Loose notes. But notes all the same."

"Unfortunately, the Internet here is shoddy at best, always dropping off." Rebecca sighs. "If I had known that, I would never have agreed to come on this retreat. An editor's work is never done." She scratches her forehead, her eyes lighting up. "Do you, by chance, have the journal with you?"

"I do," I say. "I never leave home without it. Every raw emotion, every twisted memory—it's all there in black and white, written by hand."

She looks at her watch. "My next appointment is in a couple minutes. Let's say we continue this conversation tomorrow. I, for one, would like to get to the bottom of this."

"Me too," I say, my heart thumping.

She groans. "If what you're saying is true, heads—namely mine—are going to roll. I vetted that manuscript. Thankfully, we haven't sent the first payment out yet. Paid seven figures for it."

My eyes go wide. "You thought it was that good?"

"I did. A bestseller."

I can't hide my grin. "That's amazing."

She frowns. "*If* you wrote it."

One of the Bees—don't know which one—is racing toward the gazebo. I stand up too quickly, dizzy from a head rush and information overload. "I think your next meeting is here."

"I'll see you tomorrow," she says. "Bring the journal."

"I will," I respond with a hard swallow. "Thank you for your time. And thank you for believing me."

She throws her hands into the air. "Honestly, I don't know what to believe anymore."

Me neither. But instinct tells me where the truth lies.

Queen Bee Kat Sterling is having her little hive do her work for her because she'd never, ever get her hands dirty. Now, I just have to protect myself from her sting.

SIXTEEN

(NOW)

I'm not exactly running as I cross the grounds, but speed-walking, breathless and laser-focused on my task: getting the journal. I'm winded when I reach the door. As I'm hunched over with my hands on my knees, trying to catch my breath, I hear the crunch of tires in the driveway. I look over my shoulder to see an electric-blue Range Rover pulling in. One Manolo Blahnik at a time, she steps out of the vehicle.

Kat Sterling is finally here.

For a moment, I stand in silent awe, remembering the good times we'd shared, watching her as she stretches her arms into the sky, her face shielded by extra-large sunglasses, her every movement swift and deliberate. Cat-like. She's beautiful—tall and lanky, her long black hair is smooth. I don't think she's ever had a bad hair day.

This is what I wanted, wasn't it? But not like this. I have to come up with a better plan, to take her by surprise, not the other way around. She rolls her shoulders and she's about to turn, but before she sees me, I race into the building.

I stride down the luxurious hallway of Nyx, my heart

racing. I fling the door to my room open and freeze at the sight before me. A crow—black as sin and twice as mean—is thrashing against the windows, its wings a frantic blur. The violence of its wings flapping echoes my own heartbeat, erratic and panicked. I can deal with a lot of things, but a rogue bird in my freaking hotel room is so out of my wheelhouse. The memory of the seagull attacking me in Greece hits. My hands fly to my cheeks to protect my face.

The bird's beady eyes lock onto mine, a mirror of my own terror. I should leave. I should run. I should slam the door closed, but I don't. Now that Kat's here, I really need the journal. She's always played dirty right from the start. But this is too much.

My legs give out from underneath me without warning, and I collapse into the corner of the doorway, clutching my knees as if trying to anchor myself to something. I think I'm about to have a panic attack. The only sounds are my frantic, uneven breaths and the maddening beat of wings—thump, thump, flap; thump, thump, flap—that reverberate in my head.

A sickening thud. Then silence.

I lift my head, my trembling fingers acting as a shield as my eyes explore the room. There lies a lifeless crow in a pool of blood, crimson dripping down its pointy beak, black feathers floating in the air and dropping to the floor. The sight twists my stomach into knots. I want to scream, but I can't. Nothing comes out.

Heavy footsteps pummel the hall and Mark's voice, thick with urgency and concern. "Liv? Liv! Are you alright?"

Right. My knight in shining armor has come to save the day. Except I don't trust him as far as I can throw him. I don't trust anybody. Kind of a coincidence that he shows up and, right afterwards, I find a crow in my room. Does he know how much birds terrify me? My right hand traces the scar under my eye.

Mark crouches beside me, eyes flickering between the dead bird and me. "Jesus Christ, what happened?" he demands, a mixture of alarm and amusement in his tone.

Nothing about this situation is funny.

My voice catches and I speak in broken, ragged fragments: "I-I don't..." I stutter, feebly gesturing toward the bloody mess. "Bird. Dead. In. Room."

His hand finds a place on my back, attempting circular motions to calm me down. "Breathe, Liv. Just breathe."

Tears brim in my eyes, and I whisper, "I'm trying."

"Did you leave the window open?"

My head shakes silently, and a pit of anger roils in my stomach. Yep, of course this would be my fault.

"Let's see if we can change rooms," Mark suggests.

"You're staying with me?"

"I figured you wouldn't mind."

I barely register his words, his assumption. "Rebecca... she said... my book... someone else's..." The confession spills out in a rush as I gasp for air. "She accused me of plagiarizing my own goddamn story," I manage finally, voice quivering.

I force myself up slowly, driven by the need to recover my journal—the only tangible evidence that could salvage my writing career. In a burst of frantic energy, I rip open my suitcase, scattering clothes in a disorderly cascade over the bed, panic stretching every muscle. "It's not here!"

"I'll help," Mark offers, steadying me by placing his hands on my shoulders. "Calm down and tell me what to look for..."

"My journal—the one with all my notes for my book," I

wheeze, tugging at my disheveled hair as if trying to unravel my thoughts.

I glare at him.

Like me, Mark has been under Kat's spell. He could be one of her ploys, one of her robots. Desperation drives me toward Mark's sleek leather bag; I drop to my knees and frantically search, tossing his boxers to the floor, his ironed polo shirts. "Did you take it?"

"Liv, don't be so paranoid," he says. "Your journal has to be somewhere." He heads toward the bathroom as I continue tossing cushions and blankets off the bed in a frenzy.

A second later, his voice echoes from the bathroom, "Uh, Liv, I think I found it."

My heart plummets, dread churning inside me as I join him, only to see my precious journal submerged in the toilet bowl—pages grotesquely swollen, ink bleeding into sickly streams across ruined paper. "No," I choke out, "no, no, no!"

I meet Mark's troubled gaze, my voice lowering to a harsh whisper. "Kat's trying to destroy me. She's done it before..." I cut myself off and blurt out, "Did you know this place used to be the headquarters for a cult? Kat and Sienna were part of it when they were teenagers."

Mark sinks onto the bed, his voice heavy. His eyes search mine. He already knows about this. "I was sworn to secrecy. How much did she tell you?"

My reply is grim. "Everything."

But I know Kat didn't tell me *everything*. Not by a long shot. There is way more to her story. She only told me what she'd thought I needed to hear.

Mark lets out a sigh and points at the bloodstain on the floor. "I'm grabbing Sienna. I think we should all leave. Right now."

My spine goes rigid and I squeeze my eyes shut. "You can leave if you want to, but I'm staying. I have to prove *In Her Shoes* is my story..."

"I don't understand your reasoning." He places a hand on my back. "I don't want anything bad to happen to you."

"It already has." I sniffle. Kat isn't going to take anything away from me ever again. I need to be strong. I need to find out what he knows. "Why did Kat buy this property?"

"Your guess is as good as mine," he says.

I let out a grunt. I don't have to guess. I already know because she told me her reasons once. I just didn't believe her.

SEVENTEEN

(THEN)

KAT

For the next four months, Sienna and I spent every weekend at Nexus, connecting with each other, connecting to our inner goddesses. Like addicts, we were both hooked on Tobias's lessons.

The week before we left to go back to our homes for the holiday break—the time when our parents pretended to love us by buying us more stuff—the two of us were doing yoga in the barn.

"Goddesses in the making," said Tobias. "I stopped by to wish you the happiest of holiday seasons and to give you this." He held out an envelope. "Before you pass on to the next level, there's a little issue you need to take care of. It's time to pay your dues. By my calculations, you've spent three and a half months here."

Our jaws dropped.

"Morgan said it wasn't a problem..."

Tobias tilted his head to the side, lips pursed. "I comped

you the first weekend, but you've been taking advantage of me." He grinned. "Look, you both signed right on the dotted line." He handed each one of us a bill, along with a copy of the contract. "I'm running a business, not a charity."

I looked at the paper in my hand. The number. I let out a yelp. "Fifty thousand dollars? Each?"

He nodded. "It includes the week you spent here over Thanksgiving."

"I'm not paying this," I said.

"Okay," he said, with a shrug. "Your choice. But you signed the contract, and I will make sure the debt is paid. If you don't pay, I'll send the bill to your parents. And"—his lashes fluttered—"you'll never achieve the next level of enlightenment."

We stood there numb, staring blankly ahead.

Sienna's head hung low. "This could destroy my father's political career."

Tobias made the sign of the cross. "In the name of the mother, of the daughter, and the earthly goddess, I hope you make the right decision." He turned on his heel. Before he left, he stopped in the doorway, and said, "Happy holidays. I hope to see you upon your return. We'll have your initiation ceremony. Namaste."

My hands shot to my eyes, rubbing them. In silence, Sienna and I jumped into my car and headed back to the dorms of Woodford Hall. "I'll pay," I said as we walked up the steps. "For both of us. With the inheritance my grandfather left me."

"But," said Sienna, "I thought you wouldn't receive it until you turned eighteen. And you're not even seventeen. You're on the edge of seventeen—"

"I received a percentage of it when he died."

Sienna's bottom lip quivered. "And then what do we do?"

"Play along until we burn Nexus down to the ground."

Although I loved spending time in the great outdoors, I'd never been so happy to see the concrete jungle that is New York—the lights, the honking, the yelling. Sienna and I didn't say a word on the ride home, just sang along to holiday songs, pretending like we didn't have a care in the world.

Finally, we were back in the city, pulling into my garage, located a block from my home. I parked in my spot and before grabbing our bags we linked hands, an unspoken promise between us: *Don't breathe a word about what happened to us to anybody.*

"I'll see you for my parents' party on the twenty-fourth."

"Wouldn't miss it," said Sienna. "We'll sneak a bottle of champagne and head up to your room like usual."

"Celebrating our freedom," I said with a swift nod. "By planning our escape."

Christmas came and went. So did my seventeenth birthday. My parents kissed me on the cheek, gave me another Rolex and a diamond and sapphire necklace. So very appropriate. One thing I did take away from my time at Nexus was that material possessions didn't really mean anything. But revenge did. New Year's Eve dropped like the ball in Times Square, and we hadn't really formulated a plan on how to take Tobias down.

Soon, we were in my car, heading back to Woodford Hall. Only this time I had a duffle bag filled with one hundred thousand in cash. My banker thought I was nuts until I explained I was buying my parents a surprise trip to the Maldives. He'd whistled, "Nice present. Want to get married?"

I sneered at him. "I'm only seventeen."

That shut him up.

Sienna and I spent the week attending our classes, pretending nothing was wrong. We hung out with Mouse and the boys, playing ping-pong or watching bad movies.

Finally, Friday came. We raced to my car, gunning it to Nexus. The gates opened and I parked in front of the main lodge. Tobias came out to greet us. "I'm assuming you're moving forward on your path to enlightenment," he stated.

Sienna and I bowed our heads, hiding our cringes. "In the name of the mother, the daughter, and the earthly goddess."

He lifted up his chin. "I believe you have something for me?"

I nodded and retrieved the duffle bag from the back of the car, handing it over.

"I'm trusting it's all there," he said. "Such a shame we missed the winter solstice, but we'll have your ceremony tonight and you can meet the others. Have you picked out your goddess names?"

"Yes, Tobias."

"Good," he said. "Your clothing is waiting for you in your room. Get dressed, meet me back here, and we'll get started. The ceremony will take place in Nyx's garden." He pointed toward the snow-capped mountains, to the ground. "Beautiful, isn't it? This is a real winter wonderland."

I shivered.

On the way up to the room, Sienna mouthed, "I don't think I can go through with this."

"Me, neither, but he has to be stopped," I whispered. "Don't forget. We're in this together."

We nodded.

The outfits that awaited us were not orange, but pure white—a white dress, a fur coat, with matching fur boots and headband. "I feel like we're going to be sacrificed," said Sienna.

"No," I said. "He's the one who will be going down."

We got dressed and made our way down the stairs, where Tobias waited. "Come join me in the dining room. We always start the ceremony with a tea."

"You're not poisoning us, are you?" I blurted out.

"Don't be ridiculous, Kat. If the two of you society girls go missing, what would I say to the police?"

He had a point.

He poured the tea into cups, handing us one each. "In the name of the mother, the daughter, and the earthly goddess, the ceremony shall begin." He gulped his tea down in one swallow and then met our gazes. "Drink."

Well, he drank it. Why not? We swallowed back the tea like he did.

"It tastes like dirt," said Sienna.

"Exactly," said Tobias. "We're harnessing the power of the earth. Now, follow me."

The two of us exchanged a confused look and wandered outside. On the walk to the garden, Sienna started laughing, "I'm feeling really loopy. Look at all the butterflies! So pretty! Do you see them?"

There were no butterflies.

I knew right then he'd drugged us with something,

confirmed when he said, "Magic mushroom tea. For your experience." He laughed. "Me? I'm fine. I'm here to guide you."

I wanted to run, but couldn't, because my mind whirled and my legs felt like they were made of lead. Tobias led us down the snow-covered path to the statue of Nyx.

Surrounding us were people wearing animal masks and costumes—rabbits with long fluffy ears, peacocks, deer with majestic antlers. They gently took hold of our arms and guided us toward a roaring fire, their bodies swaying to a primal rhythm while chanting, "Our new goddesses have arrived!"

The scene was surreal, almost dream-like in its haziness. Tobias beat on a drum, his voice joining in the chant as someone played a haunting flute melody.

A woman's voice whispered in my ear, "Come, dance." The warning lights flashing in my head stopped. Just like that. My hesitation melted away as the drug that Tobias had given us surged through my veins. The lights above us were mesmerizing, akin to the shifting colors of the aurora borealis in the night sky. And then everything went dark as the drug fully took hold of me.

I woke up a few hours later, groggy, the taste of dirt on my tongue, my throat parched. The fire still roared beside us. Tobias approached me, leaning over, a brow lifted. "Kat, you're on your path to enlightenment."

I swallowed, aching for water. "I'm really thirsty. What did you do to us?"

He handed me a bottle of water. "Drink."

When I recoiled, he said, "Don't worry. I promise, it's just water."

Dying of thirst, I took it and chugged, water spilling down my chin, my neck. "What did you do to us?" I repeated.

"Nothing you didn't ask for." His lips pinched into an evil grin. "Do you like your new tattoo?"

I didn't know what he was talking about. "What tattoo?"

"The one on your upper-left butt cheek. The scales—the symbol of Nemesis."

I twisted my body and pulled up the white gauzy dress I was wearing. I craned my neck to look. It wasn't a tattoo. It was a burn mark. "You branded us?"

"You're the one who asked for it... to bring you closer to Nyx and to me. You really are a wildcat, Kat."

I shuddered under his gaze. "I did no such thing."

"You howled at the moon during your initiation cere-mony. Both of you did." He grinned. "We have a video of it."

Flashes of the wild celebration came back to me. I held up my hands. "I'm out. We both are."

"You're not out," he said flatly, his beady eyes narrowing. "Not by a long shot."

"What the hell do you mean by that?"

He whipped out a folder from behind his back. "I really don't think your parents want to see what I have on you, your friend, and them."

One by one, he held a series of glossy photos in front of my face.

"What would happen if the senator's daughter is found in a predicament like this? She'd be destroyed and, well, it would probably destroy his political career. Not to mention Sienna's prescriptions, and the other things we have on all of you—the bullying, the plagiarized essays, the drug use, the insider trading, the parental abuse..."

"Our parents didn't abuse us," I said half-heartedly.

"They did. They neglected you, the reason you're here."

The world spun around me, the trees blurring into one. I wanted to vomit. We'd been set up, targeted. Drugged. Lied to. Manipulated. Blackmailed. And worse.

Tobias delivered the final blow. "I want ten million—no, make that fifteen, wired to my account within a week. Say no, and, well, your entire world is going to collapse."

"I don't have that kind of m-money," I said, stuttering.

"But your parents do. Who knows? This might bring you closer to them." He handed me the folder and grinned. "Don't worry, we have copies. Call my cell when you have the money. I wrote it down. It's in the folder. So are wiring instructions."

I raced across the lawn, grabbing Sienna. "We're leaving now."

Her eyes were glazed. "Why? I'm having fun, the time of my life."

I whipped out the photo, shoved it in front of her face. "You call blackmail fun?"

Well, the image of her and Steven sobered her up quickly. We raced across the lawn to the car, and I tore like a bat out of hell, driving straight to Woodford Hall. We needed to change, get our heads together.

On the ride back to the city, I had my parents call the Knights, explaining how Tobias was trying to blackmail the two of us. I told them to call the FBI. For once, they took me seriously. When we finally arrived at our townhouse, two agents were waiting outside. One of them said, "We've been looking into Tobias Rane for a while. We're glad your parents called us in."

As the two of us told the story to the Feds, we shielded the damning photos from our parents. They wouldn't be able to un-see them. Special Agent Murphy nodded. "OK. We've got him on statutory rape and, by your testimonies, racketeering, not to mention the pyramid scheme we've been investigating. Kat, make the call and we'll put a pin in his balloon."

The FBI had linked my phone to some device. I dialed. "Tobias Rane."

"It's Kat."

"Hello, my little kitten, I'm hoping you have some good news for me."

You're going to prison for a very long time?

"I need your account number. Wiring instructions."

"It was in the folder."

"Must have slipped out when I ran to the car."

"Hope you have a pen."

"I do. And you're depleting my trust fund."

"Poor baby." He rambled off a series of numbers that I didn't bother writing down.

"You were right, people are always after something from you." He laughed. "And another lesson. Look for your opponent's weak points. Expose them. But you already knew that, didn't you?" Click. The line went dead.

I let out an angry breath. Sienna burst into tears.

"We got him," said the other agent. "You did really well. Our people are on the way to arrest him now. And I can assure you that more of his victims will come forward."

. . .

After the two of us signed sworn affidavits, a couple of hours later the Feds left and our parents railed into us. "We love you, but we can't believe how stupid you were. How could you let that happen? You're smarter than that. We thought we'd raised you better."

Funny, they didn't raise us at all, just shucked their parental duties onto others—the nannies, the maids, anybody but them.

I stood up, nodding toward Sienna. "We're exhausted, traumatized, and we're going to my room. Victims, which is what we are, have to stick together."

Our parents slapped their hands over their mouths, and my mom shouted, "You have no right to speak to us like that."

We marched to my room. And then we fell onto the floor and bawled our eyes out, hugging one another, snot running down our noses. Reality—a brutal one—was certainly sinking in. Sienna looked up. "I'm never trusting another outsider again. It's just us."

"Just us," I agreed.

Tobias Rane's arrest was all over the news, the story of how two never-named under-aged teens led the Feds to his demise. Sienna and I did not go back to Woodford. Our parents had decided to have us home schooled, until they figured out what to do with us. We were prohibited from speaking to one another and basically put under house arrest. If I wanted to go for a walk to get some fresh air, a bodyguard, James, accompanied me.

Six months passed, and more victims of Nexus came forward. Tobias Rane was convicted of statutory rape, extortion, wire-fraud conspiracy, and racketeering, and sentenced to one hundred and twenty years in prison. Along with Rane, other members of Nexus were charged and convicted. Their names meant nothing to me, mostly because I'd never met them.

Only one name mattered to me—Morgan Rane. And her whereabouts were unknown. It was like she didn't exist. She'd never attended Woodford. There was no record of her birth. There was nothing.

You could say, she'd scarred me for life.

But I didn't want to have the scar removed. No, I wanted to be reminded of what I went through, so I'd never make those kinds of life-altering mistakes again. The photos? I gave them to the Feds... and nobody, save for people within the judicial system, would see them. The Feds found the copies, the negatives.

Soon I had more freedom. I could leave the house, although with a bodyguard tracking my every move. I could have a life—the one Morgan had taken away from me. Mostly, I just walked around in Central Park, watching the world go by.

Another year passed, and I was going to attend Columbia in the fall—close to home, yet far away enough. I'd heard it through the grapevine—my parents—that Sienna, after spending time in a mental health facility, would be attending Syracuse. I'd hoped one day we'd be able to reconnect, become friends again.

That day came two years later, and our reunion wasn't a joyful one.

My parents, wanting to see where my nightmare had taken place with their own eyes, drove up to Nexus. The property had been seized and was now owned by the government. They didn't have cars, so they took my Escalade. It was one week before Christmas and the roads were slick with ice. On the ride up, the car skidded off the road, right into the icy Hudson River. At first, the police ruled their deaths as an accident. But after the Escalade was pulled out of the Hudson, they discovered somebody had cut the brake line.

The girls came to my parents' funeral.

The police questioned me, the heiress to the Sterling fortune, for hours. I pleaded with them to track down Morgan Rane—sure the accident was meant for me. I was the one who led the Feds to her father. They didn't believe me, kept telling me she didn't exist.

A couple of years passed. I'd graduated from Columbia, and I was looking forward to the future, one I could control. When I found out the government had put the Nexus compound up for sale, the girls thought I was nuts when I said I was going to buy it, until I explained my reasons: I was going to burn that lodge to the ground and create something new, something good from the bad.

EIGHTEEN

(NOW)

Thoughts of Kat's past revelations swirl around in my brain and my gaze shoots to the window. Outside, the sky has darkened to a charcoal gray. Mark's restless pacing is driving me nuts. I clutch the sodden journal on my lap, the pages smeared, water dripping down my legs and onto the floor. I don't think Kat wanted to create something good from the bad. I think she wanted to take control of the situation. Knowing Kat, she'd wanted the power.

Mark stops pacing and stands in front of me, his hands on his hips. I can see the concern on his face, darkening his eyes. "Does Sienna know you know about the cult?"

I shake my head slowly, feeling a lump form in my throat as I recall the rift between Sienna and me. "No," I admit, swallowing hard. "We drifted apart after I moved in with Kat."

He nods, his gaze unwavering. "And things worsened between the two of you when Steven entered the picture."

"It wasn't intentional," I say with a sigh. I'm being put on the defensive. "I didn't think it would bother her. After all, she was married to Nick—"

"It did bother her. A lot," he says, and I hang my head. "Please, promise me you won't mention anything about the cult to her. It could shatter her already fragile state of mind."

"Not a problem. She doesn't even talk to me," I say, thinking she never really talked to me. "And if she's so fragile, why is she here?"

"You're right. And I think the three of us should leave. Right now," he says, frowning. "I don't have a good feeling about this."

And here we are, back to this again.

I turn my back on him. "No. First of all, you're not even supposed to be here. I have to fight for my future. I have to prove Kat stole my manuscript. I have to prove she's Lila Aiken. Don't you get it?"

"I don't. Because you won't prove anything if you're dead," he says, blowing out an angry breath. "Are you forgetting about Steven?"

"I'm not…" I begin, turning to face him. He's shaking his head, his eyes narrowed with suspicion. "What are you thinking about?"

"I don't know what to think anymore." He pulls me in for a hug, the scent of his spicy aftershave calming for a moment. He squeezes my hand and turns toward the door. "Look, I'll see what I can find out. I'll talk to her. And then we're leaving. OK?"

I nod, but I'm not agreeing with him. I'm not leaving this place until I confront Kat. Until I get what I came for.

After the door closes behind Mark, I stare out the window, watching the sky darken. A sudden knock almost has my heart leaping into my throat. A voice filters through the wood: "Liv, it's Trinity."

I mutter a curse under my breath and shuffle to the door, opening it. Trinity stands with a bright smile, a notebook clutched in her hand. She doesn't wait for an invitation and sweeps into my room, a breeze following with her scent—tea-rose perfume. "Good. Perfect timing. He's not here. Ready to commiserate?"

As much as I'd like her on my side, I'm too drained to play along. I just can't meet her halfway.

"I can't," I say, my tone sharp. I instantly regret how harsh I sound, but it's too late to take it back. "Sorry. I'm working on something, and I've gotten absolutely zero accomplished."

"Can't you carve out one hour for me?" Her eyes search mine for some sign of compromise. "It's on the schedule and we still have tons to go over."

How can I explain the urgency I feel to figure out Kat's plan? To do that, I need to filter through information like a sieve. Thankfully, Trinity hasn't looked down at the spot on the floor, hasn't noticed the feathers. But she does notice the sopping-wet journal on the bed. "What happened? Did it get caught in the rain?"

"No, it fell into the toilet. I'm a klutz. Long story," I say, trying to come up with an excuse on the fly to make her leave. "Mark will be back here any minute."

"We're supposed to be working together. It's a writing retreat, not a romantic getaway."

"I need a break. OK?"

"No, not OK. You promised that you and I would talk." Her eyes blaze into mine. "I want to know how Kat wrapped you up in her world and what it has to do with Steven Shepherd's murder."

I swallow so hard my throat burns. My hand flies to my eye, rubbing it. While I have her ear, I'll have the opportunity to pump her for information, find out what she knows. By the expression on her face, she's not going to let me out of this. "Fine. But everything I tell you is off the record."

She flashes me a wicked grin. "Let's head to my room. This place is a mess."

Begrudgingly, I follow her, closing the door behind me.

We make it to Trinity's suite, sitting cross-legged facing each other, on the couch. The words tumble out when I tell my story, just condensed into breathless phrases. She shoots me an odd look, as if she's expecting more.

I let out a breath. "I'm getting to the good part now. You'll see. I should never have moved to New York. I should never have moved in with Kat. And when Steven Shepherd came into the picture, well, that's when everything in my world turned upside down."

NINETEEN

(THEN)

There I was, standing in front of the most intimidating door I'd ever seen. Because it wasn't just a door; it was a gateway to another world—Kat's world. Even though we'd been texting daily, what if I showed up and Kat said, "Ha, ha, ha, you thought I was serious?"

Surprise! The joke would be on me.

I took a deep breath and rang the doorbell. The chime echoed inside, probably bouncing off marble floors and crystal chandeliers. The door swung open, and there she stood—Kat Sterling in all her glory. She wore a sleek black dress that probably cost more than my entire wardrobe, her dark hair cascading down her shoulders like a shampoo commercial. Her eyes? They practically sparkled with... mischief? Intrigue? World domination plans? Hard to tell.

"Liv! You're here!" she said with a grin. "Finally!"

"I am."

She snapped her fingers. "Frank, come take care of Liv's bags."

A man, around forty years old, scurried to the front landing. He was huge—at least six feet tall and built like a line-backer. "Frank, this is Liv. Liv, Frank. Frank is my all-around man, my personal concierge, if you will."

He nodded. "Welcome to Casa Sterling," he said, not one hint of emotion in his tone.

"Well, don't just stand there looking so timid, come in!" Kat purred, enveloping me in a tight hug. "Welcome to your new home!"

I managed to squeak out an "OK" while trying not to trip over my own feet.

And holy. Freaking. Chicago Cows.

Even though I'd barely stepped in the entryway, I felt like I'd just passed into what I can only describe as an alternate universe. Kat's townhouse was... well, let's just say my grandpa's entire apartment could fit into the foyer. "Thanks, Kat. This is... wow. Just wow."

Way to go, Liv, I thought. So eloquent with your words. And I was supposed to be a writer.

Kat laughed, a tinkling sound like fizzy champagne bubbles. "You haven't seen anything yet."

As Kat gave me a tour, pointing out features like she was reading from a luxury real-estate brochure, I caught my reflection in one of the many mirrors adorning the walls. Same old Liv—medium-length brown hair, athletic build from years of trying to outrun my own ambition. But now I'm Liv-in-Wonderland, tumbling down the rabbit hole into a world of luxury I can barely comprehend.

When we landed in the kitchen—all stainless steel and marble countertops—Kat turned to me with a smile. "Champagne?"

"Now?" I questioned. "It's not even noon."

She chuckled and grabbed a bottle of Dom from the

fridge, popping off the cork like a professional. "It's never too early for champagne. And, honestly, I'm so glad you're here, Liv. I have a feeling this is the start of something... special." She winked. "We're celebrating your arrival, yes?"

As she poured the champagne into crystal flutes, I smiled back, pushing down the little voice in my head that screamed, "Careful!"

Champagne in hand, we continued the tour, my battered purse from Target slung over my shoulder. I felt very out of place amongst the Picassos and Monets adorning the walls, while Kat chattered away about the history of each priceless artifact. I nodded along, trying to look like I knew the difference between Baroque and Rococo.

My words rushed out in a breathless whisper. "I can't believe I'm going to live here."

She winked. "Oh, this old place?"

After making our way up to the roof deck, with views of Central Park, we traipsed down the stairs again. "My rooms and my office are there," she said, pointing, "and *our* closet, is here." She led me into a lacquered white room filled with floor-to-ceiling clothes, shoes, and accessories galore, and where I found Frank unpacking my bags and grimacing, a sack of garbage bags beside him.

"Anything worth keeping?" Kat asked, tapping her foot.

"No," he said, throwing a sweater I'd purchased on sale at Macy's into a sack. "Nothing yet. Everything should be burned. It's bad." He clucked his tongue. "Real bad."

I stood, stunned. "Are you throwing my clothes away?"

"No," he said with a shrug. "We're donating them to charity."

"Don't I get a say in this?"

"You do." Kat laughed. "But not until you see your new wardrobe." She pointed toward the right side of the closet.

My throat constricted. "You bought me clothes?"

"You're starting a new life. And the clothes came with a no-return policy. I bought them on sale. Take a look."

A new life? I thought. I knew Kat meant well, but she had a way of steamrolling over people's feelings in the name of helping them. This time, it felt like more than I could handle, and I wasn't quite sure what to expect next.

Here's another one of those surprises. There was that job offer, the one I thought was going to launch my career in the city. I'd already envisioned my new office, bought heels I couldn't afford. Two weeks after I'd moved in with Kat, I found out the company had chosen another candidate "at the last minute," and, oh yeah, they'd sent me a rejection email that ended up in my spam folder. So I'd been waiting, hoping, envisioning a bright new beginning.

I knocked on Kat's office door, sobbing. "The job. The one I moved here for? It didn't pan out. I'm so thankful for everything, but I don't want to be a burden. I think I'll move back to Chicago—"

"No, you won't." She shrugged. "Do you really want to work for some boring company? You can work with me," she said. "I'm working on a huge project—one I'm very excited about." She lifted a brow, tapped what looked like architectural plans. "It's top secret, but I'll let you in on the surprise. I've purchased some land and I'm working on some stellar developments..."

"I don't know anything about real estate," I said. "And

you've already done so much for me. I really want to pave my own way."

"But you want to be a writer. And you'd have more time to write." She pulled out a large package wrapped in gold foil. "Open it and then we'll get back to this conversation."

I blinked when I lifted the top of the box off. Inside rested an iPhone, an iPad, and a MacBook Air. I groaned. "Kat, once again, this is too much."

"Maybe it's a sign-on advance?" She winked. "Just think about my offer."

"Kat, we're friends. I don't want anything to change that."

"Fine," she said. "I get where you're coming from." She tapped her fingernails on the desk. "I have an idea. One of my contacts runs an events and marketing company..."

"You can't force somebody to hire me..."

She laughed. "Nobody's forcing anybody to do anything. I didn't say I was getting you a job; that's on you. But I can definitely get you an interview. They used to do all the events for Sterling Spirits..."

"I do know marketing," I said.

"And, well, if it doesn't work out, you'll promise to think about plan B."

"Plan B?"

"Working with me."

My phone buzzed: Sienna. I silenced the call and slipped the phone back into my pocket, deciding I'd get back to her later.

After three incredible months of living with Kat, the city had decided to grace us with a rare patch of autumn sunshine, warming the outdoor patio of Le Petit Café where Kat and I'd claimed a coveted table—our table. Every Saturday, this had become our place, just around the corner from the townhouse.

"How's work?" she asked, twirling a lock of her hair. "Are you absolutely loving it?"

"Gretchen can be... how do I put this? Intense."

"But she's really good at what she does. Speaking of intense, remember that little taverna in Santorini?" Kat's eyes sparkled as she leaned in, her voice dropping to a conspiratorial whisper. "The one where the owner kept trying to marry you off to his son?"

I couldn't keep from sniggering, the memory vivid in my mind—right down to the owner's missing teeth. "God, how could I forget? I think I'm still finding olive pits in my purse from that night."

Kat's laughter rose in pitch, drawing glances from nearby tables. She didn't care. That's the thing about Kat—she had a way of capturing everybody in her gravitational pull.

"You should have seen your face when he-he-he...'" Kat laughed and continued, mimicking the taverna owner. "'Ah, such strong hips for bearing many sons!'"

I nearly choked on my latte. "Please, stop. I'm still traumatized."

"Oh, come on, Liv. You have to admit, it was a little flattering." She pinched her fingers together and then blurted out another laugh. "I mean, how often does one get their child-bearing hips appraised."

"Only you could make that sound like a compliment." After snorting out a laugh, I paused dramatically, lifting a brow. "I met somebody at Sienna's wedding. And he asked me out on a date. His name is Steven Shepherd," I said with a coy smile. "He's really cute. Tall. Sandy-blond hair. Thirty years old. I think you'd approve. He's in finance—"

She cut me off. "I know Steven. He went to Woodford... and he and Sienna had quite the romance in high school. It ended badly and this will put another nail—"

"Sienna and I will never be friends again because of—"

"Me. She thinks I stole you from her." Kat's smile faltered for a moment. A dark light shifted in her eyes, and she blinked slowly, absorbing this new information. "I have the best idea. Make it a double date. Mark and I will come along, too." She pulled out her phone, tapped a few keys. "I'll make the reservation. Tell Steven you set it up and have been dying to eat there."

A couple of nights later, I arrived at Luxe, the new hotspot everyone was raving about, feeling a mix of excitement and nerves. First-date jitters, you know? But the moment I saw Steven waiting at the bar, looking like he'd stepped out of a *GQ* spread, those nerves melted away.

"Liv," he said, flashing a million-dollar smile. "You look stunning."

I felt my cheeks flush. "You clean up pretty well yourself, Mr. Shepherd."

"Sorry it's taken me a while to get in touch. It's insanely hectic at work and I figured you needed time to settle in."

"Well, I wasn't staring at my phone, waiting for you to call," I quipped.

The restaurant buzzed around us, all dim lighting and clinking glasses, but I barely noticed. Steven had my full attention. But then, as I was reaching for my wine glass, I saw their arrival.

"What's wrong?" he asked.

"Um, our first date might be a double date."

"Oh," he said, looking over his shoulder, his face paling. "So that's why you chose this place. I really wish you'd warned me about this ambush."

"Ambush?" I parroted. "She's my roommate... and you're friends with Mark."

He clasped onto my hand. "Liv, life is a game of chess with Kat, and I can only take Mark in small doses."

I swallowed as the two made their approach. Kat shot me a tight grin as Mark pulled out a barstool for her. Thankfully the maître d' came over, politely interrupting, and then led us to our table, which, oddly, was set for six. As we sat, Steven tried to keep the conversation going. "So, Liv, you were telling me about your new job?"

Before I could answer, Kat chimed in. "Oh, I remember my first real job—Daddy had me overseeing a small division of our company. Nothing too strenuous, just three hundred or so employees. Liv will be fine. Event planning—not a multi-billion-dollar industry."

I nearly choked on my wine. Why was she throwing me under the bus? She was the one who got me the interview at Thunder Marketing.

"That's... impressive," I managed, my voice sounding weak even to my own ears.

"Small can be charming," a woman's voice interrupted. "I'm sure you'll learn... something, Liv."

Steven's face turned a whole new shade of red. Oh, yes, I picked up on *that* innuendo and I knew the voice of the person who said it. The hair on the back of my neck bristled and I turned my head in shock. Sienna stood behind me, her smile razor-sharp.

"Sorry I'm late, got caught up at a modeling shoot. Nick couldn't make it." Sienna sighed, sitting in the open chair next to Steven. "He's always out of town."

Right about then I wanted to shoot her in between her eyes. OK, maybe that's a bit dramatic. But seriously, who invited Sienna? Oh right, it was Kat, and she just showed up like some sort of perfectly coiffed nightmare.

"Steven," I said, probably a bit too loudly. "Tell us more about that project you mentioned earlier. The one with the sustainable energy startup?"

His eyes lit up like I'd just offered him a golden ticket. "Oh, you remembered! It's fascinating, actually. We're looking at innovative ways to..."

As he talked, I nodded along, asking questions and making mental notes. Take that, Sienna. I can talk shop with the best of them. But the real surprise? Steven. He kept bringing me back into the conversation, even when I could feel my confidence shrinking with every backhanded compliment Sienna threw my way.

"What do you think, Liv?" asked Steven.

Replaying Sienna's quips in my head, I'd missed part of the conversation. I blinked and took a sip of my wine. "Think about what?"

"With your PR background, I bet you'd have some great ideas for our client's campaign. A little social media push?"

Sienna's laugh came hard and furious. "Social media? Liv? You've got to be kidding."

My perfect first date was now a smoking wreck, thanks to Hurricane Sienna. She left before dessert, eyeing me and saying, "Some people should really watch what they eat."

Finally, this torturous evening came to an end. Kat was sleeping over at Mark's, so Steven walked me outside to hail a cab. I stared blankly at a flickering streetlamp. I couldn't shake the feeling of Sienna's eyes boring into me all evening. It was like being under a microscope, every flaw magnified. Did my laugh sound too loud? Was my dress too casual? But here's the thing: Steven's gaze kept drifting from me to Sienna as if he was deliberating, as if questioning whether he'd made the right decision.

"Liv?" Steven's voice snapped me back to the present. "Everything OK?"

I turned to face him. Might as well get this over and done with. "Kat told me about your history with Sienna."

"We were so young. In high school," he said.

"Why did you break up?"

"You'll probably find out anyway." He cleared his throat. "I cheated on her. But that was a lifetime ago and a lot has changed. I've changed. Don't let a young boy's mistake in the past ruin his future." He gulped. "I really want to see you again—the next time alone. Just us."

"I'll think about it," I said.

I hailed a taxi, slid into the cab and closed the door, leaving him standing on the curb.

TWENTY

(THEN)

Even though our first date was a complete disaster, I did see Steven. Again. And again, and again.

He was everything I had hoped for: intelligent, funny, and, more important, genuinely supportive of my writing aspirations and appreciative of my quirks. And I appreciated his. He remembered all those little things, like the way I took my coffee. The way he made up silly songs about us. The way he talked to random animals on the street as if they understood him.

Half a year had slipped by, and Steven and I began to spend more and more time together. Our dates turned more regular, at least twice a week, with me often staying over at his place on the weekends. One night, after we made love, we lay in bed, my hand resting on his chest, and Steven said, "There's something I need to tell you."

Confused, I looked over at him, his face serious.

"I think you should move in with me," he said, grinning. "And I'm also thinking we should get married. Your thoughts?"

Thoughts? Mine were spinning around in my brain. I stared at the ceiling, deliberating. He was everything I'd wanted in a partner, wasn't he? It felt like a natural next step, like we were slowly building something solid. Yet, I couldn't ignore the small voice in my head telling me we were moving too fast. That I was moving too fast.

"Liv," said Steven, kissing my nose. "I love you and I see a future for us. And you haven't answered me."

My throat tightened. "Yes," I whispered, figuring things between us would only get better. "Yes, I'll marry you."

He turned on his side, opening up the drawer in his nightstand. My heart pounded when he held out a small velvet box and opened it, revealing a white-gold ring with an enormous square-cut diamond. He took my hand and slid the ring onto my finger.

Of all things, as I stared at the ring, I wondered how I was going to break the news to Kat.

The morning after the proposal, I walked into my bedroom to find Kat sprawled out on my bed, flipping through the pages of my journal like it was a fashion magazine. She looked up when I entered. "I feel the same way about you, too," she said. "Sisters."

I stood there, stunned. "You're reading my private thoughts? Completely unacceptable," I growled. "You've really crossed a line. Do you have any boundaries at all?"

"Don't be so dramatic. Boundaries are for strangers. You said it yourself. We're sisters." Kat sat up, swinging her legs over the side of the bed. "Plus, I feel like I don't see much of you anymore. You're always with *him* now. Honestly, I didn't peg you to be one of those girls," Kat said, her tone sharp.

I swallowed hard, feeling a knot form in my stomach. "What girls?"

"The kind that blows their friends off for a guy." She shook her head in disapproval. "Truth be told, I'm not a fan of his. Never have been, especially after what he did to Sienna."

"Kat," I said, hesitating before I held out my hand, wiggling my finger. "He proposed last night."

Her face twisted in a mixture of emotions, none of them happy. Her eyes narrowed. "And you accepted?"

"Of course I did. I'm in love—"

"I take it that you're moving out of here, and moving in with him."

"That's the plan." I'd expected her to be upset by the news, but I didn't expect the pangs and feelings of guilt pinching my heart. Kat had done so much for me—too much.

"When?"

"In two weeks, after Valentine's Day." I paused. "With the exception of reading my journal, you've been a really great friend. You know how much I appreciate everything you've done..."

The look in her eyes scared me. "Been?"

I corrected myself quickly. "You *are* a great friend."

She nodded slowly, as if considering something. "That's more like it."

"You know how much you mean to me," I said, putting the focus back on her. "This doesn't change anything."

"Doesn't it?" She sighed and gripped a pillow tightly to her chest. For a moment, I thought she was going to lob it at my head. "Look, I just want you to be happy, you know that. Just make sure you're making the right decision. Marriage is a big step."

I nodded, relieved but still tense. "I'm just trying to balance everything. It's all happening so fast."

"Yeah, life has a way of doing that," she murmured and then her face lit up. "I have the best idea. Before you move out, we'll have a little bon voyage party."

For the next two weeks, it felt like Kat was going out of her way to make me uncomfortable or to exclude me.

The number of people in attendance at the party she threw for me was staggering, and I felt overwhelmed from the moment I walked into the living room. Faces blurred together and I only recognized a handful of the guests—the architect, her hairdresser, the personal shopper. It was as if the entire city had descended on us with loud conversations about the symphony or fashion or music, and the ever-present who-knows-whom. Aside from Mimi, Sienna, and me, Kat didn't have friends, and Mimi wasn't in attendance. When I'd asked Kat who all these other people were, she'd just laughed and said, "I know how to throw a party."

As Mark and Steven chatted in a corner, I tried to mingle, holding a crystal glass of champagne and wandering from group to group, but I couldn't shake the feeling of being an intruder at my own celebration. Just as I was about to suggest we call it a night, Sienna ramped things up to an eleven on the Richter scale with her arrival.

"Oh, Steven," she purred, her hand sliding across the table to rest on his forearm. "You have to try this crème brûlée. It's to die for."

She'd scooped up a spoonful and held it to his lips. Momentarily stunned, it wouldn't have surprised me if she'd made airplane noises, puffing out her plump lips.

Steven leaned back slightly. "I'm good, thanks, Sienna."

"Well, you're missing out," she replied, shooting me a look. "Big time."

My upper lip curled. "Where's Nick?"

"Do you care?" she spat out. "You don't know what's going on with me anymore. I mean, a 'Hey, nice to see you, what have you been up to?' would be nice…"

"Sienna, you never call me back."

"You blew me off for Kat." She sniggers. "How's that working out for you?" She holds up her hand in the stop position. "Wait. Don't answer. I really don't care."

The next morning, I woke up in my bed feeling like absolute shit—chilled and shaky. I threw out my arm, patting the other side for Steven. He wasn't sleeping next to me. I headed downstairs to the living room, finding a lot of people passed out on the floor, in chairs, on the couch. No Steven. After chugging a bottle of water, I meandered slowly upstairs to Kat's floor. Her bedroom door was open, so I walked in.

My jaw dropped open in absolute horror. Kat's arm was slung over Steven—the monkey in the middle—and there was also another woman on his other side. I whipped the ring off my finger and lobbed it at Steven's forehead.

"Clearly, the engagement is off."

Kat opened one eye and sat up in bed. "What's going on, Liv? You're so loud. My head is pounding. Last night was fun, wasn't it?"

"How dare you!" I cut her off. "You've been trying to sabotage my relationship with Steven from day one. What's your problem? Are you so insecure that you can't stand to see someone else happy? You have to take my happiness away? Well, congratulations, you win."

I was trembling, but it felt good to finally say it out loud. I wasn't sure who I was angrier with—Steven, Kat, or myself for being so damn stupid. Kat opened her mouth, closed it, then she abruptly stood up.

"I don't have to listen to this nonsense," she hissed, eyeing Steven.

Steven jolted out of bed, his face a perfect mix of confusion and concern. Like he'd just witnessed a car crash and wasn't sure if he should call 911. "Liv, I can explain..." he began, wrapping a throw blanket around his naked body, and then he frantically searched for his clothes.

I held up his boxers. "Explain this."

I stormed out of the room, racing to "our" closet and quickly grabbed the suitcase with the rest of my belongings. As I bolted out the front door, I could feel Kat's eyes on my back. I could hear Steven's pleas. Outside, the frigid morning air hit my face, and I took a deep breath, hailing a cab. I'd lost a friend. I'd lost my fiancé. I'd lost my cool. And, well, something in me snapped and, for a brief stretch of time, I lost my mind.

TWENTY-ONE

(NOW)

Trinity just listens to me ramble on, occasionally nodding along, her expression a mask of calm interest. Because she's a journalist, I'm expecting her to whip out a pad of paper, a pen. She doesn't.

"It sounds like Kat was grooming you," she says. "It's the way she was programmed to keep you in line, to keep you under her spell."

"Programmed?" I spit. "I'm not a robot."

"Sorry, but in my opinion, after what you've told me, you acted like one—taking all her gifts, allowing her to mold you into the person she wanted you to be."

I hold up a hand and stand abruptly. "Enough with the judgments."

"I don't blame you for being angry," Trinity replies calmly. "But I just figured you'd want to know how she works. Clearly, I was wrong."

I turn to face her, my mouth twisted into a scowl. "I know exactly how she operates. I lived with her for two years—"

"You're not giving me a chance to tell you what I know. Thought you wanted to hear it."

"I do," I admit, slumping into my seat.

"I've been doing some research into this place, into the cult that was based here. I know that Kat was here as a teen, and her mind still works with a cult-like mentality. See, nobody actually sets out to join a cult; they're recruited with promises." She pauses. "The leaders tend to have extremely narcissistic behavioral patterns—"

"You're explaining Kat to a T," I interrupt.

"You were vulnerable and she preyed on you." Trinity pauses. "Think about it. The death of your grandpa. The move to a big, bad, and scary city. She saw you as an easy target to recruit—"

"Where are you going with this?"

Trinity's eyes meet mine, unwavering. "Let's just say when you're digging into stories that powerful people want buried, the past gets covered up." Trinity's expression darkens. "And sometimes people end up getting buried, too."

Her gaze flickers to the window before returning to mine. "You briefly mentioned the girl who recruited the two of them into the cult—the daughter of Tobias Rane, Morgan." She shrugs. "But she doesn't exist. No birth records. Nothing."

I swallow. "That doesn't make sense."

"Right? Nothing does. And two of the girls that brought Tobias down are here—Kat and Sienna." Trinity leans forward. "Look, I know Kat owns this place. But why would somebody buy a property if they were tortured—as stated in their affidavits to the police and FBI—here? And what she told you."

"I don't know." I clench my teeth. "Maybe to find power over what happened to them?"

"Exactly. And I'm thinking Kat is starting a new cult, one she's in charge of. My advice," she says with a low laugh, "don't drink the Kool-Aid."

Trinity's eyes narrow as mine go wide. "Let's break it down. We have a luxury resort, a bunch of writers, and a cosmetics brand. Add in the alcohol and clothing lines. Seems like an odd mix, doesn't it?" She taps her fingers on her thigh. "What if Foster Literary isn't just sponsoring this retreat? What if they're linked to this new cult... testing something?"

I swallow back my disbelief. "Testing? On us?"

Trinity shrugs, but her eyes are sharp. "It's just a theory I'm working on. But us writers... we're a desperate bunch, aren't we?"

I laugh, but it's hollow. "God, that's dark."

"Like I said, I have a theory," Trinity admits.

I rub my temples. "And this theory of yours involves me how exactly?"

"I don't know. Maybe Kat wants her control over you back," says Trinity. "You said, and I quote, 'Kat always gets what she wants.' Right now, she wants to play you."

She's right, and Steven was the first person who saw through it all. My stomach twists as Trinity's words hang in the air between us. I can almost envision Kat's smile—that perfect, calculated curve of lips that never quite reaches her eyes.

"She's got her hooks in you," Steven had said one night. *"And you don't even feel them anymore."*

"By killing Steven? That's one twisted game..."

I feel like such an idiot. I never listened to any of his warnings.

"He ruined her relationship with you. She'd wanted you to depend on her. And then you didn't. Maybe it's a form of twisted revenge?" Trinity shrugs. "Kat seems to like collecting broken people, making them rely on or worship her like she's some kind of goddess."

I glance toward the window, noting a flock of geese taking flight in the sky, and then I take in a deep breath, forcing myself to exhale evenly. I stand up and brush my hands against my thighs. "Let's go look for that statue of Nyx, the one I told you about."

The words come out firmer than I'd intended, but I don't care. I refuse to let Kat get inside my head again. That's exactly what she wants from me.

TWENTY-TWO

(NOW)

For what seems like an eternity, Trinity and I traipse along a winding dirt path, our steps heavy with purpose. Above us, the clouds have darkened to a steely gray and a light rain trickles onto our heads, droplets running down our cheeks like tears. Although we're protected by the canopy of the trees, I lift the hood of my sweatshirt over my head.

A creek burbles on our left, the water splashing on rocks, and the squawks of birds come at me from every direction. I fix my gaze on the rhythm of my footsteps, trying to drown out the paranoid thoughts in my mind. Behind me, Trinity hums. The tune, catchy as it is, only intensifies the reminder of how Kat had blinded me. But guess what? I can see her clearly now. I see everything.

I stumble to a halt and Trinity, in her own world, bumps into me.

"Why'd you stop?"

I point, my eyes darting sharply to the side. "Through there."

"Have you been here before?" Trinity asks, her tone laced with suspicion.

"She told me about the garden," I say, pointing. "And instinct. There's an opening."

We press forward, pushing our bodies through a dense wall of hedges. Leaves brush our clothing, branches tangling in our hair and we burst into a secret garden. Trinity's eyes widen, absorbing every vivid detail, and her mouth drops open. "It's quite the contrast to the rest of the grounds—like stepping into another realm."

She isn't wrong. While the rest of Nyx flaunts pristine, manicured lawns and gleaming modern amenities, this secluded garden revels in a wild, chaotic madness. Flowers in deep purples, midnight blues, and vibrant oranges burst from the ground, their colors and forms breathtaking.

"It's absolutely beautiful," I say in a whisper. "But it's the kind of beauty that should come with a warning—like don't eat anything here."

Trinity lets out a soft chuckle. "Still thinking about lunch, I take it."

I'm thinking about everything. I'm thinking about Steven. I'm thinking about her. I'm thinking about betrayal.

Now walking side by side, we venture further into a clearing. Every twisted vine and concealed nook offers inspiration.

"Holy shit," Trinity breathes, coming to an abrupt stop.

There, amidst unruly blooms, stands Nyx—the Greek goddess of the night—chiseled from obsidian so dark it seems to absorb every stray ray of the remaining light. Her outstretched arms silently command us closer. At her feet lies a delicate carpet of white, lace-like flowers mingled with bursts of brilliant reds, regal purples, and fiery oranges.

"Well, this isn't ominous at all," Trinity whispers.

"She's... mesmerizing," I murmur and then point. "Those flowers? Queen Anne's Lace?"

"The white ones? No, that's hemlock," she corrects, her voice a blend of warning and resignation. "And they're definitely poisonous—not something to be touched or eaten."

I blink rapidly and turn to Trinity, my voice lowered. "OK. You've got to admit, something here is definitely off."

"She's keeping up with that cult vibe, don't you think?" Trinity whispers, her gaze never leaving the dark statue. "It's like she truly believes she's a goddess."

"Oh, she does," I agree.

Thunder rumbles in the distance.

With a determined lift of her chin, Trinity declares, "I can't wait to break this story wide open. We should probably head back now. The weather is going to get a lot worse very soon."

I offer Nyx's statue one final look before nodding. "Agreed."

As Trinity and I retrace our steps back to the main lodge, the rain comes down harder and our feet slosh in mud and fallen pine needles, the scents of the earth. My heart stutters as I think about Steven and how he's going to be buried in it soon.

When we cross the meticulously kept lawns, our feet sloshing, my eyes are involuntarily drawn to the surface of the pond where a pair of swans glide gracefully across the waters. Beauty, it seems, is tangled with danger, with the unknown.

"You OK?" Trinity asks.

"I'm fine," I reply. "Just thinking."

She clasps my hand, squeezing it. "Thank you for sharing what you know."

I nod. I didn't tell her the whole story. "Thank you for listening."

Swallowing hard, we step into the main lodge where the once comforting hallway now appears transformed—no longer a sanctuary. Every shadow and every closed door sends my internal alarms into overdrive.

Then, as if drawn by the anxious plotting in my head, I see Mark striding casually down the hall. His unhurried gait and too-easy smile only amplifies the conflict within me.

"Hey," he greets me, his voice echoing off the walls. He shoots Trinity an annoyed look. Odd, considering he's the interloper.

Trinity raises a brow and mouths, "See you later," as she heads toward her room.

I pause in front of my door before opening it, needing a moment to gather my resolve. Mark follows me in. I kick off my muddy shoes and whip my hoodie off, heading to the bathroom. As I wrap my hair in a towel, Mark eyes me curiously.

"Where have you been?"

"With Trinity on a nature walk," I answer defensively.

"Explains all the mud."

"And you? What did you do?"

"Not much. Took a steam in the spa."

I grab my brush from the bathroom. "Did you talk to Kat?"

"I couldn't find her," he replies, tilting his head. "You didn't tell Trinity about the..." His words trail off.

"I just confirmed what she already knew," I say with a shrug, and he shoots me a scowl.

"What the hell? The records were sealed and now a nosy reporter is poking around?" Deep, angry breaths punctuate his words, and his face contorts with anger. I don't like this side of him. "Damn it, Liv, you talk too much."

"The truth, as they say, always rises to the surface." I sit on the bed, pulling off my wet socks. I meet his angry glare. "Who are you trying to protect? Kat or Sienna? What about me? What about us? I'm trying to protect my book. You know how much writing means to me…"

"You really are a piece of work, you know that?" His eyes narrow into a death glare. "I need to check in on my sister."

He turns to leave, and my hand instinctively reaches out to grab his shoulder, but it falls uselessly to my side. I call softly after him, but there's no point. I want him to leave. I now know where his loyalties lie, and they aren't with me. His footsteps echo down the hall. I watch until his silhouette disappears around the corner, a cold sense of dread knotting inside my stomach.

Sienna's words echo in my mind. *Mark does and always will belong to my friend, Kat.*

Maybe he still is hers. I'd only been to his place a couple of times. When we went out (on the rare occasion), he always seemed on edge, and he always wore a baseball cap. Like people were going to recognize him in Brooklyn? Plus, I only saw him on Mondays and Wednesdays, and the occasional Friday night.

Which makes me wonder what he'd been doing with the rest of his time. I close my eyes, willing the world to stop spinning. Images flash through my mind: Mark's piercing blue eyes, cold as a winter sky. His expertly styled hair, always just so. The way his perfect lips quirked into a sneer when I asked him about us.

I'm not an idiot.

Maybe there never has been an "us." One thing is certain, he could mess up all my plans.

TWENTY-THREE

(NOW)

Before dinner, I head down to the business center, needing to do a little research—something I can't do in my room. Like the rest of the resort, the room is modern and well equipped, a coffee and drinks bar in the corner. The computers are all iMacs, the desks slabs of travertine, and the chairs a buttery, ivory leather. Clean and simple lines, everything works together, the lighting soothing. A couple of other retreat members greet me with warm hellos as I sit down at an open station—one of the Bees is using the computer next to me.

"Hey, there! It's Liv, right?" she asks, her voice bubbly and bright. She smiles, her teeth even brighter than her tone. "I'm Brittany!"

A deep sigh escapes my lips as I rub my tired eyes. I'm so not in the mood for small talk. "Nice to meet you."

"I seriously can't believe we don't get Wi-Fi in our rooms." She rolls her eyes and flashes another blinding smile. "I loved, loved, loved your query letter. *In Her Shoes*. What a great title!"

"Thanks."

She lifts a manicured brow. "Maybe when we're ready to query, you can give ours a look? I mean, seriously, yours was so, so good."

"Sure," I reply, wanting to nip the conversation in the bud.

"Ahhhh-mazing!" she chirps. She scribbles something down on a piece of paper. "Here's my email. What's yours?"

Somebody kill me now.

"Olivia dot montgomery dot thrillerauthor at xmail dot com," I say, giving her a slight smile.

"Thanks." Her eyes light up and she nods with exuberance. She jumps out of her seat, the chair rolling backwards. "I can't wait to tell the rest of the girls. They are going to die."

"I hope not," I say.

Brittany snorts. "You're funny."

I force a smile, thinking my life is a joke.

After she bounces away, in a moment of supreme frustration, I pull up a browser to find Foster Literary's most recent *Publisher's Weekly* deal announcement.

In a pre-empt, in a major deal, executive editor Rebecca Stiles at SilverGate Publishing has acquired World English rights to Lila Aiken's IN HER SKIN from Victoria Foster at Foster Literary. The publisher calls it "an extraordinary debut thriller of betrayal and deception with 'Single White Female' meets 'Mean Girl' vibes. Publication is slated for spring 2026.

I choke back an angry, frustrated sob. With a shaky finger, I google the author, Lila Aiken, to find she's an enigma —no social media presence, no website, no photos. Nothing. It's like she doesn't even exist.

Kat Sterling.

She's tethered me to her messed-up world and it's time to cut the line. I place my elbows on the desk, my hands cradling my head, thinking, when somebody lightly taps me on the shoulder. I turn to find Mimi standing behind me. She points to the screen and raises a brow. "I see you found the announcement."

"I did," I say, my lips twisting into a frown. "Who is Lila Aiken?"

She shrugs. "Rebecca thinks she's you."

"I'm not." I meet her concerned gaze. "Did you read the manuscript?"

She nods and then clucks her tongue. "I read yours today. It's much more polished. Aiken's reads more like the draft before the final draft." Mimi's eyes flash to the other retreat members, especially the ones edging in to hear more salacious gossip. "Let's take a walk and talk."

A shiver of dread scurries down my spine. I suck in my cheeks, biting down on them. "I just need to grab a sweater from my room."

"We'll walk there."

I close out of the browser and we leave the business center, heading up the stairs.

"Seems there's a lot of duplicity going on," says Mimi, her voice strained. She stares straight ahead. "I can't believe you and Mark are together."

I go silent, my back rigid.

"Look, Liv, you know all about Kat's weird on-again-off-again thing with him," she continues casually, placing a hand on my shoulder. "Don't worry, your secret is safe with me. But if there's a chance of you and Kat finally burying the hatchet, I wouldn't mention that you're seeing him."

A surge of anger rises within me. I hiss through gritted teeth. "Hatchet? Like the one she threw in my back?"

"Well, I guess you're even then," she quips with a smirk.

I turn around in a huff and open the door to my room. Mark, thankfully, is not in it.

"No, we're not even," I say, my voice hardening. "Our friendship ended because she slept with Steven."

Her gaze meets mine. "And now Steven Shepherd is dead."

I suck in a breath. "What do you know about that?"

"Kat told me the police questioned her and Sienna. She told me everything." She raises a brow. "Leave the door open. I'm not coming in."

"If you're inferring that I'm like Sharon Stone's character in *Basic Instinct*, think again. *In Her Shoes* is fiction."

"But there's truth in your fiction. I recognized all the characters." She tilts her head to the side. "Even me." Mimi looks down and points a shaky finger to a spot on the floor, her mouth dropping open. "Is that blood?"

"Probably," I say, explaining the crow fiasco.

Her face pales. "How did it get in?"

"It's a mystery," I say, eyeing the bloodstain on the floor, the rogue feathers scattered like a scene from a scary movie. "But somebody is definitely messing with me. Stealing my manuscript. The crow. Sabotaging my journal with all my notes in it by dropping it in the toilet." I lower my gaze from hers, my mind racing like a spin cycle set on high. "I'm pretty sure it's Kat. And I think she killed Steven..."

Mimi sucks in her breath and shakes her head slowly. "Kat may be a lot of things, but she's not *that* vindictive. She's certainly not a murderer. And she definitely wouldn't touch a crow."

I raise a brow.

"Maybe we have a prankster in the group," she offers, halfheartedly. "Or maybe you did something to piss somebody off."

"Well, they're not funny at all; they're sick and twisted," I say, spitting out the words. "Aside from you, Sienna, Kat, and Mark, I don't know anybody else here."

She eyes my suitcase, the clothes strewn on the bed and the floor. "Are you leaving?"

I hesitate, the uncertainty of everything pressing down on me. I'm not sure what I'm doing anymore. "It's just a lot right now, trying to get my writing career, if I even have one, on track, everything with Steven..." I gulp. "I'm at my wits' end. But I need to prove to Rebecca the book is mine."

"There's probably a logical explanation for everything. If you're staying, you definitely need to clear things up with Rebecca." She points to the spot on the floor, shuddering. "And the staff will clean that up." She looks at her watch. "I have a meeting set with Victoria and Anna. I'll see you at dinner."

Dinner? No way. I'm not ready to come face to face with Kat. Not until I come up with a solid plan. I hunch over a little, feigning a stomachache. "I'm not feeling so well. I'll just order room service and wait for the cleaner. Eat with Mark."

I think of the hemlock I'd seen in the garden, my stomach churning. There's no way I'm eating anything tonight— unless everybody else is eating the same thing I am. I think I have a couple of granola bars and an orange in my purse. That'll have to do to tide me over until morning. And I'm really hoping Mark doesn't come back to the room.

"OK, I'll see you at breakfast," she says, squeezing my

shoulder. "Don't worry. This will all blow over. And I'm truly sorry about Steven."

After Mimi leaves, I lock the door behind her and step over to the gift basket. I reach for the perfume labeled Nemesis, the light glass bottle etched with the logo of a sword. I twist the cap and breathe the fragrance in. Sweet like oranges and citrus, jasmine, and a bit of musk, the scent reminds me of Kat, and I want to vomit.

A knock comes a few moments later and Jenn greets me, holding a mop and a bucket. She eyes the floor, the feathers. "Well, Vicki didn't do her job. Sorry," she huffs, snapping on gloves. "I guess if you want anything done right you have to do it yourself."

I sit at the desk, trying to think clearly. While she's here, I figure I can pump Jenn for information. "How long have you worked at Nyx?"

She's on her hands and knees, scrubbing. "Since the beginning. I'm the general manager."

"Do you like working for Kat Sterling?"

"I'd do anything for her, including cleaning up crow blood..." Jenn looks up, a purple streak of hair falling over her eyes, her mouth dropped open. "How did you know Kat Sterling is one of the owners?"

I shrug, wondering who the other investors are. "We used to be friends. And the other owners?"

Jenn's lips pinch together. "Sorry, I signed an NDA, and I've already said too much."

Kat's having other people do her dirty work for her. And it's the reason she'll mess up. My eyes flicker to the side. It's then I notice the note on the desk:

Staying in Sienna's suite tonight. She's really upset about our relationship and you know how she can get. Sorry about storming off like I did. See you in the morning and we'll talk. Mark

I shake my head. I've been ignoring all of the warning signs when they are practically flashing right in front of my face. Perhaps I'm looking at the wrong person, but if Kat isn't after me, who is?

TWENTY-FOUR

(NOW)

I stare at the ceiling for hours, listening to the rain hitting the windows, thinking. I should never have gotten involved with any of these people. Back then, I'd thought having the shiny bright light that was Kat in my world would give me the sense of belonging I'd desperately craved, how being in a relationship with Steven would fill the void in my heart. I'm so mad at myself because you'd think I'd learn from my mistakes, especially since I keep making the same ones. It's not that I search for trouble; it just keeps finding me.

In the morning, I groan when my alarm goes off and I look at my phone. I didn't sleep one wink last night, wondering if I'm truly a horrible person or simply misguided. The truth? In my own way, I'd loved Steven, the life he'd promised me when we'd been together. But I'd loved Kat more. She'd become an obsession—the woman I wanted to be. I'd wanted to live in her shoes, see life through her eyes.

My shoulders shake and I start bawling my eyes out. A good fifteen minutes later, I roll out of bed and stumble to the bathroom, splashing cold water on my face. The woman in the mirror is a stranger. Her eyes are red-rimmed and blood-shot, hair a tangled mess. Yesterday she had her act together —sort of. Now she looks like she belongs in one of those cautionary pamphlets they hand out on the street. Don't do drugs! My fists clench involuntarily.

"Congratulations," I say to my reflection. "Well, Liv, you've officially hit rock bottom. What are you going to do about it?"

The question hangs in the air, obviously unanswered. If I did get an answer, I'd check myself into a psychiatric ward. Before I burst into ragged tears again with snot running down my nose, I jump in the shower, trying to come up with a new plan. I have to set things right before everything gets out of hand.

Not quite fresh, but looking a hell of a lot better, I pick up today's schedule.

Day 2: Thursday—Creative Flow & Nature's Inspiration

7:00 AM—Sunrise Bird Watching

8:00 AM—Breakfast

9:00 AM—Papermaking Workshop or Perfume Making

11:00 AM—Writing Block #2

12:30 PM—Lunch

2:00 PM—Canoeing on the Pond

4:00 PM—Meeting with Editor/Agent #1

6:30 PM—Dinner

8:30 PM—Evening Meditation and Yoga or Free Writing Time

The storm has ramped up this morning, the rain coming down hard. Such a shame. They probably canceled bird watching.

Aside from the windows rattling and the lights occasionally flickering, breakfast is a non-event, still no sight of Kat. Over our eggs, Trinity and I try to keep the conversation light and casual, setting up a plan to work on our project after papermaking. Mark sits there, mashing his eggs with his fork. He doesn't eat one bite.

"How is Sienna doing?" I finally ask.

He glares at me and mouths, "Not good." Right. I talk too much and he doesn't want to reveal anything in front of her.

"So, Liv tells me you went to Woodford Hall," says Trinity, shooting me a concerned look.

"I did," he replies, his upper lip lifting into a sneer. "And I graduated two years before Kat and Sienna went through their experience."

Trinity's eyes widen. "What experience?"

He shoots her a closed-mouth smile. "The one you're obviously investigating."

She lays a finger on the table, her eyes brightening. "Care to answer a few questions?"

"I don't." Suddenly, Mark stands up, pushing his chair back. "I'm going for a run."

"It's raining pretty hard out," I say.

"So what? I'll just get wet."

I go silent as I watch him walk away. "Something is off," whispers Trinity. "What do you really know about Mark?"

Good question. I only know what he wants me to know about him, which is basically nothing. I know he's an attorney. I know he's Sienna's brother. I know he's Kat's ex. I know his dad is a senator. And I know his family is insanely rich. What I don't know is if he's been playing me. I'm so sick of all the games, yet I keep gambling with the hopes I can win.

Before I'm able to respond with anything remotely on point, Rebecca Stiles stops by our table, shooting me a pointed look. "Liv, I hope we're still on for our meeting later today."

Without my journal, I might as well stamp the word "plagiarist" on my forehead. "Yes," I say, nodding my head with force. "Can't wait."

"I'm having our tech team look into the email communications I've had with Aiken." Rebecca holds up her phone. "We're getting to the bottom of this."

There are multiple versions of the manuscript backed up on the cloud. "Can we meet in the business center?" I ask.

"Sure?" Her upper lip lifts with confusion. "Although I really like the setting of the gazebo."

No, I really need the Internet. "The storm is coming in. And it's raining out."

"I love storms. In fact, I was headed off to watch the weather shift before it hits hard," she says, lifting up a brow when my eye twitches. "But that could be a me thing." As she turns on her heel, she looks over her shoulder. "See you in the business center. Bring the journal."

I sit numb, shoulders rigid.

Shit.

"The journal? The one you dropped in the toilet?" Trinity scoffs, once Rebecca is out of earshot.

"Yep. The very one." I gulp. "Let's get to papermaking. Maybe I can make a new one?"

We cross the lawn toward the papermaking facility, no

geese in sight. Before we make it to the barn, though, we pass a donkey with silver-gray fur and tall fluffy ears. He brays a hello and Trinity backs away. "I hope that's Pedro," she says in a low whisper. "Jenn said the other ones bite." She stops in her tracks. "You know what? I need to do some research. And, well, when you mentioned the business center, I—"

"I get it. Go."

"You sure?"

"I'm sure. I can fend for myself."

After Trinity and I part ways, I meander down a flagstone path and walk into a large barn, the facility humming with the steady sounds of machinery and the gentle slosh of water. Dominating the center of the room is a huge cement vat, filled with a thick, milky mixture. The air is slightly humid, carrying a distinct, earthy smell.

Towering racks and tables hold sheets of freshly made paper in varying stages of drying, from damp, soft sheets that glisten in the light, to large, stiffened slabs of finished paper that await cutting and inspection—some stacked high into piles.

An employee, wearing rubber gloves and a stained apron, turns and greets me. "Good. I guess everybody else has chosen the perfume making symposium. And I was wondering if anybody was going to join me today." She grins. "I'm Carol. And I'm here to introduce you to the magic of papermaking. Aprons and gloves are over there." She points. "Suit up and get ready to get your pulp on!"

I do as instructed, staring at the murky water churning.

Carol gestures toward the vat and explains the process. "So, the pulp you see here is the starting point. It's a mix of wood fibers, recycled paper, and water. This machine"—she taps a large blender-like mechanism—"keeps it moving so the fibers don't settle, then we pour it onto screens in thin layers to drain out the water, forming a basic sheet of paper."

She reaches for a metal frame, lowering it gently into the vat to scoop up some pulp, repeating the process a couple of times. "Once you've got the right amount on the screen, press it to squeeze out the water and let it dry before it's pressed flat." She points to metal rollers in the distance. "You have to be careful with the pulp consistency, too," she adds. "Too much water, and the paper won't hold; too little, and it'll come out thick and uneven. Any questions?"

"I have a question," says a voice behind me.

A voice I recognize. A voice that fills my heart with dread.

"Sorry," says Carol. "I didn't see you come in, Ms. Sterling. I can go over everything again..."

I turn to face Kat, her eyes blazing into mine, Sienna standing like a well-groomed guard-dog by her side.

"That won't be necessary," says Kat with a low growl. "The only thing I want to know is why this traitor is standing in front of me. What the hell are you doing here?"

Carol gulps. "S-should I leave?"

"Nobody is leaving but her. I want this woman off my property." She raises her voice. "Radio security! Now!"

Sienna snickers. "Mimi invited her."

Kat growls, "Why would she do that when she knows how I feel about her—"

"Feel about me?" I interject. "How about the way I feel about you? What I know about you! What you did!"

"You stupid girl. You ingrate of an imbecile." Kat glowers at me. "I tried telling you that I crawled into my own bed that night... but you wouldn't listen, wouldn't even give me a chance to explain. For all I knew, he could have been one of my goddamn pillows."

I lower my head, shaking it. "Who was the third woman?"

Kat's eyes meet mine, her lashes flickering, her cheeks twitching into a nasty grin. "You may want to ask Sienna that question."

Sienna coughs out a wicked laugh.

I force one foot in front of the other, walking toward her, shaking, my jaw clenched. "You bitch!"

"Oh, I'm the bitch? We were never really friends." Sienna lifts up her chin. "You proved that when you dumped me for Kat, when you got involved with somebody I'd warned you not to get involved with just to hurt me."

"You were married to Nick. And you only dated Steven in high school."

"And then you went after my brother, knowing full well how much that would hurt Kat."

Kat whips her gaze onto Sienna's. "What?"

"It's true. Mark told me everything on the ride over."

Kat's eyes blaze with a fury I've never seen before. She gets right up in my face, enveloping me in her scent. She doesn't smell sweet; she's bitter. "After everything I did for you, after everything? You and Mark? What, to get back at me?"

In hindsight, she's telling the truth. I don't say a word. I just tilt my head to the side.

"Mark always has his meaningless flings and then comes running back to me like a dog with its tail between its legs," Kat hisses. "Pack your bags, I want you off my property. And I'd move out of the city if I were you."

She doesn't scare me. Not anymore. "Or what? Are you

going to off me like you did Steven? Put another crow in my room? Try and ruin my writing career?"

She shakes her head, my words clearly blindsiding her. "Steven? His murder? The police questioned me yesterday morning..."

"They questioned me, too," says Sienna. "But I think we're looking at his killer."

"I knew there was something different about you. You're not right in the head. I'm filing a restraining order." Kat locks Carol in her gaze. "Any luck with security?"

Carol gulps and rubs her eyes. "Ms. Sterling, there's a problem. A bunch of the big pines have already fallen, blocking the road..."

"I want her gone this instant."

"I don't think that will be possible. They told me to tell everybody to hunker down. Until the trees are cleared, nobody can leave. And, worse, nobody will be able to get here. The Hudson River is already flooding..."

"This is a nightmare," whispers Kat. She opens the barn doors and we all stand in shock.

Dark clouds have gathered overhead, snuffing out what light was left in the sky just ten minutes ago. Powerful gusts of wind whip the once serene and tranquil landscape into a frenzy, and the usually calm pond has turned into a churning mass of waves. A flash of lightning illuminates the sky, followed by deafening claps of thunder that shake the ground beneath us. And then the rain comes down even harder.

"We better get to the main building," Kat finally says. "Now."

The four of us race across the lawn, slipping and sliding. Drenched, we finally make it into the lobby, our clothes leaving puddles, our footprints muddy messes.

Kat turns toward me, shaking a finger. "No matter how I feel about you, you're lucky I'm not a monster. Don't come within fifty feet of me or it won't be Mother Nature's wrath you'll have to worry about."

Not a problem, especially with the way I feel about her. Right now, I'm thinking about wrapping my hands around her skinny neck. Only problem? Too many witnesses.

TWENTY-FIVE

(NOW)

KAT

I make my way up to my suite, snickering to myself. I'm finding it absolutely hilarious that Liv actually thinks that she'd surprised me. I'm playing my part well, acting the way she's expecting me to. Even funnier? I've known about her and Mark for months. I'm the one who sent him to the bookstore. I'm the one who paid for that ridiculous old book. I'm the one who told Mimi to invite her on the retreat. And I'm the one who wants her back in my life. I miss our friendship. And I'm hoping one day she'll forgive me the way I'm willing to forgive her. Now that she thinks she's gotten her revenge, perhaps we'll call it even.

However, Steven's murder has blindsided me and wasn't part of my master plan. And the fact he'd left everything to her makes her a prime suspect. The police told me as such when they questioned me yesterday. I wonder if Mark has told her that they'd questioned him and Sienna, too. As for the crow, I have no idea what she's talking about. She probably left her window open.

Before plopping down on the couch, I kick my shoes off and turn the fire on to a blaze. Comfortable, I'm just about to pull up my iPad to read when Mimi saunters out of the bathroom. I grin. "Thanks for sending this on."

"I'm not sure you're going to like how she writes your character." She pours herself a glass of wine. "Spoiler alert. You die at the end."

I'm intrigued. "How?"

"After you stab Seth to death with a letter opener, your yacht blows up. Boom!"

My lips twitch into a smile. "She's pretty creative."

"And she could be a murderer," says Mimi, her voice just above a whisper. She takes a sip of wine.

I roll my eyes. "I don't think she killed Steven."

Mimi plops down next to me. "And how can you be so certain?"

I shrug. "Let's just say I've been keeping tabs on her."

"You've been spying on her?"

"Not me," I say. "I hired somebody to watch her—nothing too outlandish."

"You really are a control freak." Mimi chortles and then her face turns serious, her mouth twisting to the side. "She really pegged your character. Why are you so obsessed with her?"

"I always watch over my investments." I pop my lips. "And I invested in her."

"But if she didn't murder Steven, who did?"

I tap a finger on my chin, deliberating. "I honestly don't know."

"Kat, that has me really worried." Mimi shakes her head.

"Somebody is seriously terrorizing Liv, and they might come after us."

I laugh. "They wouldn't dare."

"What about Liv?"

"Oh, I need her for my plans," I say. "I'll make sure she's safe—but she's going to have to beg for my forgiveness."

TWENTY-SIX

(NOW)

I'd waited for Rebecca for over an hour in the business center, but she didn't show up for our meeting. Now, I'm worried about what she found out and whether she doesn't want to meet with me at all. Dragging my heels, I head to my room, surprised to find Trinity with Mark.

"I didn't want to be alone," says Trinity, by means of an explanation. "So I bribed Mark."

This is an odd turn of events.

"With what?"

"Gin rummy, of course," says Trinity, holding up a deck of cards. "And gin."

"Along with promises not to ask questions about my sister or Kat," he says. "Or the cult."

Trinity grins. "Believe me. I tried."

"Deal me in," I say, eyeing Mark and then Trinity. "Why are you wearing a towel on your head?"

"Dropped my phone in the papermaking barn and ran through this nightmare of a storm to get it. I crossed paths with Mark on the way back."

I eye her with suspicion. "You didn't go to papermaking."

"I changed my mind, but by the time I got there everybody was gone."

She certainly offers logical answers to everything.

Hunkered down in the room, we're about to play a hand while listening to the storm getting louder and more severe in pitch. The windows rattle. Tree branches scrape the glass. I'm jumping at every thunderclap, and the wind is howling.

"Well, papermaking was fun," I say, glaring at Mark. "I learned a lot."

"Sorry I missed it," says Mark with a shrug. "Why are you looking at me like that? What happened?"

"Kat happened," I say and then whisper, "And I'll tell you all about it later."

Trinity's eyes dart from side to side. "I, for one, am champing at the bit."

"Keep on champing." I shoot her a smirk, still finding it odd she's in my room with Mark. "Because I'm not getting into it right now. I'm in serious need of a break." I grab the bottle of gin, pour a glass. "I'm also in the mood for this."

I take a good look at them, the way they're both swaying. I'm thinking both of them are wasted. I look at the bottle. Half of it is gone. "How much have you had to drink?"

Mark laughs. "Before or after they closed the bar?"

OK. This explains everything.

"I downloaded some music before I came here." Trinity links her iPhone to a portable speaker and plays Billie Eilish's "All the Good Girls Go to Hell" and I cringe.

"Turn that off."

"Just trying to lighten up your mood."

"Oh, I'm in a great one," I say, clenching my teeth.

"Be positive," says Trinity with a laugh. "At least we have electricity."

She says this as web lightning flashes in the sky and the lights flicker. Trinity's lips quirk into a wry smile. "You have a really nice complexion, Mark."

"Thanks, I guess," he says.

I have no idea where this conversation is headed, but I pick up on Trinity's ulterior motive: disarming Mark with something he clearly likes to talk about—his appearance. Maybe she's not as buzzed as I thought.

As Trinity and Mark banter, talking about the latest beauty treatments, Sienna and Kat's words echo in my ears, my fingers twitching to grab the gifted journal and a pen. I want to write everything that's happened down, mostly so I can make sense of the events.

Mark nudges my side with his elbow. "Liv, tell me what's on your beautiful mind."

Oh, he really doesn't want to know about the theories running around in my brain.

A knock sounds at the door. Trinity leaps off the floor and opens it to find Jenn standing in the hallway, the lights flickering. "Good, I found the three of you. I was getting worried there for a moment. Everybody's gathered in the dining room. Over dinner, we'll be giving updates on what to do if the storm intensifies."

I'm now thinking about Kat's anger. Her threat. Sienna's laughter.

"I don't think I should go," I say.

"You have to. This is not a drill. It's obligatory. The dining room is safe—we've closed all the shutters. I suggest you all do the same thing." She steps over to the window and opens it, bringing in a gush of water. She grabs the shutters and turns. "There, done. See, that wasn't so bad."

I hunch over, my pulse quickening.

From a bag, Jenn reaches in and hands out battery-operated candles. "Just in case. We're always prepared here at Nyx. Follow me."

Nothing could have prepared me for this shitstorm I'd stepped into, the fury taking on a whole new meaning when we step into the dining room. Attendees are talking over one another, the Bees the loudest. Kat sits next to Sienna, their eyes blazing into me. Mimi shoots me an apologetic smile.

This is truly a nightmare.

Mark and Trinity stagger to seats at a vacant table, and I join them.

My eyes scan the room, searching for Rebecca, eventually landing on Kat again. She stands up, nostrils flaring. Before I know it, her hand is squeezing my arm, leading me out to the lobby. I look over my shoulder, shooting Trinity a pleading look. "Don't worry. I've got you," she mouths.

"How could you?" she hisses. "What kind of friend are you?"

I meet her stone-cold glare. "We are no longer friends. You made sure of that."

Her mouth twists. "You're just his sidepiece. Sometimes he likes to slum it. Like I said, he'll come back to me. He always does." She leans forward and whispers in my ear, her angry breath hot on my neck. "And, by the way, your writing is shit."

Her words hit me like a punch to the gut, but I stand strong. "Shit? I thought the whole point was to write what you know. Maybe the book is about you."

Kat chuckles, "It's over for you, Liv." The words hang in

the air between us. Sharp. Final. Her expression hardens, her green eyes turning icy cold. "Don't forget. I know you, even loved you like a sister, and, well, honestly, if I was in your shoes, I'd probably have done the same thing to get back at me, but you're taking things too far."

Shoes. I look down at hers—black Christian Louboutin boots. "You're Lila Aiken."

"No, I'm Kat Sterling and damn proud of it." Her nose scrunches. "Who is Lila Aiken?"

My mind spins. "What book are you working on?"

"It's a memoir—very private right now."

My throat hitches. "The title of your book. Is it *In Her Skin*?"

Her lips twist to the side. "No, it's called *Under the Influence*. Why?"

My breathing picks up and my eyes sweep the dining room again. "Where's Rebecca?"

"*My* editor?" Kat sucks in a breath and places a hand on my shoulder. "I don't know."

"We have to find her. Now. I think she may be in trouble. The last time I saw her she was heading to the gazebo..."

Jenn hurries up to us. "Some of the guests are—"

"Missing," says Kat, cutting her off. "Have you seen Rebecca Stiles?"

"I knocked on her door to tell her to close her shutters and to head down for dinner. She didn't answer. So I went into her room to close them myself. She wasn't there."

Kat's face visibly pales. Her eyes lock on mine. "Let's go. Jenn, grab a walkie-talkie and a flashlight."

We race out of the resort, the rain pouring onto our heads and pricking into our skin like sharp needles, Kat's heels sticking in the mud. The only sound I can hear is my panicked breath. When we get to the gazebo, we all stop, frozen in our tracks.

A glimpse of silver hair. A body splayed out on the wooden floor.

Jenn's eyes go wide. "I'm radioing for help."

Kat and I race up the steps. Rebecca is still breathing, but there is a pool of blood beneath her head. Her eyes meet mine and then dart to Kat's, her lids flickering. "I-It happened so quick. I forgot my iPad and went to get it. For a moment, I sat, watching the storm clouds roll in." She wheezes. "I love the smell of rain on the grass, the earthy freshness, the colors changing from blue to gray to black in the sky, the birds flying off to wherever they take cover."

"Who did this to you?" asks Kat.

"I didn't hear her come up behind me. But I felt the rock or whatever she hit me with crack against my skull. I heard her threat. S-s-she said, 'This is not a warning. You are not publishing Kat Sterling's memoir. Understand?'" She takes in a shaky breath. "I was dazed; I nodded and then she ripped my iPad from my hands and ran."

Jenn and another Nyx employee push Kat and me to the side. "Gary used to be a nurse," says Jenn and he starts asking Rebecca a barrage of questions regarding her neck, her head, her vision, as he gently moves her onto a stretcher.

"I'm freezing," she says.

"We'll get you to your room and put a fire on," says Gary.

"Wait. One more thing. Where's Liv?"

"I'm here."

"You're Lila Aiken," she says with a wheeze.

She must be delirious. "But I'm not!"

"We've got to get her inside," says Jenn. "The wind's picking up and the pond is about to flood."

The next few minutes pass by in a haze. Kat links her arm in mine and, together, we fight the elements, finally getting back to the main building. Soaked to the core, I should be freezing, but I'm not. The blood is rushing through my veins like fire. In a daze, I let Kat lead the way, surprised to see that we're in the Nyx boutique, Kat ripping off her clothes. I blink. She's bending over, pulling on pants when I notice the tattoo on her butt. She looks over her shoulder. "Stop staring at my ass and pick out something to wear."

I point. "Your tattoo? I mean, I've seen it before. I forgot the meaning—"

"The scales. A symbol of Nemesis, the goddess," she says, throwing me a long-sleeved t-shirt and a pair of pants, which I catch, followed by a pair of yoga slippers, the latter hitting me in the shins and thudding to the ground. "I told you Tobias Rane branded us. And I'll tell you more about him later. Right now, get changed. You're dripping water all over the floor."

Still reeling from waves of shock and nausea, I do as I'm told. There are so many questions I want to ask her, so many things I want her to expand on, but the little voice in my head is screaming *it doesn't matter what she says*. Actions speak louder than words and hers have been more than treacherous.

TWENTY-SEVEN

(NOW)

There's an audience of gaping authors waiting for us when we exit the boutique, all breathing heavily as if they themselves had been caught in the storm, as if they are the ones with targets on their backs. Mark races up to us. "Are you OK, Liv? What's going on?" he demands.

"Not now, Mark," barks Kat, her sharp pitch cutting through the rising chatter and shocked cries. "A piece of debris knocked Rebecca on the head while she was watching the storm come in," she lies smoothly. "But she'll be fine. I'm just glad we found her when we did, or the outcome would have been less than favorable. Please, everybody, go to your rooms, have a coffee or tea in the dining room, or go to the yoga symposium in the spa. We'll have updates on the storm and Rebecca in the morning."

I watch the concerned faces, feeling a mixture of panic and relief. One of the Bees groans, "This retreat is the absolute worst. I need something a lot stronger than coffee or tea."

Understatement of the century.

"You'll all be refunded," says Kat, locking her gaze on Victoria's dropped jaw. She mouths, "I'll pay."

"That's it?" somebody grumbles. "I feel like I've been kidnapped."

"There are many things I can control, but, unfortunately, I can't control the weather. Help yourselves to anything in the bar." Kat shrugs and then turns to me. She mumbles, "A storm. A bunch of drunken writers channeling their inner Bukowskis. Probably not the best mix." She gives me a tight smile. "Let's continue our conversation in my room."

"Your room?"

"Mark is staying with you. And I don't want to look at his smug face." Her eyes glint. "Or I may kill him."

"Please tell me you're kidding."

"Of course I am, Liv." She holds up her hands, wiggles her fingers. "I spent three hundred on my manicure, and I don't want to ruin it."

"Fine," I say. "I just need to grab the gifted journal."

"Why?"

"I'm trying to figure things out and to do so I like writing everything down."

I fumble with the doorknob, hands shaking, and the door swings open. At first, I'm hit by the comforting scent of lavender—the sanctuary's signature aroma—but as I step inside, my breath catches in my throat. There, like the scene in a slasher film minus the blood, scrawled across the mirror in vivid red lipstick and on the walls, are the words: "Watch Your Back, Fraud. FAKE, POSER, IMPOSTER," and "NOT ONE OF US, CON ARTIST. MURDERER."

I approach the mirror slowly, as if the words might leap out and attack me. My reflection stares back, pale and wide-eyed.

"Fuck," Kat whispers, her voice barely audible over the pounding of my heart. "Who did this?"

Ignoring the fact that Kat rarely swears or perhaps that she may be more concerned about the ruined walls, I'm about to dart to the bathroom to grab a towel, wanting to erase the damning messages, when a thought stops me cold. What if this is evidence? What if erasing it makes me look guilty? Instead, I sink onto the floor, my gaze locked on the walls. The words blur as tears fill my eyes, but I blink them away. I can't afford to be weak now. Kat wriggles down onto the ground next to me.

"What's going on? Did you do this?"

"Why the hell would I terrorize myself?" I meet her stunned expression. "You heard Rebecca. Somebody hit her on the back of the head. Somebody put my journal in the toilet. Put a bird in my room..." Get it together, I think, running a hand through my wet hair. Think like a writer. What would your protagonist do? The irony isn't lost on me. How many times have I written scenes like this, reveling in the tension, the fear? Now that I'm living it, it's far from entertaining. "Sienna. It has to be her," I say. "She hates me as much as you do."

"I don't think so," says Kat. "And I don't hate you."

"You don't?"

"Never have. And, honestly, I've been hoping for this day. To reconnect."

I shoot her a wary look.

"Go on." She crosses her arms over her chest. "Why Sienna?"

As I explain everything about Steven, ending with an apology about Mark, Kat paces the room with the restless energy of a caged animal. Her hands flit from her hair to her hips and back again. "I don't care about Mark. Honestly, you did me a favor. You finally woke me up." Her voice is firm, almost angry, but there's a hint of relief buried in her words. "Look, I know Sienna hates you to the moon, stars, and back again, but she wouldn't set you up for murder, mostly because she's an idiot and wouldn't get away with it. Plus, it would damage her social media influencer status." She tugs her bottom lip, examining a sore I hadn't noticed before. "Why did Rebecca mention this Lila Aiken? You did, too. Who is she?"

"Somebody who's stolen my story."

Kat turns to face me, her eyes sharp and questioning. "And your story is about?"

"Us. Sort of. Us with a couple of twists."

I expect her to explode, to accuse me of betrayal, but instead, she just stands there, motionless, as if the news has paralyzed her. I can almost see the wheels turning in her head, trying to piece together how this revelation fits into everything else I've just told her.

"I get it. You were writing through your pain. Like I did." Her lips purse. "Does my character die in the end?"

"She does." I close my eyes, preparing myself for her answer to my next question. "You're evading my question. Tell me. Are you Lila Aiken?"

"You know me, I like a bit of drama, but, come on, if I were to use a fictitious name, I'd come up with a better one than that." Kat lets out a laugh and then gasps, looking down at something on the dresser. She points. I stand up, ambling over to her. My eyes lock onto a letter opener, the one I'd given Steven. The one the cops are most certainly looking for.

"Somebody is definitely trying to set me up for Steven's murder," I say, my eyes bugging out. "Or drive me crazy."

The going crazy part is working because all of this is absolutely insane.

Kat picks up the letter opener, stuffing it into her pocket, and heads to the door.

"What are you doing?"

"Protecting you."

"I don't need your protection—"

"But you do. And nobody is setting you up. Not on my watch." Her expression turns serious. "We're getting out of here. Don't touch anything else. It's all evidence. Leave your suitcase. You're staying with me in my suite."

"What about Mark?" I ask.

"Right, him," she says, her eyes flickering from side to side. "I'll have one of my staff members bring Sienna's things up. He can stay in her room and she'll stay with us. I have a two-bedroom suite with a living room. Mark can stay in her room or in the barn."

"He won't agree."

"He won't have a choice," she says with a lift of her shoulders. "This is my resort. And we need to talk."

"Talk about what," says Mark, barreling into the suite, his eyes scanning the walls. "Fuck. Who did this?"

My lips involuntarily pinch together. "It wasn't Kat. Was it you?"

"Why would I trash a room I'm staying in? And, clearly, we can't stay here."

"Exactly," says Kat, turning toward Mark. "I can't stand to be around you, can barely look at you, but we're all going up to my suite."

"This is a nightmare," says Mark.

"My thoughts exactly. And, lucky me, you're in it," says Kat.

"Let me grab my toothbrush," I say, heading to the bathroom. Once again, I find a word scrawled on the mirror, written in red smudged slashes. Psychopath, but they'd spelled it wrong. Sykopath. I let out a surprised yelp and Kat comes running.

"Oh, boy," she says, tsking. "Time to figure out who is going to be locked up."

My eyes scan the vanity. "That's not the only problem." I tap the counter. "I placed it right here. Right here. My necklace is missing. The one I won in Santorini when we played that ridiculous game."

Kat swats at my hand. "Don't touch anything. Everything is evidence. Fingerprints."

"But I was staying in this room—"

"Not your fingerprints. Whoever is doing this to you, to us."

"To us?" I ask, still doubting her. "I don't know how you're maintaining your composure. I feel like I'm losing my mind."

"For a while, I did, too. When it first started happening. The notes slid under the wipers of my car, in my mailbox. 'I know what you did. And you'll pay.' The feeling I was being watched, followed."

"Somebody was stalking you?" Mark asks.

"Not was—is. And I'm thinking that whoever this person is, she's definitely female and she's here, watching. Waiting."

Before we leave the room, I grab the gifted journal from the basket and shrug. "I need this so I can write everything down to make sense of things."

She shudders. "Good luck with that."

Kat pulls out a key card and I hear a click. Stunned, I take a step backwards. "I thought the doors didn't lock from the outside?"

"They do when you have a master key."

"You really should rethink that system," says Mark.

"Believe me, I am." She sighs. "As much as I wanted to believe in it, there's no such thing as a safe place." Kat saunters down the hallway, the lights flickering, and my knees lock. I don't follow. She turns to face me. "What?"

"You know, I don't trust you."

"I don't trust you either." She sighs. "But I know you're not a killer."

"I've thought about it." I swallow. "Killing somebody."

"I've thought about it, too, but thinking and acting on that notion are two different things." She pauses. "Especially when you're a writer."

Despite the circumstances, the dread pounding in my heart, I have to grin. "You know me so well."

"And you know me."

She doesn't know about the micro-recorder I've placed in the pocket of my cargo pants. To be safe, I surreptitiously click it on. The dynamics of this retreat have shifted like the weather, and I'm still waiting for the other shoe to drop.

TWENTY-EIGHT

(NOW)

KAT

As we walk to my suite, I'm happy that Liv and I will have a chance to finally sort out our differences, all those petty little things that drove us apart. OK. Fine. What drove us apart wasn't little; it was huge. Still, it's true, I never slept with nor seduced Steven Shepherd, as Liv has accused me of. He was way under my pay grade, as most people are. Even Mark, who I've kept around for my own convenience. He'd lost his luster a long time ago and, regardless of how good he looks in suits, he can't be polished up.

I look over my shoulder, watch her slow and deliberate movements, the way she's eyeing my back. She's watching me, just as I've been watching her, but she's being blatantly more obvious about it right now.

Me? I operate in stealth mode.

For the past two years, I've kept a close eye on Liv through a surveillance team. I've seen her sad smile as she sold books in that even sadder bookstore in Brooklyn, still wearing all the clothes I'd purchased for her. I'd liked her from the moment I'd first met her, because she didn't ask anything from me. She'd been honest, to a point.

Liv is the only person who truly knows me, what makes me tick. Way back when, she didn't judge me when I'd told her about my past; she'd simply accepted it. And I'd accepted her. I still remember her words, replay them in my head: "We can't let the past define us, but it can surely shape us."

I miss her friendship like the night misses the sun—the way we used to laugh like hyenas, the late nights watching bad movies, the way we'd connected. I know, once she hears me out, Liv will come around. Because I'm about to tell her something I've never told anybody—a dirty and very ugly truth—hoping she'll also confess her truths to me.

I know everyone has secrets they'd rather keep buried, but this tango of ours has to come to an end. I can't wait to lead the next dance. The question now running in my head is: which song shall I play?

TWENTY-NINE

(NOW)

We enter Kat's suite and once my eyes adjust to the dim lighting from wall sconces, I take in my surroundings. She'd really downplayed her quarters, because it's not *just* a suite; it's an entire apartment, complete with a spacious living room with a fireplace. This space exudes a sense of minimalism with clean lines and a mostly white color palette accented by pops of vibrant green. Everywhere I look, plants hang—potted ferns, succulents, cascading vines, and orchids in every color.

Mark heads over to the gas fireplace, turning it on. Then he walks to the bar, grabbing a bottle of whiskey, pouring a glass, like he's been here before. He shoots me a look. "This is way too uncomfortable for me," he says. "I'll let you two talk. I'll be in the office. Just scream and I'll come running."

I watch him vanish round the corner. Can't he hear me? I'm already screaming on the inside.

Kat sighs. "I'm glad he left."

"I am, too," I mutter and her lips twist to the side.

"Please, get comfortable. We've got a lot of catching up to do," says Kat, gesturing toward a set of plush chairs and a couch arranged around a carved wooden coffee table. "I'm going to open a bottle of one of our finest eaux-de-vie."

"Eau de vie?"

"It's something I wanted to do here, seeing that I grew up in the spirits industry. I'm still a major stockholder in the company my grandfather founded." She glides over to the bar, her feet swishing softly against the wooden floor. "But I'm doing things a little differently. All of our ingredients come from the gardens and are processed right here in our distillery—small batches," she explains, looking over her shoulder.

I blink back my surprise and straighten my posture. "Are you trying to poison me?"

She gives a soft laugh. "If I were, I don't think I'd tell you."

I watch her hands as she reaches for several glass bottles, each filled with a jewel-toned liquid. She handles them with the care of a craftsman, or perhaps an alchemist. "Peach? Pear? Cherry? What are you in the mood for?"

A sense of unease settles in the pit of my stomach. Then again, I'm the one who mentioned poison, mostly because I saw the hemlock in the garden. My mind races as I struggle to find the right words. Finally, I blurt out, "I'm in the mood for the truth."

Kat's smile falters for a moment. "The truth?" she echoes, her voice laced with surprise. "What are you driving at, Liv?"

"I didn't kill Steven, and somebody is clearly trying to set me up," I say.

"Yes, I know. And I believe you. I didn't kill him either. Your point?"

My heart pounds in my chest as I blurt out my suspicions. "I know you were involved in a cult. And everything about Nyx feels very... cult-like."

A heavy silence hangs in the air as Kat considers my words. Finally, she says, her tone serious, "You're not wrong, but you're also not right."

I swallow. "You tried to change me, convert me—"

"Change you?" she guffaws. "No, I liked you the way you were. Sweet. Nice. Honest."

"What about all the clothes? The gifts?"

Her jaw clenches. "Liv, I only did all those things for you because I could. Never, ever did I think changing your outer layer would change the inner mechanics of who you are as a person."

I hang my head. "I was just trying to fit in with the rest of you."

"Sometimes it's good to stand out." She tsks. "I'm sorry if what I did changed you—the real you. I just wanted you to feel good about yourself." She uncorks a bottle and takes a swig directly from it. "I chose peach." She licks her lips. "Because life is just so damn peachy. Back to the cult accusation, which, as you know, is true," she says, her voice trailing off. She sits down next to me on the couch, placing the bottle and two glasses on the coffee table. The fire flickers, warming my body, Kat's gaze just as intense as the flames. "Remember that secret project I was working on? The one I'd wanted you to be a part of?" she asks, and I nod.

A chill shimmies down my spine. "Starting another cult?"

"Don't be silly. Nyx isn't a cult. All proceeds from the products we sell, well, after paying the staff and operating expenses, go to a women's charity I founded—women who have suffered abuse." She clasps my hand. "This is my way of making sure nothing like what happened to us happens to any woman. Ever again."

This is not computing. "What about your memoir?"

She nods. "It's entitled *Under the Influence*, and how we—Sienna and I—became enamored with Tobias Rane when we were teenagers." Kat's voice rises into one of hopeful optimism. "Anyway, we're doing great things here at Nyx. We're creating something truly special by telling the world how we got out, raising awareness." She lets out a heavy sigh, her shoulders slumping. I look up toward Kat, trying to read her.

"What happened to your parents?" I ask cautiously.

"Somebody from the Nexus cult killed them—probably ordered by Tobias himself," she says bitterly. "He wasn't the only one we sent to prison." She sighs. "Unfortunately, we don't know the exact reach of Nexus." She gulps, her eyes flickering with pain. "I'm sure whoever that person is, they're after me, after all of us. Whether you like it or not, Liv, you're connected to us."

Her words hit me like a cold wave.

So does her honesty.

A clap of thunder interrupts our discussion, almost as if emphasizing the gravity of her words. Even though the shutters are closed, a crack of lightning illuminates the room. The rain beats down on the roof like bullets. We sit in tense silence, staring at the fire.

"Unfortunately, until we stop whoever is threatening us, the situation is probably going to get worse."

I can already feel the panic building in my chest. "How much worse?"

Kat hands me my drink, and I take a sip, feeling the burn of alcohol coat my throat.

"A lot worse," she replies grimly. "But, before I get into all of the sordid details, I need to know something. Mark told me that Steven warned you about somebody. A week before his... passing."

My hand tightens around my glass. When did Mark speak with Kat alone? "I thought he was warning me about you. Maybe Sienna."

Kat leans forward. "What did he say? Exactly?"

"I can't remember his exact words. Something like 'She was crazy in high school. She's even crazier now. She's stalking me. And it's gotten so bad over the past month that I'm moving to a new place with a doorman, security.'" I shudder. "He also said, 'You don't know what *she's* really like...'"

Kat shakes her head, her mouth twisting with disbelief. "He wasn't talking about me or Sienna. He could have been talking about *her*, but that doesn't make any sense."

I feel like I'm going to internally combust. "Who are you talking about?"

"I'm getting to that," Kat says as she refills my glass. "Trust me, you're going to need this because you'll learn why I never really talk about the past." She shakes her head, a rogue strand of black hair falling in her eyes. She lets out a long breath. "The story I'm about to tell you is going to blow your mind."

Too late. My mind has already been blown to smithereens. I place my hands on my knees, bracing myself for whatever she's about to reveal... or not reveal. I lean forward, meeting her eyes. "I'm listening."

Kat goes silent and takes a sip of her drink. "Earlier, I told you I'd thought about killing somebody. And, well, I did. Kill somebody..." Her voice trails off and she locks her gaze onto mine. I can't quite read the light in her eyes—defiance, maybe, or a twisted form of pride. "I killed her with my own two hands."

THIRTY

(THEN)

KAT

It happened after our initiation ceremony at Nyx. Sienna and I raced out of the garden, the wind blowing our hair, the snow crunching under our feet, the trees dropping clumps of fresh powder on the path. Our faces were red and our fingers numb, our bodies shivering. And yet, we couldn't stop. We had to keep moving, keep running.

The scent of pine infiltrated our noses as we inhaled clean mountain air. Behind us, I heard a snap, the sound of a twig breaking, thinking it could be a deer. Two peacocks strutted into the driveway, their trains fanned out in all their glory, the plumes sparkling in the sun. We gasped in awe as we watched them march into the brush.

Like nothing bad could ever have happened here.

As we raced down the driveway, we were both surprised to see a lone figure, sitting in the gazebo on the edge of the pond. This person's gaze snapped onto ours. Morgan Rane. I'd have recognized that mop of strawberry-blond hair anywhere. I stormed toward her through the snow, Sienna following me.

"I thought we were leaving this horrible place," Sienna shrieked. "Where are you going?"

"Before we leave, I'm going to tap into my inner goddess," I mumbled.

I was about fifty yards away from Morgan when she held up her hand like a gun. She grinned. "Bang! Hunting season has started."

Anger raged within my entire system and I picked up my pace. Sienna tried to grab my arm, but I whipped it away. I ran through the snow, stumbling a few times. I couldn't hear a thing, save for the pounding urgency in my brain. My feet were numb. My mind, too.

Finally, I stood in front of her, her icy-blue eyes locked onto mine. And then she laughed. "Enjoy your initiation ceremony? Did it work wonders?"

Not able to control my impulses, my arm whipped out and I grabbed her by the hair. Thanks to years of studying Krav Maga, I'd learned some serious moves. I kicked her legs out from under her and then grabbed her arm, dragging her to the pond, her body thrashing. She could put up a fight. But I was stronger. Sienna was screaming, "Kat! What are you doing? Stop! Stop! You're going to kill her!"

It was my intention. I ignored her cries. Crows scattered into the sky, as if they knew something horrible was about to happen.

Morgan's eyes met mine. I saw something spark inside them: fear. She pleaded with me, gasping for air. I couldn't hear her words, didn't want to. I was waist deep in the pond, the water freezing, sloshing around my body.

I pushed her underwater, through a thin layer of ice,

holding her down until she went still, until the air bubbles no longer popped up to the surface in rings. I gave her one quick look, the ice crackling on the pond in snowflake patterns. Little crystals. Then I turned and ran as fast as I could to the car, starting it up with a trembling hand. Sienna jumped in and we tore out of there like a bat out of hell—our own hell.

Shivering from adrenaline and the cold, I turned up the heat. Finally, I spoke. "I had to do it."

Sienna stared blankly out the window. "I think we should call the police."

"And say what?" I snapped.

"But—"

"No buts."

"What if somebody saw you?"

"*Me?*" I snorted. "We're in this together. Her death is on your hands, too. You just stood there and watched. You didn't stop me, which makes you an accessory to murder. Do you want to go to prison?"

Sienna sank into her seat, knee on the dash. I gripped the steering wheel, my knuckles turning white, trying to block everything that had happened out of my memory.

It worked, for a while.

ACT THREE

THIRTY-ONE

(NOW)

When Kat finishes recounting her twisted story, I am speechless. She has just confessed to murder. It takes effort to catch my breath. I wasn't expecting her to be this brutally honest. The sound of the storm outside only adds to the chaos rocking my mind. "I think I need another drink," I finally say.

Kat gives a sad chuckle and refills my glass. "Hate to say I told you so," she says, her full lips pressed into a thin line. "But I told you so."

I down the eau de vie like it's a shot, feeling the burn in my throat. How much of what she's told me is true? Like me, she knows how to spin a story. It takes me a moment to gather my thoughts, to find the right words. "I'm sorry you had to go through all of that," I finally say. "I can't imagine what it must have been like."

"Well," says Kat with a heavy breath, "what doesn't kill us makes us stronger. And sometimes you have to strike first."

I'm not quite sure I can mask the impact her statement has made on me. I tap my foot, my legs drumming their own beat. I can't meet her eyes. "I think I'd need therapy for the rest of my life."

"Been there, done that. Nobody really understands what I went through." Kat shakes her head and lets out a soft laugh. "That's the reason I'm writing my memoir about what happened." Her chin lowers. "It's really been a painful journey, writing everything down, but, honestly, a part of me—a huge part—has healed along the way. It's my own way of... moving on."

I swallow. "I have so many questions."

"I'm sure you do." She squeezes her eyes tight shut as if she's sorry. "Obviously, there's a very good reason why I never shared the last part of my tragic tale with you. But now that my memoir will be published, everything will be out in the open..." She swallows. "Well, everything but *her*. That stays between us."

"I, uh, I don't know what to say. Why did you tell me this?"

"I thought you might understand."

I clench my hands together, digging my nails into my palms. "Do you regret what you did?"

She leans forward as if she's expecting a different response, her head tilting to the side.

"Every day." She shrugs. "I know Tobias had Morgan target Sienna and me because of our families' wealth. I think, in a severe lapse of judgment, a moment of insanity, I took my anger out on her."

"In the worst of ways," I say, gulping.

"I know." She bites down on her bottom lip. "Don't kill the messenger."

Is she for real? I'm wondering how damaged and delusional Kat is now. And I don't feel sorry for her at all. "I think you should tell the police what you did."

Her eyes spark up and she leans forward. "You can't kill somebody that doesn't exist."

"But she did exist."

"Not for me."

The finality in her tone chills me to the bone.

A loud knock startles us, cutting off our conversation right when we're getting somewhere. Kat squeezes my hand and then lifts herself off the couch. My eyes follow her as she opens the door, waiting for her next move. It's not only Sienna, but Mimi, who is supporting her by the arms.

Sienna stumbles into the room, slurring. "Are we ready to continue the party? The Bees are fun. They like tequila shots. The storm is madness. Who came up with the expression it's raining cats and dogs? I haven't seen a dog. But I do see a Kat." She tilts her head back and laughs, pointing at Kat.

"Sorry, she's wasted." Mimi frowns. "Went *way* beyond her two-drink limit."

Kat shakes her head. "She's not supposed to be drinking at all. Interferes with her medications…"

"Medications?" I ask.

"Sienna's head, if you haven't ever noticed, is wildly messed up. Has been since…"

She doesn't need to finish her sentence.

Thunder booms. Sienna jerks her arms away from Mimi, her eyes wide and frantic. She bolts over to the bar, her ankles threatening to give out beneath her.

Kat's lip curls with disgust and she points. "Go to bed."

Sienna crosses her arms over her chest. "I'm not tired."

"Then sit down and sober up," says Kat, handing her a bottle of water from the bar. "I told Liv everything."

Sienna's eyes go wide as she takes in my presence. Her jaw drops and she shakes her head. "What the hell is she doing here? Hasn't she caused enough trouble already?"

I do what any normal person would do in this situation. I step up to Sienna and wrap her in a tight hug. Because that's a normal reaction, right? "I know why you hate me," I say softly, "and I don't blame you. I'm also sorry I wasn't a better friend..."

Sienna's eyes flash with awareness. She pushes me away, cringing, and turns to face Kat. "What did you tell her?"

"Everything," confirms Kat with a lift of her brows.

"Everything?"

"Well"—Kat pauses for a moment—"almost everything."

I straighten my posture. I knew she'd left something out of her twisted tale. And I'm wondering if she'll tell me the rest of it. Knowing Kat, she's waiting for the perfect moment to strike.

"She's not one of us," Sienna declares with force. "Never has been. Never will be." Arms flailing wildly, she swaggers up to Kat, poking her clavicle. She hiccups. "You had no right to tell her what happened. No right."

"Why not? My memoir is going to be published anyway. I don't use your real name. Only mine—"

"People will make the connection. You're bringing me down with you." Her head and her voice lowers. "Your memoir shouldn't be published. I'm not happy about this at all."

"Uh, Sienna," says Mimi, "I urged Kat to write her memoir. She was a victim. You were a victim—"

"Blah, blah, blah—enough with the victim mentality. I'm over it."

Mark peeks his head around the corner from the hallway, his sandy hair tousled and eyes bloodshot. He's wearing sweatpants and a faded college t-shirt that's seen better days. "I thought I heard my darling sister," he says with a lazy smirk, leaning against the wall with feigned nonchalance. His gaze darts between Sienna, Kat, and me.

Kat's entire demeanor shifts in an instant. "Go to Sienna's room. Or go to the barn. Sleep with the other animals." She shrugs and then meets Mark's widened eyes. "We women need to talk. Out."

Mark glares at Kat and shakes his head. "Kat, have you lost your common sense?"

"I've never lost my senses. They're my power when it comes to perfume making. And they're alive and awake right now." Kat sniffs the air, looks over her shoulder. "Liv, why don't you tell me how you reconnected with Mark? Were you following him around? Stalking him? That's what he told me."

Once again, Kat is changing the narrative.

"No," I say, not knowing where this conversation is headed. "He came into the bookstore. And asked me out."

"And you accepted because you thought it would hurt me?"

I grimace. "True."

"Good. I like the truth."

I have no idea what her intentions are, but she's clearly madder at Mark than she is at me. We're all just chess pieces to her. We're the pawns and I want to see this game she's playing to the end.

"Mark," I say, placing a hand on his shoulder. "Kat's

right. You should go. We need to talk. We're trying to clear the air."

Mark's eyes darken. His mouth twists into a sneer. "I can't believe this," he mutters.

"Believe it." Kat shrugs and then she flicks her fingers up and down in a robotic wave. "You know where Sienna's suite is. Buh-bye."

Silence settles over the room, save for the hiss of the fire and the thunder booming in the distance.

"Liv, have fun clearing the air with your *good friend*, Kat. She destroys everything in her path. And she'll make you pay." Mark's lips curl into a nasty sneer. "But not with money. She'll find something on you and keep using it against you. Just like she did with me. She's out-of-this-world insane. Don't say I didn't warn you."

I watch as he huffs and puffs, slamming the door behind him. I don't chase after him because he is no longer part of *my* plan. I'm one step closer to winning the war I have with Kat.

"And I'm the crazy one?" Kat's chest heaves up and down with quiet laughter. "Who needs a drink?"

"I do, but Sienna is definitely cut off," says Mimi, stepping over to the bar. "And then I'm going to bed."

"Back to your questions, Liv," says Kat. "And we'll move on from there."

"OK," I say, wringing my hands. "I'll start with a basic one." I pause. "Kat, are you Lila Aiken?"

"Why do you keep bringing up this person?" Kat replies, looking at me like I'm nuts.

"You want to destroy my writing career..." I start.

"Kat is *not* Lila Aiken." Sienna grimaces and then lets out a long groan. "I am. Well, technically, Liv, *you* are..."

I feel the blood drain from my face. The room tilts slightly, the chatter in my brain fading to white noise. My jaw tightens, my voice sounding distant, even to my own ears. "Sienna? What did you do?"

"OK, so I might have gotten onto Mark's computer one day. And I might have found your manuscript. And I might have forwarded it to myself. I hated the book, the way you portrayed all of us. Me? The ditzy, gold-digging sidekick." She gives Mimi a look. "Well, you, you were fine—"

"Sienna, get to the point," says Kat, her eyes darkening.

The betrayal feels physical, a knife twisting between my ribs.

She hiccups. "I set up an email using the name Lila Aiken—queried the hell out of the book. I wasn't expecting an offer so quickly—or one at all—but one came in and I may have signed it." Her eyes go wide. She shoots me a sloppy, wicked grin. "I wanted to hurt you the way you hurt me. I wanted to destroy your career."

"I never hurt you..." I begin.

She stands up and points a shaky finger at me. "But you did. When you traded in my friendship for Kat's, constantly blowing me off. When you went after Steven, knowing full well I'd had a thing for him."

Mimi lets out a caustic laugh. "You're acting like you're still in high school. What you did was illegal."

"Not as illegal as murder," I mutter, focusing my attention on her. "Did you set me up for Steven's murder? And what about Rebecca? Somebody whacked her on the head. You know what, forget this, I'm calling the police."

"No phone service and the radio is on the fritz," says Kat with a shake of her head. "No Internet."

"I haven't killed anyone." Sienna sinks onto the couch.

"Don't you understand? I'm their next target. Last week someone left a threatening letter in my Pilates bag. I didn't think much of it at the time, thought it was one of my fans. But it was a threat."

The way she blinks and won't lift her head up, I sense she's lying, or not telling the full truth. With what I now know, I'm certain she's responsible for the lipstick threats in my room and dumping my journal in the toilet. Before I can rail into her with accusations, Mimi clears her throat. "You're not the only one. Right after we announced Kat's publishing deal, I got an email. It said, 'If *Under the Influence* sees the light of day, you're going to regret you were ever born.'"

"You didn't tell me about that," says Kat.

"I didn't take it seriously until now," she replies, setting her glass down. "And I can't take much more of this. I'll see you in the morning."

After Mimi shuffles to her room, I don't know where to focus, not with the massive headache threatening to split my head wide open. The gravity of the situation hangs thick in the air, punctuated by the loudest of thunderclaps. I sit tense, alert, waiting.

THIRTY-TWO

(NOW)

My mind is tweaked to the point of no return. I just want to write everything down, get to the end of this twisted story. Though all I want to do is sleep, we continue the discussion, trying to put the puzzle pieces together, comparing notes.

"Liv," says Kat, "this isn't good. The police know about your relationship with Steven. They know about his texts to you. You must be a person of interest."

I hang my head, my mind swirling to the past. What do the police know?

The end of my relationship with Steven came in a fiery explosion. When I went back to retrieve my belongings from his place, my vision blurred and all I could see was red. Mugs and glasses shattered. The fight escalated and we were so loud one of his neighbors called the cops. The next few hours were a blur.

The piercing sound of sirens, of stern voices; the vision of flashing lights pass through my mind as the police hand-cuffed and escorted me away, cold, hard metal biting into my wrists. They took my fingerprints and then snapped a mugshot of me looking disheveled and unhinged. Steven eventually chose not to press charges, but he did file a restraining order against me.

"I know it looks bad, but I didn't kill him."

"I think you did," says Sienna. "And I think you should leave."

"Liv's not going anywhere," says Kat, shooting Sienna a steely glare. "Let's think. The police said Steven was killed on Sunday—found by his cleaner on Tuesday morning."

Sienna throws her hands in the air. "Ha! I was in India until Sunday."

"Why'd you go to India?" I ask.

"I wanted to do some research for the sanctuary."

I blink. "But Kat's the founder."

"Mimi and Sienna are private investors in Nyx. Sienna is in charge of the clothing lines, the food and beauty products. And me, I told you about the spirits and perfumes. Mimi, obviously, is paper and marketing. Proceeds from our sales go to our foundation, which helps women escape from abusive situations."

I know bullshit when I hear it. "What's it called?"

"Selene's Light—inspired by the goddess of the moon, and representing guidance, hope, and illumination in dark times," says Kat.

I raise a brow and shake my head. "Fine. If Sienna didn't kill him, we have to figure out who did. Tell me, did they ever find Morgan's body?"

Sienna swallows and then screams, "You told her about *that*?"

"I did, and calm down," says Kat, staring blankly ahead. She swallows and then meets my eyes. "We were never questioned. The bears would have found her. The Catskill

Mountains have the densest population of black bears in New York State. Sometimes we see the cubs playing in the pond. They're quite cute, the way they roll around on the banks or try to catch fish."

My eyes bug out. Kat's brain really needs to be rewired, neuron-to-neuron, synapse-to-synapse. Sienna sits in her chair, rocking back and forth and mumbling swear words to herself.

"What about your staff? Could one of them be involved?"

"It's a possibility," says Kat, "and it's the reason I have James and Carol here. They're my watchdogs, here to alert me if they see anything shady going on or if trouble comes knocking on the door." Her eyes dart to mine. "Both of them are ex-military and, well, they've been married to each other for ten years and like living in the country. I still have my bodyguard living with me in the city. You know him."

"I do?"

"Frank."

"Oh," I say, clearing my throat. How could I have forgotten about him? I need to recover quickly. "I didn't see Frank around much."

"His job is to slip into the shadows, not to be seen." She tilts her head to the side, shooting me the strangest of looks.

"I remember how he searched my things the day I moved in with you," I say, nodding. "You bought me a whole new wardrobe. And it made me very—"

"Happy," she says and then she pops her lips. "Well, once you realized I was only looking out for your best interests."

We sit in silence for a moment, heads down. "What about your new bestie, Trinity?" asks Sienna. "I think she's the person we should be looking at. Last name Powers. Could be her goddess name..."

"Or her parents really loved the film *The Matrix*," says Kat with a laugh.

"Whatever." Sienna taps her chin. "She's interviewed me before for one of her stories on influencers. Isn't it weird she happens to be here now?"

"Yes, Sienna, we know how important you are." Kat lifts up her chin. "Trinity freelances for some of the big magazines. She's doing a piece on the resort for *Vanity Fair*. A photographer was supposed to arrive today or tomorrow, but... the storm really put a big old kybosh on that."

"She's also investigating you, Kat," I say, wondering how she'll react. "She knows about the cult, that you were a part of it."

Kat reddens. "Whatever," she says. "Find out what she knows. But don't tell her anything. We can trust absolutely nobody—not the writers on the retreat, not even the staff. The only people we can trust are sitting in this room."

We'd already decided that the four of us will stay together— safety in numbers. Sienna and Mimi will take the second bedroom and Kat invites me to sleep with her in her California king, enough room for all of us. But I'm not sleeping with the enemy.

"I'll just sleep on the couch," I say.

Kat squints. "You sure?"

I nod toward the fire. "Positive."

Finally, we all settle in for the night to the music of the rain pelting on the roof, the windows. My mind is in overdrive and I can't stop thinking about her messed-up story—

I'm still envisioning Kat holding Morgan down in the pond, Morgan's blue eyes losing their light. Chills, a coldness, sets in. I wrap the blankets around me tighter. They smell of Kat, her perfume.

No, I won't be sleeping tonight.

About an hour later, I hear footsteps pad into the room and I jolt upright, on the defense. My eyes search the darkness for a flash of light on a blade, completely paranoid.

"You're still awake," says Kat.

My heart settles down. Sort of. "I can't sleep."

"Neither can I." She turns on a light in the kitchen. She's wearing a nightgown, her lanky silhouette glowing pale yellow, her hair smooth on her back. "Water?"

"Yes, please."

I hear the sound of water being poured and she joins me on the couch, handing me a glass. "If you'd never met us, this wouldn't be happening to you," she says. "That's what's keeping me up. I'm sorry."

She doesn't sound sorry. No, her tone is flat, devoid of emotion. She's angling for me to say something. Her eyes meet mine.

"Once the storm has subsided and the roads are clear, I won't hold it against you if you leave."

"Nope," I say. "W-whether I like it or not, I'm in this. Actually, I learned a lot from you… when we spent time together."

And there's so much more I need to find out.

She nods thoughtfully. "I told you that I saw something special in you. I meant it. It was some weird, cosmic connection."

"Uh-huh," I agree. "Why did you buy this place? I mean,

it's beautiful, but... I don't get it. You lived through a nightmare here. And now..."

"It's an ongoing nightmare." She shakes her head and blows out a breath. "Regardless of everything, my goal, as mentioned, was to take something from the darkness and make it bright and beautiful." She squeezes my hand. "I learned a lot about myself here." She stands up abruptly and lets out a deep yawn. "I'm exhausted. I'll see you in the morning," she says, padding back to her room, humming a haunting version of "You Are My Sunshine."

As I think about the lyrics, the true meaning hits me— they are not about love, but about obsession and possession. This is the Kat I know, manipulative and dangerous. The Kat who needs to be followed, worshipped. The Kat who has confessed to murder. As much as I'd love to give Kat the benefit of the doubt, she thinks she's fooled me with her sob story.

Think again, Kat.

THIRTY-THREE

(NOW)

In the morning, the storm has dwindled to a drizzle, no longer assaulting the roof like an overzealous marching band on parade. Kat unfastens the shutters, peering out with hopeful eyes. She points toward the horizon, her finger tracing an arc. "I see the makings of a rainbow and a slash of blue cutting through the gray," she says, turning to me with a smile. "Get ready, Liv. I had the boutique send you up a fresh change of clothes. Today is a new day."

"Thanks," I say. "I'll pay you back."

She sniggers. "As if."

As I take a quick shower and dress, the only thing I'm getting ready for is the next circle of hell.

An hour later, Mimi and Sienna saunter into the living room. "Oh good. We're all here," says Sienna, shooting me a smirk.

"I never want to share a bed with Sienna ever again," says Mimi with a groan. "She snores like a buzz saw. She tosses and turns, hogging the blankets and wrapping herself up like a burrito. I really need coffee."

I let out a yawn. "Aside from getting a caffeine fix, do we have a plan?"

Kat tilts her head to one side, contemplating, and then she strikes a pose, her finger bobbing up and down as she shifts her weight to one hip. "'Staying Alive'?"

"Ah, ah, ah, so funny," says Sienna.

"It is," she insists, the corners of her mouth quirking. She places her hands on her hips, striking a confident stance. "I'm wagering that whoever wants to sever our—what's the word I'm looking for?"

"Ties," I offer.

"Yes, not heads, ties," she says, her voice taking on a more serious tone. "I may be making a lot of assumptions here, but after what happened to Rebecca, they know about your book, Liv. And they definitely know about mine."

We fall silent, each of us lost in our own thoughts.

"I'm going back to bed," says Sienna with a groan. "I don't feel so well."

Poor baby. Sienna is likely facing a monstrous hangover and I don't feel bad for her. Not one bit. Leaving her to her fate, Mimi, Kat, and I make our way down to breakfast. We pass Mark in the hallway; he grunts, "Liv, we'll talk later," and then he shoulders past us with a green smoothie clutched in his hand.

Kat shoots me a look.

"I can't deal with him now," I say.

At the entrance to the dining room, Kat pauses. "Just pretend everything is normal," she says in a low voice. "And find out what Trinity knows."

I nod, making my way to my assigned table, journal in hand. I glance around the room, taking in the familiar yet now ominous surroundings. The tension is palpable, and I hope my face doesn't betray me.

The Bees are having an animated chat at their table, as are the other writers. I start to write, then pause, tapping the pen against my lips. What is my next move? Who is responsible? None of the writers look like a threat. Kat? Mark? Sienna? I'm in the process of underlining Trinity's name five times when the scrape of a chair startles me out of my spiraling thoughts. I freeze, heart pounding, as if caught in some illicit act.

"I see you're working on something," says Trinity, her eyebrows raised.

Shit. I glance at the incriminating scrawl in my notebook, and slam it shut. My throat constricts.

"Just getting into my research," I say.

Trinity's piercing brown eyes scan my face. "I knocked on your door this morning, but you didn't answer." She pauses, tilting her head, assessing me. "Are you alright? You look like you've seen a ghost."

"We all have our ghosts. The trick is to make them work for us, not against us." I laugh, the sound a bit overzealous, and she recoils.

"I thought we'd made plans to meet up before breakfast to talk more about"—her eyes dart to Kat—"her."

"I stayed with Kat in her suite," I say with a shrug. "We worked through our differences."

"Sure that's a good idea?" she whispers. "I mean, I was worried when you didn't answer."

A server comes by, pouring freshly squeezed orange juice into our glasses, and I've never been so thankful for an interruption. I need to keep my wits about me. Is Trinity's obsession with Kat merely professional interest, or something else?

I take a swig of my juice. "Sorry about that."

"Right," she says. "After we're done here, come to my room. I want to show you something. You need to see my research. I worked on it all night."

Begrudgingly, after a light breakfast of fruit and a much-needed dose of caffeine, I follow Trinity, catching Kat's eye in the foyer on the way. She's speaking with Victoria Foster, and the discussion looks heated. I mouth, "Her room."

"Be careful," she mouths back.

Trinity leads me down the hall and I stop in front of my room, wiggle the doorknob. The door is still locked. "Did you need to grab something from yours?" she asks.

"No, I'm good."

While she's distracted, I flip the pocket recorder on.

Trinity opens the door to her room and ushers me inside. I let out a gasp.

Every square inch of one wall is covered with a collage of faces—photographs and newspaper clippings—mostly of Kat and, as I step closer, of me. It's disturbing. Red threads connect Kat to me, to Sienna, to Mark, to Steven, to Mimi— all of our faces more haunting in print. I watch her, trans-fixed by the manic energy radiating off her in waves. She points to the center image of Kat. And then she taps a picture of a girl with blonde frizzy hair and blinged-out braces. "This is Morgan Rane. She's the girl who recruited them into the cult."

It's taking every ounce of self-control not to launch into a coughing fit. I'm not sure if I should protect Kat now, but proving Kat killed somebody who'd never been found, presumed eaten by bears, would be hard. "I thought she didn't exist."

"Oh, she did. I'm the one who took her picture." She

raises a finger. "I told you I had my reasons for not wanting to let this story go. I was there at Woodford when everything went down. I always wanted to be part of Kat's group. Back then, I was an easy target for her bullying, but I was still captivated by her. By all of them. I always listened in on their hushed conversations. I heard them talking about all that goddess stuff, choosing a goddess name, Nexus, Tobias. When I left school, I totally reinvented myself. It drove me to be successful, to become who I am today. I was formerly Zuri Williams. And now I'm me."

Her declaration resonates in the silence that follows. She's not going to let this story go.

"I get it," I finally say, my eyes laser focused on the picture of Kat. "I completely understand reinventing yourself."

"Right? But somebody is not reinventing the wheel." She nods. "I think Kat's continuing Tobias's work, hiding behind the façade of a real business. She's starting a new cult. And I'm going to bust this story wide open."

She has been watching all of us, studying us like lab rats. Part of me wants to scream at her, to tell her to leave everything alone. She brushes off my shocked expression, the way I'm looking at her like she's nuts. "It's just research. I hired a private investigator."

"You're wasting your time," I say, judging her reaction. There is none. "Kat comes clean about everything that happened with Tobias Rane in her memoir."

Trinity's upper lip and eyebrows lift at the same time. "She told you about it?"

"Last night."

"I need to get a copy of that manuscript," she says, her tone more urgent than it needs to be. She taps the photograph of Kat. "I bet anything she wouldn't have told you or anybody the whole story."

Yes, Kat never tells the whole story. In her eyes, it's her world and we all revolve around her. I can't fall for her act all over again. We've always had a toxic and delusional friendship.

"We need to watch her closely." Trinity's gaze flickers over to me, and I can see the suspicion flashing in her eyes.

"I think we should be looking at everybody here. Even you," I say, but, again, Trinity doesn't flinch.

"Liv, I'm an investigative journalist. You're seeing connections where there are none," she says, but her words lack conviction. "In my experience," she continues, her voice low, "nobody is ever truly innocent. Especially those who try too hard to look it."

Why do I feel like that statement is directed at me?

"But for my story, I'm focusing on one person. Kat Sterling. It's... tricky material. She's tricky. I guess it will be a race to the finish line."

As we're leaving her room, my eyes catch sight of a metallic gleam tucked under her pillow. It looks exactly like the edge of an iPad. The truth has a way of flashing right in front of your eyes even when you're not supposed to see it. Is it hers—or the one stolen from Rebecca?

One thing is certain. Trinity is not only after a story, she's after Kat. Guess what? I am, too.

THIRTY-FOUR

(NOW)

The higher powers must be looking down upon us favorably. Forget about the goddess of night and bring on the sun. Right before lunch, our phones buzz and chirp like cicadas. Finally, the storm is clearing.

I walk into the dining room. Trinity follows, and we take a seat at our usual table. I'd like to talk with Sienna privately, but it's impossible with Trinity and her sharp ears and probing eyes—also impossible because Sienna's not here. Victoria stands, clinks her glass. "Ladies, as our lunch is served on what's looking to be a beautiful day, I'd like to play a fun game. Get this writing retreat back on track." She smiles. "My question. Are you a plotter? Or are you a pantster?"

"What's a pantster?" one of the Bees asks.

"Somebody who, when they write, flies by the seat of their pants."

"Oh, we're all definitely that," says another Bee with a giggle. "But we're usually unzipping them."

Anna Hale rolls her eyes. Mimi tries to hold back her sneer. Victoria lets out a small laugh and then directs her attention onto the literary group, who lift their chins up. "Obviously, we're all plotters with some minor pantsing. Outlines are our friends."

They all nod. "True. Everything starts with a plan."

Everybody's gazes lock onto our table.

"I agree," says Trinity. "Especially in journalism. We take fact checking seriously."

I'm now in the hot seat. I clear my throat. "I used to think I was a plotter, but I think I'm a pantster, too." My eyes meet Trinity's for a brief moment. "Sometimes unexpected things happen. You see new things. You come up with new ideas. I don't know. I guess you could say I'm a plantster. I'm always adjusting to the circumstances—to all the plot twists."

"Well said," says Anna. "That's the way I approach writing, too."

"Us, too," agree the young, cool girls. "We're totally plantsters."

Lunch is served and the chatter in the dining room is more vibrant, happy even. Animated. After dessert is served, Trinity looks at her watch. "I'm going to head to the spa. Want to join me?"

As if she's cued, Mimi walks up to the table, as Trinity is about to leave. "Liv, Rebecca is feeling better. She'd like to speak with you."

Trinity stands, her expression unreadable. "See you, Liv. We'll brainstorm more later."

I turn to face Mimi. "Where's Sienna?"

"She's still in Kat's room on her phone, arguing with Nick. From what I heard, trouble in paradise... but you didn't hear that from me. And, yes, she'll be joining us, too. Let's go get her."

Together, we make our way upstairs, one steady foot at a time. We enter Kat's suite and Sienna looks up from the couch, her cheeks tearstained. I almost feel bad for her, the way she looks like a child, hugging her knees to her chest.

Mimi walks over and squeezes her shoulder. "Are you OK?"

Sienna shrugs Mimi's hand off her back. "I'm fine. Just got something in my eye."

"OK then," says Mimi, her tone laced with exasperation. "You're going to come clean to Rebecca about what you did with Liv's book."

"When?"

"Right now."

She groans. "Fine."

Any empathy I may have had for her vanishes. Like I'm the one who has put her in this position. Down the stairs we go again. At least I'm getting in a good workout.

Mimi knocks and Victoria Foster opens the door. "You've got some serious explaining to do, Ms. Montgomery," says Victoria, her eyes locking onto mine.

"That's why I'm here," says Sienna.

"OK," says Victoria, and she sighs. "This should be interesting."

Rebecca is laid in her bed, propped up on pillows, a bandage wrapped around her head. Her eyes blaze into mine and my stomach drops to new depths. "Well, well, if it isn't Lila Aiken a.k.a. Olivia Montgomery. When I'm done with you, you'll never work with SilverGate or any other publishing house ever again. I hope you have a good attorney because we will be coming after you. I mean, who did you send after me?"

My throat constricts. "Nobody. I-I..."

Mimi nudges Sienna and growls, "Ms. Stiles, she can explain."

"And you are?"

"Sienna Knight."

She coughs. "And you're here, why?"

"Because I'm Lila Aiken. Well, technically Liv is because it's her book, but I'm the one who sent it in to Victoria without Liv's knowledge."

Victoria sinks into a chair, sighing loudly. Sienna paces in front of Rebecca's bed. "I didn't think anybody would take her book seriously."

"I thought I'd heard it all," says Rebecca.

"If we can find out who stole your iPad," I say, "we can find out who hit you on the head. And, well, find out who is trying to terrorize all of us."

"Miriam, Victoria, and Sienna." Rebecca stares blankly at the ceiling. "Can you please give Olivia and I some time alone to hash things out?" She clucks her tongue. "And, well, after what you pulled, Sienna, I don't want to look at you."

Victoria stands up, scowling at Mimi and Sienna. Rebecca calls Victoria over, whispering something in her ear. Victoria nods. After they leave the room, my gaze meets Rebecca's. "Wait a sec. Are you still considering publishing my book?"

"I'll have to run everything through legal, of course." She lets out a low chuckle, understanding etched in every line of her face. "And we'll have to survive the rest of the weekend, but yes. The real question is: which name do you want to use?"

"Mine."

"OK," she says. "Save for the murders, I'm thinking *In Her Shoes* is a story about your relationship with Kat, when you were roommates. Am I correct?"

I nod.

"If SilverGate moves forward with the book, which I hope we do, your version will be the one we will be publishing. Of course, I'll have edits."

"Of course. And I'll be looking forward to them." I grin and then snap back to attention. "If we get to that point."

Rebecca exhales. "Do you know what Kat's memoir, *Under the Influence*, is about?"

"Yes, she told me about it last night."

"Some serious stuff in it. Which is why I wanted to speak to you both." She pauses, takes a sip of water. "I instructed Victoria to send her to us. She should be here any minute," she says just as a knock comes.

Rebecca gestures, an expectation for me to let Kat in.

Slowly, I make my way to the door and take a deep breath before turning the handle. Kat wraps me in a tight hug, her spicy perfume making me woozy. She leans in, her lips brushing my ear. "Not a word about what happened at the pond," she whispers, her tone laced with malice.

I'm expecting her to say, "or else."

"Obviously," I whisper back, fighting the wave of nausea gnawing at my insides.

Kat's confidence is unshakeable, her sense of entitlement infuriating. She thinks she can get away with anything and she has—even murder. A bitter taste fills my mouth.

I watch Kat's expression, looking for signs of guilt, but she's unruffled. "We're trying to figure out who attacked you, Rebecca," says Kat, eyeing me. "Right, Liv?"

My mind races while trying to decipher the layers in her words. Sometimes I marvel at how she's able to deceive people without even trying. Maybe that's why I'd become obsessed with her whole persona.

But I'm over it now. I'm over her.

THIRTY-FIVE

(NOW)

After meeting with Rebecca, I want to get away from Kat, maybe carve out some plotting and planning time. To my relief, Kat seems to be on the same page. She hands me the Woodford Hall yearbook she managed to find online and printed off, then she tells me she's going for a power nap.

I clomp down the stairs, thinking about how messed up everything is. I'm not paying attention to my surroundings, and I should be on high alert. Somebody taps me on the shoulder. I turn around, my heart racing, to find Mark glaring at me. He's dressed in expensive running clothes, right down to his designer sneakers. I scan his face, searching his eyes for any signs of emotion. And there is one: pure anger.

"You're doing exactly what you did to Sienna, to me," he growls. "You've made your choice. You're choosing Kat."

His words hang in the air, pulsing, and hitting me in the heart.

"I didn't choose her," I say.

"But you did. And you've made a huge mistake."

"I really don't have time for this," I say, heading toward the lobby.

He follows, grabbing me by the wrist again. "Liar. Fake. Con artist," he spits, his words flying through the air like shrapnel. "Sienna is right about you. You're pretending you're someone you're not—to take advantage of people. Guess what, Talented Mrs. Ripley, I have you all figured out. And Kat's going to find out who and what you really are. A nothing—not even worth the air we breathe—"

I rip my arm from his grip. I can't believe I'd ever seen anything in him. He's showing his true colors now. "This conversation is over."

Over his shoulder, our argument has caught the attention of the people sitting on the terrace, including Sienna. He shoots his sister a look. "This time, Kat won't play around, she'll finish you off. Just like you did with Steven."

My blood runs cold.

"Is that a threat?"

His eyes meet mine and then he stomps off, heading out the door and down the steps toward the gardens. Before he rounds the corner, he turns to face me and yells, "It's not a threat. It's a promise."

Sienna's sitting at a table on the terrace, her perfect blonde hair veiling her face as she refreshes her manicure, but she looks up when I make my approach, my heart slamming against my ribcage. Last time I checked, potential murderers didn't paint their nails stark white. Blood would be too visible. Her piercing blue eyes—the same color as Mark's—lock onto mine.

"We need to talk," I say with force.

"No, we don't. I'm on a mission. And it seems to be impossible."

"What mission?"

"Avoiding you," she says, smirking. "I saw you talking"—she pulls her fingers into air quotes—"with my brother. He looked very pissed off. I'm really hoping he ended things with you."

My nerves are already on fire... and she's getting on the last of them. "I'm not playing games, Sienna. People are dead. People are getting hurt..."

"Honestly," she says, tilting her head with infuriating calm, and then blowing on her nails, "I'm hoping you're next."

I want to scream, but I force myself to breathe. In. Out. Channel that rage into words. The pen is mightier than the sword. But before I can formulate a retort, a thunderous boom echoes in the distance, sending a flock of geese into frantic flight. We both whirl toward the direction of the sound, united in our confusion. Sienna's eyes go wide. "What the hell was that?" she whispers, more to herself than to me.

My jaw tenses. A Nyx worker steps onto the terrace. She raises her voice. "Sorry about the commotion. A tree must have fallen. The good news is"—she smiles—"the roads should be cleared soon."

A cheer resounds from the Bees' table.

"Thank God, I can't wait to get away from you. I'll book your car, pay for it," begins Sienna, and then she sucks on her bottom lip, glaring at something behind me.

I turn my head to find Trinity staring at us from another table. Sienna shudders. "That reporter really gives me all of the creeps." She stands up, her lips quirking into a tight smile. "Glad we had this little chat. I'm going to tap into my inner goddess. I'd ask you to join me, but I don't want to spend one more second with you."

Ditto, I think, watching her amble down the steps.

Trinity steps over as Sienna sashays round the corner. Her eyebrows lift curiously. "I saw you arguing. What happened with Mark?"

"Well, we definitely broke up."

"Because of Sienna? Or because of Kat?"

I go quiet.

The sun finally manages to burst through the clouds, warming up the doom and gloom, if only for a moment. As Trinity tries unsuccessfully to pump me for more information about Kat and Sienna, I look at the fractured reflection of the mountains in the pond, thinking about my own fractures, thinking about the circumstances in which people can crack.

THIRTY-SIX

(NOW)

Fake it until you make it away from Nyx has become my new motto. I don't want to go back to Kat's suite to grab the gifted journal, so I head to the boutique to buy a new one, hoping they can charge it to my room.

To my right, a wall of glass shelving catches the recessed lighting, transforming ordinary perfume bottles into objects of art. The Nemesis collection commands the central display, each bottle a different shape but unified by their smoky glass and gold accents. The names are etched in an elegant script: "Vengeance" in a tall, dagger-like flacon; "Retribution" in a round vessel with sharp edges; "Payback" housed in something that resembles an elegant poison bottle from another century.

Vengeance. Retribution. Payback. I can almost hear Kat's voice peppered with seductive intonations as she describes each scent with precise, cutting adjectives.

The sales associate—a young woman with a practiced smile—notices my gaze and takes a half-step in my direction, waiting to see if I need assistance.

"We're looking for more sales reps," says the woman, whose nametag reads Silvia. She's petite, bright and bubbly. "Are you interested?"

I smile. This is getting interesting. "Actually, I am, Silvia. How does the process work?"

"OK. So, you have to buy the entire line in the beginning, but think of it as an investment..."

She babbles on, explaining the high commissions and that if I'm connected, the more representatives I bring in, how I can make a fortune. I nod along, thinking how Kat is using her influence, how she's a liar, and how she's creating the ultimate in pyramid schemes.

Kat is definitely creating a different kind of cult, one that only serves her.

Silvia shoots me a grin, her eyes wide, handing me a stack of papers. "Should I sign you up?"

"Let me think about it," I say. "Read everything over."

"OK," she says. "But don't take too long. We're capping off level-one members soon—that's the highest."

"How many levels are there?"

She shrugs. "Five."

I nod, grabbing a journal. "I'll take this for now. Can you charge it to room seven? Olivia Montgomery."

I'm sitting in the common room, studying its sharp contrasts —plush armchairs and rustic wooden beams, modern art next to country chic lamps—and trying to write. I chew on the cap of my pen, deliberating. And then the words flow, raw and unfiltered. I pour out my anger, my thoughts onto the page until my fingers cramp. I don't stop. I can't stop. This act of putting everything I'm feeling into words feels like a lifeline and my fingers can't keep up with my torrent of thoughts. Soon, I'm working on character studies. As I write, one particular character begins to take shape—she's flawed, she's angry, but she's strong.

I take a deep breath, blinking at the words. I realize I'm writing about me. I flex my fingers, enjoying the ache, but then my eyes dart around, taking in every detail, every face in the room. A nauseating cocktail of uncertainty.

My blood runs cold. What would Stephen King do? How about Agatha Christie? My mind races, cataloguing every interaction, every sideways glance I've received since arriving. I must be staring because the two younger girls hesitantly step toward me. I scan their faces, looking for any signs of danger. There are none, unless you count big wide smiles. I force what I think is a friendly grin.

"You're Liv, right? I'm Emily and this is Sarah. Stiles is our mentor, too. We couldn't help but notice you scribbling away in your journal." She grins and wiggles her brows. "Working on the next great American thriller?"

I let out a soft laugh. "Maybe the next American disaster."

"Rebecca was tough on us, too," says Emily, head nodding, eyes focused on the ceiling.

"But she was right," agrees Sarah. "Man, do we have our work cut out for us."

"I heard your book is a mash-up," I say. "*Big Little Lies* meets *True Blood?*"

"Now we have to mash it up less." Emily gives a soft laugh. "Care to share what you're working on? You look completely focused."

"Sorry," I say. "Right now, I'm just trying to figure out what's going on. Rough notes. Nothing is making sense."

"Oh, we get that," says Sarah. "Yep. Yep. Yep. Sometimes it's back to square one. If you need to run anything by us, feel free."

"Thanks," I say. "I may take you up on that."

But I won't because I'm not writing fiction.

I watch the girls walk back to the couch they'd secured by the window, with a view of the mountains. Soon, they're back in an animated discussion. "We need to circle back to the main plot. That's what Rebecca told us, that and to go through the twelve beats of *Save the Cat*."

Save the Kat? I hold back my laughter and scribble the words in my notebook.

I'm about to delve further into Kat's character when Trinity taps me on the shoulder. Like a bad penny, she just keeps showing up. "What are you working on, Montgomery?" She leans over my shoulder and I close my journal. "You want to be the next Nancy Drew?"

"Something like that," I say in a low voice.

"Take a break. We can talk more," she says. "The sun is shining. The birds are—"

I glare at her.

She holds up her hands in mock defense. "Sorry. Forgot about the bird drama. Let's grab a coffee. We're supposed to be brainstorming now. It's on the schedule."

In this place, even something as innocuous as perfume or coffee could be deadly. My fingers involuntarily shoot to my temples. I eye the Bees, buzzing around an irritated Anna Hale, as Trinity calls a server over.

Trinity plops down in the chair across from mine, tapping her nails on the table. A couple of minutes later, the server sets a carafe of coffee in front of us, pours. I take a sip, savoring the bitter and rich taste on my tongue.

Bitter. Rich. Two words that describe Kat.

"I'm going to hit the spa," says Trinity. "Wanna come along? We can continue our discussion about you-know-who while unwinding in the jacuzzi."

I can't help but grimace. "No, thanks. I'm not much of water person. And I really don't want to talk about her."

Trinity's composed mask slips for a fraction of a second. I catch a glimpse of something raw, almost animalistic, in her eyes before she blinks it away, flashing one of her wide "nothing bothers me" grins and she's already rising to her feet with fluid grace.

"We're supposed to be working together," she says, turning on her heel. "But I get it. You do you."

As she walks away, I realize what's driving her; she's way more obsessed with Kat than I am.

THIRTY-SEVEN

(NOW)

The clock on the wall ticks relentlessly, each second mental torture. I look through the printouts Kat gave me earlier of the Woodford Hall yearbook. People change in appearance. Look at Mimi. She's like a new person. Look at me. I've changed.

Before I can examine the photos, Kat races up to me, breathless. "Liv, come with me."

"Where?" I ask.

"You'll see."

Kat grabs me by the wrist, and we race out of the common room to the terrace and down the stone steps to the papermaking facility.

Carol and James stand by the large vat.

"I think we found your necklace," says Kat, pointing.

I take a step closer to the vat. There, submerged, is a body, sloshing around in viscous pulp, a sapphire and diamond necklace linked in between stiff fingers. It takes me a few seconds to realize who it is. Mark. His blue eyes—wide open—stare blankly at nothing, clouded in a milky haze. His black hair fans out in the pulp, undulating like snakes. Slivers of wood and pulp residue stick to his skin.

My legs give out from under me and I slide to the floor. I feel the fight leaving my body, draining out of me like a punctured balloon. As I sit there, a crumpled mess on the ground, Kat's eyes meet mine. "A bunch of people saw you arguing with Mark and James thinks he's been stabbed—"

"I was in the common room for hours. There are at least half a dozen witnesses." I hunch over, shaking my head. Why isn't she more upset? Does she have one ounce of compassion? "Where were you?"

"Working on my memoir." She eyes the vat, her lips pinched. "I can't believe this is happening. Did you—"

"Are you freaking kidding me? I faint at the sight of blood. You know that." I gulp. "Can't even get my own drawn without being on the verge of passing out."

Kat nods with remembrance. "I used to have to hold your hand when the doctor came over."

James looks over toward us. "Carol, send Gary and call an ambulance. I think I've got a handle on this. You should go."

I stand up, edging closer to the vat to take one final look at Mark. My eyes sweep his form, his blood-soaked t-shirt, the rip in it, and the cut across his heart. I hear a slight clink. And then I see the shimmer of a blade, floating in the viscous murk beside him. My heart races. Somebody is doing their best to set me up—now for Mark's murder. Not going to happen on my watch. I feign like I'm really upset over his death, and then I surreptitiously stuff the letter opener up the sleeve of my hoodie.

"Are you OK?" asks Kat, placing a hand on my back.

"Not really," I say, sniffling. "But who is?"

"Nobody." She stares off into space, a single tear sliding down her cheek. "Could you all please give me a moment?"

Kat, Carol, and I head into the resort to the sounds of pants and cries. *What now?* I see Jenn leading Trinity toward the infirmary. Trinity's body is as bright red as a cooked lobster. She screams, "It was her! It was her! I saw her arguing with her boyfriend, Mark Knight." Trinity gasps for air. "About twenty minutes later, I heard her. I was in the sauna. She said, 'Stop sticking your nose in where it doesn't belong.' She did something to the lock and then turned up the heat. To boiling. I couldn't get out. Thankfully, Jenn found me."

By this time almost every person on the retreat—some of the staff members, all of the writers—have assembled in the lobby, jaws agape.

Trinity points an accusatory finger in my direction. "She murdered some guy in New York. And now, because I know too much, she tried to kill me."

Kat gently grabs me by the arm and whispers, "Just go with this."

"Until we assess the situation and the police arrive," says Carol with force, "I'll be keeping an eye on Ms. Montgomery."

"But you're a papermaker," somebody says.

"I'm also ex-military." She leads me toward an office, looking over her shoulder. "Obviously, papermaking is canceled."

Hushed gasps and mumbles follow my every step. I run a shaky hand through my hair, tugging at the roots. Whoever did this played their hand well. And I'm now thinking that person definitely isn't Trinity. Didn't she say it's always the person you least suspect?

Let's just chalk this retreat up as the biggest mistake of my life. I'm sitting in the Nyx office, replaying everything over in my head—Steven's murder, Mark's murder, Rebecca being whacked on the head, and Trinity's recent scare, not to mention the crow. All four people are linked to me, but they're also linked to Kat and Sienna. I think of Sienna's earlier words. *I'm going to tap into my inner goddess.*

"Carol!" I call out. "Have you checked in on Kat?"

"I think she's with Sienna, why?"

My mind is racing. At first, I would have pointed the finger of blame in Kat's direction, but Sienna probably found the letter opener when we'd left her alone in the suite. I don't know how to explain this gut instinct of mine, so I just blurt out, "I think Kat may be in serious danger."

"I'm going to radio James, loop him in." Carol clicks on her walkie-talkie. She only receives a crackle, no response. I jump up, bolting out the door. "Where are you going?"

I don't have time to explain. I just run with my hunch, clicking on my ever-faithful pocket recorder. "Nyx's garden," I yell over my shoulder, my breath coming hard and fast. "Sienna was headed there earlier, tapping into her inner goddess."

I have no idea what I'm expecting to find as I race down the path to the hedge. But I know who I expect to find. And I know I can take Sienna down. I've got at least thirty pounds on her. When I arrive at the clearing, I find Sienna pacing in front of Nyx's statue, mumbling to herself.

A twig snaps under my foot and Sienna turns, flashing one of her mega-watt smiles. "Oh, the con artist user is here. Good. We can get this over with."

"You were responsible for the lipstick threats."

"Obviously," she says. "I suppose I should apologize for ruining your journal and for the crow, too." She tilts her head back in laughter. "Sorry. Not sorry."

Worry pumps through my veins and my eyes scan the garden. "Where's Kat?"

"I sent her a text a while ago with the exact time," she says, looking at her watch. "She should be here any minute." Her gaze shoots up toward the sky. "I had something to take care of first."

"Trinity?"

"You're smart, Liv. I wanted to scare her to back off. Rebecca, too. I can't let what happened all those years ago get out. Period." She paces in front of Nyx, tugging at the roots of her hair with one hand. "It would ruin me."

My mind reels, trying to reconcile the broken woman before me with the passionate, bubbly friend I thought I once knew. And it hits me. I've never really known her. She just told me things she thought I'd wanted to hear. Kat, on the other hand, told me the truth, whether I'd liked hearing it or not.

"Ever since my experience at Nexus, I haven't been the same person. That girl is dead. She's been dead inside for a very long time. I thought you might have been the person to revive her... but you're just like everybody else. The moment Kat showed up—you blew me off. And then you went after

Steven. Who the hell does that? What kind of friend are you?" she pants. "I'll tell you what kind. A bad one. Both of you are. You know what? I think I hate you even more than I hate Kat," she mumbles. "Funny, I used to think we were sisters."

"Sisters don't destroy one another," I say with a gulp. "They build each other up."

"Get that from a Hallmark card? I'd expect better from such a *talented* writer." Sienna lets out a wicked cackle. "I'm glad Steven is dead. He... he told Nick I was crazy. He told Nick about that night. The stupid fucking party. Steven urged Nick to divorce me. H-he deserved to die." She glowers at me. "Voilà. Nick and I are getting divorced. And it's all your fault."

I can see Sienna spiraling further now, the flip of the switch I'd noticed before but didn't really pay attention to. How could she be bubbly and effervescent one second and manic the next? My heart pounds against my ribs—like a caged bird, of all damn things, desperate for freedom. Her eyes flash with malice, something dark swirling in the depths.

"What about Mark?"

"What about him?" she scoffs.

"Somebody stabbed him... and then threw him in the papermaking vat."

Her eyes flicker to the side. "Pathetic. Stop making stuff up."

"Liv isn't making anything up." Kat appears in the opening to the garden, her green eyes wide. "Your brother is dead."

"Both of you are liars!" She nods toward the statue of Nyx. "And I know exactly what I'm going to do." Sienna saunters closer to me, her movements fluid and predatory.

"What do you think, Liv? You're the writer. You tell me. I read your stupid book. How do you see this story ending?"

"I'm hoping you calm down," Kat whispers. "This is insane."

"Insanity? Genius more like. Such a fine line of distinction between the two, don't you think? Kat deserves to be punished. She admitted she killed Morgan. She's a killer! And I loved Morgan. I loved everything I'd learned at Nexus. She ruined everything. Morgan was my friend..."

"I'm your friend..." I begin.

"If you were my friend," she spits out, "why would you write about me like that? You think I'm so stupid. But don't worry. I'll help you make your little book a reality." She motions toward a jug of gasoline and then points at the hemlock and then at Kat. "You're going to kill Kat and then you're going to kill yourself. The end." Sienna points a gun at me. "The safety's off and it's very much loaded. Now, do it."

Kat just blinks. She doesn't say anything. I can't read her expression.

I swallow hard, suddenly aware of how mad she is and how isolated we are. Until I figure out what to do, I need to keep her talking. "That depends. What exactly are your intentions here, Sienna?"

"Liv, I'm not joking around," she says. "Nyx told me what to do."

With sinking clarity, I realize there's no reasoning with Sienna. Any words I might be able to manage die in my throat when our eyes lock. My mind races with ideas of how to get out of this situation, my brain prickling. I could try to make a run for it, but I know Sienna's gone hunting before. She's bragged that she's a good shot, probably how she'd wounded the crow.

Before I know what's happening, I hear a whoosh and Sienna falls to the ground. Carol comes running into the clearing. "Tranquilizer darts," she says, holding up a gun. "You know, for the bears. James has called the cops. Along with an ambulance, they should be here soon. Let's go."

"I should have seen her breakdown coming," Kat mutters.

We follow Carol down the path, leaving Sienna prone. My stomach churns as we walk away from Sienna, the weight of what I know about Kat pressing against my chest, the weight of what Sienna has done. To think, I'd almost been tempted to tell Trinity the rest of my story.

THIRTY-EIGHT

(THEN)

My birth certificate listed my name as Olivia, mother Diana Montgomery. Father unknown. But I knew who he was—and Tobias called me Morgan, after the shape-shifting Celtic war goddess the Morrigan, the patroness of revenge, magic, and witches, who oftentimes took the form of a raven or a crow.

Kat Sterling tried to kill me, and she would have succeeded if I hadn't practiced apnea—challenging my mind, my body. After Kat left, I'd clawed my way onto the bank, where my mother found me lying in the snow, my lips a whole new shade of blue, before I sucked in what seemed like my last breath—suffering the effects of extreme hypothermia. The shivers coursing through my body couldn't be controlled. Seizure-like. My mom ripped my wet clothes off, wrapped me in warm blankets, and sped straight toward the hospital in one of the Nexus jeeps. Apparently, my heart stopped for three minutes in the emergency room—any longer and I would most likely have had permanent brain damage. I did see the light—a flicker, telling me to change.

Perhaps they were only my thoughts, guided by my subconscious.

Mom told the nurses we'd been ice-skating on a pond... and the ice cracked and caved in.

The hospital staff believed her. "It happens every year," somebody said.

I was coming in and out of consciousness in my room, Mom by my side, when the news came on: *Tobias Rane's Nexus Compound Raided*.

The story the reporter recounted really woke me up. As a fifteen-year-old, I realized life—especially the one I'd been leading—wasn't a game. I suppose I got caught up with trying to win *his* approval, would do anything to get it. When he'd asked me to scout out the girls at Woodford Hall, I'd thought it was my chance to fit in with other teens. It's true that I never attended the school. The uniform was easy to find at a second-hand shop. Somebody from Nexus would drop me off just before lunch and pick me up a couple of hours later. Of course, a couple of people like Mimi questioned why I wasn't in their classes, and I had my response ready. "I'm in advanced placement," and then I'd change the subject. Right back to goddesses and tapping into your full potential. It was almost too easy. People heard what they wanted to hear and saw what they wanted to see.

I didn't blame Kat for trying to kill me. I'd blamed myself for bringing her to Nexus.

Mom gripped my hand, hers shaking. "If he'll have us, we'll live with your grandpa in Chicago..."

My heart clenched.

"We'll change our names, even our appearances, just in case anybody is looking for us. And you're never to mention the name Morgan or Tobias Rane ever again."

. . .

Mom and I took the bus from New York to live with her father in Roger's Park, Chicago. I was on the edge of sixteen, ready to take the world by storm. But, as before, I was home schooled, even though I still wanted to fit in with people my age.

"Gangs! Drugs! Monsters! They're everywhere!" my mom would argue. "I want you to be safe."

Grandpa didn't seem too happy to see us at first, but eventually warmed to me. There were a lot of hushed conversations between him and my mom, some of which I overheard.

"This is your fault, Diana," he said. "And you put a child —your child—in danger."

"Maybe if you'd been a better father I wouldn't have run away."

"We can't change the past, but we can change the future." Grandpa sighed. "I'm glad I'm finally able to get to know my beautiful granddaughter."

Although we had a computer, as most of my lessons were online, my view on the "outside world" was limited. We didn't have a television, so I found fun in books and using my imagination. Sometimes I'd watch the neighborhood teens from the window seat of the apartment or from a corner in the library, aching to connect with people my age, but by this point the rumors about me had started.

"That's the garbage man's granddaughter. She stinks."

"She doesn't go to school. There's something wrong with her."

"She's a freak."

"Her clothes are from the Salvation Army."

They were.

Needless to say, I had a three-block radius to roam—the corner store and the library. I did make friends—in books and, well, the head librarian, Mrs. McNulty, an elderly woman with kind blue eyes. She always wore a "practical" dress that hit below the knee and ballet flats—no matter the weather. She must have changed her shoes at the library in the brutal Chicago winters. Mrs. McNulty always had a stack of books waiting for me until one day she said, "I don't know what to do with you, Olivia. You've gone through all the young adult books." She lowered her glasses and eyed me, tapping her chin. "I know. I have the college curriculum. You're an advanced reader. That's what we'll do. How's that sound?"

"Great, and some thrillers, too," I said, and she placed a pile of books in front of me.

And thus my induction into the adult literary world began, moving on from classic authors like Steinbeck and Austen and Rand to Gillian Flynn, Paula Hawkins, and Liane Moriarty, to name a few. One night, I'd looked at my grandfather. "I think I want to be a writer," I'd said, haphazardly twirling a strand of spaghetti on my fork.

Grandpa smiled. "A good profession."

"For those who make it," said Mom, rolling her eyes. "She's good with computers."

Grandpa ignored her and took my hands. "Liv, you should spread your wings and go to a university—"

"She's not going to university," said Mom. "Period. End of story."

"You can't keep her under lock and key forever," said Grandpa. He stood up and slammed his fist on the table, rattling our water glasses. "I've had it with you, Diana. You're too overprotective. She's not living a good life."

"I have my reasons," said Mom, her cheeks flaring red.

And so the fight of the century went down—a screaming and yelling match, along with a couple of broken dishes. Finally, my mom sat down, breathing heavily. "Fine. Liv can go to university... *if* she can get into a school and *if* she can pay for it."

My eyes bugged out wide and I raced to the computer, googling universities with the best writing programs. Mom dwindled down my list, wanting me to focus on the University of Chicago or Northwestern because they were closer to home. I wanted to get far, far away.

"Look, Liv," Mom said. "Syracuse has this S. I. Newhouse School of Public Communications—very well respected for their advertising, public relations, and journalism degrees."

"But I want to be a writer..."

She scoffed. "We googled the chances of becoming a successful author. You need to stop living in a fantasy world and start thinking about living in the real world, because that's what you want to do, right?" She tapped the screen. "The campus looks safe, and they have security."

One thing I'd learned from Tobias was how to hack—it was how he got a lot of leverage on people, and I was quite good at it. A couple of hours and a thousand keystrokes later, I'd hacked into Sienna and Kat's email accounts. I watched their social media posts with an eagle eye. That's when I found out Sienna was gunning for Syracuse.

For weeks I worked on my essay, took all the required tests (a near perfect score in English), and prayed. I got into every university I'd applied to. But only one stood out. Not only did Syracuse accept me as an early admission, I qualified for financial aid—the big decision maker.

The tuition was still steep, but Grandpa and I went to the bank, applying for student loans. "I'm proud of you, Liv," he said. "Your life is going to change."

Even though I'd gone through so many changes, I was ready for another. I was ready to start making amends. I wanted to prove to myself that I was a good person—that I wasn't like my dad, although his lessons proved to be invaluable and would help me. I had one last play—hacking into the Syracuse system using an LLM agent (it worked) and ensuring I became roommates with Sienna. Finally, I found my way back to Kat.

THIRTY-NINE

(NOW)

The storm has lifted, and the sun is glowing over the Catskills Mountains, painting the main building of the Nyx Sanctuary in hues of amber... and, well, blood. As much as we all want to, nobody can leave. Working with the local authorities, a detective from Manhattan will be questioning everybody.

I stand on the terrace, the air seeming to thicken with an electric undercurrent of tension. And it is so tense my back is aching. I look toward the pond. At first, I'd wanted to forgive Kat for what she'd done to me. It's always been weird with her—like Tobias, she has a way of putting you under her spell. And, if I'm being honest, I'd wanted forgiveness, too. For what I did to them. I'd wanted to belong. To fit in. To be something. I'd wanted to set things right.

But I've never really forgiven her and there's one last thing I need to do. One final play. One more truth to reveal.

. . .

I race up to Kat's suite and grab the micro-recorder, my sunglasses, and, while I'm at it, I change into something more comfortable. Then, I stand on the terrace, watching the geese take flight over the pond, their honks soothing for once. A few minutes later Mark's body is loaded into an ambulance and Sienna is led to a police car in handcuffs, the lights flashing.

I hear footsteps and I know it's Kat coming up behind me. I smell her signature scent—orange, jasmine, and musk, know the click of her heels. *In Her Shoes. In Her Skin.* I tense, my fingers gripping the railing. "Don't sneak up on me like that. I may snap, do something I don't want to do. You know I hate surprises."

She lets out a melancholy laugh. "You and me both."

An intimidating male cop with bulging muscles reads Sienna her rights. She looks so tiny next to him, her hair a wind-blown tangled mess, her face tearstained. Before they shove her in the back of a cruiser, she looks up and then it's as if she looks right through us, like we're not even there.

"Such a tragedy, really." Kat looks down toward the ground, shaking her head. "Are you wearing my shoes?"

"I'm not." I lift my sunglasses to the top of my head and meet her gaze, raising my chin. "Thing is, Kat, I definitely wouldn't want to be in your shoes right now."

I'm expecting her jaw to drop. I'm expecting her to clasp her chest and have a heart attack. I'm expecting anything except her lips twitching into a grin.

She blows out a breath and then releases a soft laugh. "I've always known you were Morgan, Liv, whatever you want to call yourself. I knew who you were the moment I laid eyes on you in Santorini."

I feel like all the air is going to be sucked right out of me. She's been playing me for years, screwing with my head and messing with my life.

FORTY

(THEN)

KAT

The moment I saw Liv walking down the sandy beach toward the tender in Santorini I knew exactly who she was—Morgan Rane, the woman I thought I'd left dead in the icy-cold waters of the pond. Although she'd slimmed down and her hair and eye color had changed, I knew her by her walk, her mannerisms. Her tics, the way she straightened her spine, bit down on her bottom lip. And I really gave her a lot of credit for trying to pull off the act of not knowing me. I'd tried to dig for information, namely how she knew Sienna, but she wouldn't break. Just kept going on with her sweet, innocent façade—told me things about herself, just things I didn't really care about.

I wanted to know why she was back in our lives, and I couldn't come out and say, "I thought I killed you."

I wanted to know what she wanted, what her endgame was. So, I invited her to live with me in the lap of luxury. Spoiled her rotten. Made her feel worthy. Thought one day she'd break down and tell me everything. Even though I'd dropped many hints along the way, told her my story about Nexus, that didn't happen.

Naturally, Sienna was furious that I had taken Liv's friendship from her. Self-centered as she was, Sienna never realized that Liv was actually Morgan. When she'd witnessed what happened at the pond that day—the day I killed Morgan—Sienna lost it. Her PTSD wasn't caused by the cult or the blackmail—her mental illness swirled into madness because of me.

Sienna had loved Morgan, thought she was the bomb—cool and unshakeable. Sienna had lost all semblance of reality after Morgan died—closed herself off from me, and became a danger not only to herself but others as well—until Liv came along.

And then Liv ruined her when she'd moved in with me and started dating Steven.

Sometimes when worlds collide, there are catastrophic outcomes, but like the roots of trees communicating under the earth, Liv and I share a connection.

FORTY-ONE

(NOW)

KAT

My gaze snaps up to her eyes, to the ice-blue colored contact lenses she's now wearing. "Did you think I'd confess what I'd done to just anyone?"

Liv's eyes dart to the side. She takes a step toward me and growls, "You tried to kill me and..."

"Clearly, you survived and came back even stronger." I clasp onto her hand. "And if you were in my shoes, wouldn't you have done the same thing?"

Her book is more on point than she thinks.

Liv blows out a breath and then lifts an eyebrow. "No, I'm not a murderer."

"Neither am I. You're not dead," I say with a shrug. "I think we both got what we wanted from each other. I've forgiven you for bringing me to that cult. And you've forgiven me for the day at the pond."

Her jaw clenches. "You took so much more away from me..."

I puff out my bottom lip into a pout. "Are you really upset about Tobias? That I was the one who sent him to prison?"

She scratches at her ear. "No, he deserved to go to prison. He's the one who sent me after you and Sienna. But, in the process, you also took away my mom—"

"Abandonment issues." I pull Liv toward me. "We're both orphans, Liv, and, honestly, that's why I need you and, perhaps, it's the reason you need me," I say, hanging my head. "I'm reading your book."

Her eyes blaze with anger. "What the hell? Who sent it to you? Sienna?"

"Mimi did. And, if we're finally being honest, I was as obsessed with you as you were with me. But we have each other now. We have a deep connection. A bond. And it goes far beyond family." And then I whisper, "After all this blows over, I may have an offer for you—one you won't be able to refuse."

She lifts her chin. "Oh, I'll probably refuse."

I shrug my shoulders. "Name your price."

Her eyes survey the land, the mountains in the distance. She points, circling her finger. "I want what is rightfully mine."

"I figured as much. I've already had my attorney draw up the contract. Do we have a deal?"

She doesn't say a word, just turns to face the mountains, steadying her hands on the railing. I watch her back expanding and contracting with her breath and then I continue, "I truly believe in what I'm doing here. I believe in the products I'm creating. I believe in female empowerment, especially when I felt it was taken away from me." I pause, swallowing hard. "I believe in Nyx. And I'd really like you by our side—with Mimi."

"And what would my role be?"

"We'll need to change the narrative if word gets out about what happened here. And it will get out." I place my hands on her shoulders. "Liv, you don't have to answer me today, not even tomorrow. I'll give you some time to think things over."

I can see the wheels churning in her head. I'm getting bored. She's almost too easy to play. The challenging Liv I know has gone into hiding.

"Because, at present, you know what my answer would be…"

"No," I say, releasing her from my grip.

"But it might be yes," she says. "If…"

My sour mood brightens. "If what?"

"I want ownership."

Bingo. I've been expecting this answer. "I'll have Sienna's shares transferred to you. With what she's done, she's in breach of contract."

She twists her upper lip into a sneer. "Not good enough. All of us should have equal shares."

Always ten steps ahead of everybody, I'm also prepared for this request. I'm prepared for everything. I pull out my phone, tap a couple of keys. "Done. My attorney will send you the paperwork to sign."

She eyes me with trepidation. "What's the catch?"

"There isn't one." I grin and then whisper in her ear, my breath coming hot and heavy on her neck. "As long as you don't tell the police what I did to you. And I won't tell them what you did to me. That, and nobody can find out that you're Morgan Rane."

She smiles in turn. "What if I tell them everything?"

I know she's bluffing. "Do you really want to play that way? You'd become a pariah, Morgan. Your writing career would be finished—"

"First of all, my name is Liv, and second,"—she holds out her hand—"we have a deal."

Right when we're shaking, an officer steps onto the terrace. "Ms. Sterling, please follow me."

I watch her shoulders cave in as I'm walking away, knowing I have her exactly where I want her. A hunter always knows its prey—and waits for the perfect moment to strike. The thrill isn't in the chase, but drawing its target closer.

FORTY-TWO

(NOW)

KAT

Detective Shaw leans heavily against the wall. A massive, rugged figure with a noticeable paunch, he's clad in nothing like a designer suit—a raw, unpolished presence, an eyesore.

As I answer questions about the past few days, the recent terrifying experience with Sienna, and how Carol found Mark, Shaw scrawls sharply in his battered notebook, the pen scratching fiercely against the paper. He looks up. "Which brings us to Steven Shepherd's murder. Ms. Sterling, a couple of days ago, you mentioned you had a... connection to Ms. Montgomery. You implied she'd killed Steven in our initial meeting and that you two weren't on speaking terms, but I just saw the two of you having a deep, seemingly meaningful conversation. Is there something you want to tell me?"

I maintain eye contact, keeping my voice level. "Liv is upset. I was making sure she was alright, especially after what happened with what Sienna pulled on us."

He paces with a simmering tension, shooting me pointed looks. "You dropped Ms. Montgomery's name in our initial meeting..."

"I did tell you then that I know Liv," I respond coolly. "She's reckless, theatrical even, but she's no murderer."

"And now, as if Mr. Shepherd's death wasn't enough, Mark Knight has been murdered, too." Shaw's tone is edged with disbelief. "Weren't you involved romantically with Mark Knight?"

"I was," I say.

His eyes widen. "And then one of your former friends, as you put it, got involved with him."

I let out a sigh, dab my eyes with a tissue. "Clearly neither one of us is attached to him anymore."

"Right. Because somebody killed him." His lips twist into a tight grin. "You?"

"Detective, Sienna basically confessed that she'd killed Steven Shepherd. She'd said I'm glad he's dead and, after today's event, I wouldn't be surprised if..." I allow myself a small sigh. "Detective, Sienna wanted to set Liv up for everything."

"Sienna. Right." Shaw stops pacing and plants his hands on the chair opposite mine. "What motive would she have to kill her own brother?"

I lean forward. "He knew too much about our past and Sienna wasn't happy about it."

"And how would you know this?"

"People talk to me, detective." I hold his gaze. "Sienna has a temper. A lot more to lose than Liv does."

"You seem very invested in Ms. Montgomery's innocence."

"I'm invested in the truth." My voice remains steady

despite the tension I feel. "And in protecting people who deserve protection."

"If you're withholding evidence from me…"

"I'm providing evidence, detective." I stand, smoothing my skirt. "I protect my friends. All of them. Even from each other when necessary."

His eyebrows rise slightly. "Isn't Sienna a friend of yours?"

"Was. She wanted Liv to burn me alive. She killed Steven to get back at Liv. And she killed Mark. She told me she has always hated me."

"And how do we know Ms. Montgomery didn't kill Mark?"

"Because she was with me. We used to be close, like sisters, and we were burying the hatchet."

He flashes a tight grin. "Interesting choice of words."

"Look, I won't let Liv bear the fall for something Sienna did. Sienna, clearly, is seriously unhinged." I lock eyes with him. "Is there anything else, or can we end this conversation? I want to close this chapter once and for all."

But it's not over—at least, not for me and Liv. Our story is far from finished; it's on the brink of being rewritten.

FORTY-THREE

(NOW)

Kat saunters back onto the terrace with a cop and rolls her eyes to the man in blue by her side. "This is Officer Abrams. I guess they're saving the best witness for last."

"Please follow me," says Abrams and I do as I'm told.

As I sit, I watch Detective Shaw arrange his notepad on the polished oak table between us. The resort's library—with its floor-to-ceiling bookshelves, linen curtains, and perfect lines now frames a different kind of scene. This could be my chance to take everything away from Kat, but I'm going to play it cool, because she also has the opportunity to take everything away from me.

"Ms. Montgomery, I appreciate you agreeing to this interview."

"I really don't have a choice, do I?"

"You don't," says Abrams.

His voice is measured, practiced in its neutrality, but his eyes betray a suspicion that cuts right through me. "We've been wanting to speak with you, and left you several messages, but..."

"The storm. I'm sorry. And there is really bad cell service here. We're out in the middle of nowhere."

Shaw leans forward. "Can you tell me more about Sienna Knight? Her state of mind? I understand you roomed with her at Syracuse."

"She was fine at Syracuse," I say, bristling a bit. "We were close."

"How close?"

"Very," I lie, knowing that we'd used each other so we weren't alone, knowing that I'd targeted her again. "But I suppose I never really knew her that well—just the surface stuff."

He grins, his eyes lighting up. "I understand you've had... complicated romantic relationships with both Steven Shepherd, one of her ex-boyfriends, and Mark Knight, her brother."

Complicated. Such a bloodless word. I smooth my hands against my thighs, feeling the rough texture of my jeans against my palms. The tactile sensation grounds me, a technique I'd learned during those years after my father went to prison. After Kat's testimony sent him there.

"Who told you that?"

"Ms. Sterling did."

He taps his pen on the table. "And we've read the police report—the one Mr. Shepherd filed against you."

"Then you'd know he dropped all charges against me." I swallow and place my hands in my lap, rubbing my thighs. "And you'd also know Sienna killed him."

"We won't know that for certain until we get all the evidence," he says, jotting something in his notepad. "I understand you've also had a strained relationship with Ms. Sterling in the past, used to be her roommate. And now you're here on a writing retreat at Nyx. Coinciding with Ms. Katherine Sterling's presence as the sanctuary's owner. And coinciding with a murder—two of them."

The accusation hangs in the air, unspoken but palpable.

"I didn't know Kat owned Nyx," I say, though the lie tastes metallic on my tongue. Of course I knew. I'd tracked Kat for years, watching from the digital shadows as she transformed the compound of my childhood into this haven. Watching as she built a life from the ashes of what she'd destroyed.

"Ms. Montgomery. Olivia—"

"Liv," I correct him automatically. "Everyone calls me Liv." The diminutive, the persona I'd constructed after everything fell apart. Olivia was the fifteen-year-old who believed her father's promises about building a better world. Liv is the woman who survived what came after. And, well, Morgan is truly dead.

"Liv it is," says Shaw. "When did you recognize Ms. Sterling?"

The question lands like a punch. When? Immediately. The moment I saw her shoes stepping onto the driveway, her laugh still the same, her hair perfectly styled. I clamp my lips together and breathe through my nose.

"It took a few days," I lie again. "She's changed a bit from when we were roommates."

"And once you recognized her—why stay? Most people would find that... uncomfortable—especially since you were dating her ex."

Most people. As if either Kat or I fell into that category anymore. As if either of us had been 'most people' since that fateful day when I first brought her to Nexus.

I swallow. "Mark has absolutely nothing to do with Kat and me."

"But he does. He's dead." His eyes glimmer. "Do you think Ms. Sterling killed him because of you?"

I shift in my seat. "No, she's happy we've rekindled our friendship."

"So the two of you were working together?" asks Abrams.

"On what?" I reply, head down. "Look, I came here because I wanted to get an editor's eyes on my book," I say, blinking, and this, at least, is true. The book that had brought me here—ostensibly a thriller about female friendship and betrayal. A book I'd been writing in my head ever since I'd met her.

"We've read some of the chapters, especially the ending. Some pretty dark passages in there... and, well, a lot of coincidences with what's happened."

Shaw leans back, creating space between us. His technique is good—alternating pressure and release, waiting for me to fill the silence. I've studied interrogation methods extensively for my novels. I recognize the choreography of this dance. His fingers drum against the table with increasing urgency.

"Sienna read the book, too," I say, clearing my throat. "And, well, I suppose she took things a little too far."

I cringe and place my hands on my lap, picking at my cuticles.

"Interesting choice of words. Tell me about your relationship with Trinity Powers," he says, shifting gears so abruptly I almost flinch.

"We're friendly," I say carefully. "Fellow writers. We had some interesting conversations about research methods."

"Research." Shaw repeats the word, infusing it with

doubt. "The story she's been working on is about a cult. This land used to be home to Nexus, run by Tobias Rane. She told me she's been researching Kat and Sienna's involvement."

He can't find out about my past. Not now. If he makes the connection I might as well stamp guilty on my forehead.

"Many writers, especially journalists, draw from real events," I counter, meeting his gaze. "True crime is popular. And Kat's memoir is about her experience here."

"Indeed. And your book is about what?" The detective taps his pen against his notepad three times, a tell that I catalog automatically. He pulls out a page from a file and reads. "Two hours later, the news breaks like a storm: Emily and Seth have been found dead, their lives extinguished in a catastrophic explosion on the deck of her mega yacht. The screen flickers with images of twisted metal and burning debris." He pauses. "I believe you based Emily's character on Katherine Sterling. Now which one is Seth? Steven Shepherd or Mark Knight?" He lets out a short, caustic laugh. "Should we expect an explosion?"

The accusation lands on my head, heavy and unmistakable. I feel my heart quicken but keep my breathing steady, my face neutral.

"N-n-no," I stutter.

"In addition to the copy of your book, we also have your journal," Shaw continues. "And I quote, 'She's flipping out right about now, probably thinking she's going crazy or being targeted. She is. And I'm enjoying every minute of torturing her. Just like she's tortured me. For now, I'm sitting back, waiting for the perfect moment, calculating my next move. The circle is complete... and I'm thinking more people are going to be pushed out of it—especially the one who doesn't belong.'" He leans forward. "Pretty dark stuff. Care to explain?"

This is so bad. I squeeze my eyes shut. "I'm a writer. Thrillers. I was trying to get my mind into that of a killer. Crazy as that may sound."

He rubs his chin. "It does."

"But it isn't. As I told you, I came on this retreat to write. I have a lot of material—Steven's death. Everything that's happened here. I've been a target. I was trying to figure out who was coming after me. And that person was Sienna. She wanted to destroy my career. She wanted to kill me. She wanted me to kill Kat. And, obviously, she killed Steven and Mark."

Detective Shaw tilts his head to the side. "I'd like to ask you some questions about your relationship with Mr. Shepherd."

Of course he would. Because my ex-fiancé—the one who broke my heart, crushed my dreams, and left me a shell of my former self—couldn't have the decency to die without dragging me into it.

"I don't have a relationship with him," I huff, hanging my head low. "Not anymore."

"Then why did he list you as the sole beneficiary of his estate?"

I lift my shoulders into a tight shrug. "I don't know. I'm assuming he felt bad about the way things ended with us."

Detective Shaw snorts. "Right. When he filed a restraining order."

"I saw him a week ago," I begin, explaining how he'd come to Brooklyn Bound to warn me.

"Yes," he replies. "We saw his texts to you."

"Then you'd know I didn't respond to any of them."

"While you've been away, we obtained a warrant to search your place. Care to explain why you have such a large collection of letter openers—"

My heart is about to leap out of my throat. I can feel every muscle pulsing and throbbing. My ears are ringing. I take a moment to collect my thoughts, gather my nerves.

"I'm a writer. I collect letter openers, fountain pens..." I pause, my mouth dropping open. "Wait. Was Steven stabbed with a letter opener? Is that how he died?"

Detective Shaw raises a brow, the answer clear. A long stretch of silence settles between us, Shaw watching me closely. He taps his knuckles on the table. "We believe Mark Knight was killed the same way, too." He pauses. "If there's anything you want to share with us, the time is now."

His words blur together as realization hits. I've read enough thrillers over the years. And I know my best move is not to say anything without an attorney present. I've probably already said too much. I clench my teeth together. I used to be so grounded, level-headed, until *she* infiltrated my life. My thoughts race inside my mind, tripping over one another.

"Kat Sterling collects letter openers, too. I know this because I lived with her. She's the one who turned me on to them. You're wasting your time with me," I snap.

The words slip out of my mouth, a whole lot sharper than I'd intended and way too wrong. Damn it. Why did I say that?

Detective Shaw clears his throat and eyes me warily. He's watching me too closely. Does he see the story behind my eyes? The deleted scenes, the alternate endings? "We've already spoken with Ms. Sterling." He pauses. "How would you classify your relationship with her?"

"It's complicated," I say, using the same word he'd used.

The next hour is beyond uncomfortable. Sweat pools at the nape of my neck as Detective Shaw paces around the room, shooting me pointed looks and spouting off a barrage of questions. Back and forth the conversation goes, always landing on the restraining order.

I shift in my chair, the backs of my legs sticky. "As you can imagine, this news has me shaken up. I've been pushed into a story I really don't want to be in."

Detective Shaw's lips twist into the tightest of smirks. I swear he rolls his eyes before directing his gaze to me. By his laser-focused stare, he's telling me that he thinks he's found their killer. "Thank you for your cooperation," he says. "Until we conclude our investigation, you're not to cross state lines. Understand?"

I sink into the chair, my head lowered. "Understood."

He and Officer Abrams make a move to leave, pausing in the doorway. Shaw shoots me a curt nod.

"Before you go, I have a question for you," I say hesitantly, and he waits. "What's going to happen to Sienna?"

"While we process the evidence and crime scenes, her parents are sending her to the Central New York Psychiatric Center in Marcy because of her actions toward you and Ms. Sterling. She's been there before—after her first experience here when the property was called Nexus. She'll be evaluated," he says, his voice distant. "The courts will decide after that."

I nod, as if I understand, as if I'm not complicit.

As they leave, the blade presses against my ribs and a sense of relief floods my system. I'm thankful they didn't frisk me. I know I've taken a huge risk by hiding evidence, but I'm not going down for a crime I didn't commit.

FORTY-FOUR

(NOW)

KAT

After searching my car and rifling through the contents of my suitcase, a hulking officer watches with feigned boredom as I rearrange the mess of clothing, his other hand lazily scrolling through my phone, scanning for what he thinks will make the big catch.

There's no privacy here, not even for Nyx's closest thing to a celebrity. I can't believe these people are treating me like some common criminal, as if I'm one of their everyday hicks. Don't they know who I am? Don't they know I'm a goddess compared to their paltry lives? Although I do enjoy spending time in nature, I can't wait to leave this podunk town in a cloud of dust and get back to the city where I belong. I'll have to put all this countryside drama behind me, get everything back on track with Liv firmly by my side. I can't wait to talk to her, to hear her voice and know she's in on this wild ride. I'm wondering what she told the detective, if she kept her cool like I'd told her. She can't go soft on me now; I need her.

One thing is certain: I have to squash the news before it gets out. Steven's murder was bad enough, but Sienna will take the blame for that one—probably Mark's, too.

Before the officer leaves, he hands me my phone and I collapse onto the couch, scrolling through pictures, searching for shots of me and Mark, reliving the moments when we burned bright and hot. He was a beautiful man, more like a pretty boy, really, and we were such an Instagram-worthy couple. We'd met at that awful gallery opening my parents had dragged me to, the one I didn't even want to go to. But the minute I saw him, brooding in the corner by the giant abstract monstrosity they'd called art, I'd been smitten. A few drinks, a few smiles later and we were sailing off into the proverbial sunset, him playing rich.

Anything to please me, Mark must have cycled through three cars, from Ferrari to Lamborghini to Porsche. After I'd discovered he padded his hours at the law firm, I'd threatened to tell all of his clients, most of whom I knew, and we came to an agreement of sorts. Of course, when I'd told him to go after Liv, she would be the thing that killed him. Killed him, or killed us. I'm not sure which.

Part of me will miss him, the way you miss a favorite pair of shoes. But he'd served his purpose and in the end he doesn't matter. I'm moving onto greener pastures.

FORTY-FIVE

(NOW)

Kat's nowhere to be found when my interrogation finally ends. Chaos has erupted at Nyx—everyone's losing it. In the common area, I can see a mass of jittery bodies huddled together, their whispers laced with panic as they shoot me wide-eyed, apprehensive glances. Mimi paces like a caged animal by the fireplace, her phone clutched tightly against her ear as she speaks in frantic, broken bursts.

The Bees are pressed into a tight cluster in the corner, their heads leaning in conspiratorial whispers, eyes flaring with distrust. Suddenly, the room's clamor dies down, replaced by a suffocating silence where twelve pairs of eyes bore into me. I shrink further under their relentless scrutiny, desperate to vanish. Walking out front, I silently plead for escape and I'm about to send Hank a text to pick me up when Kat's Range Rover screeches onto the driveway. The passenger window rolls down and she calls out to me. "Liv, get in."

I take a deep breath. "I just want to go home."

"I'll take you there. Williamsburg. Above a book shop,"

she says, winking, and my jaw goes slack. "We've already hammered out our deal, and there's no more room for debate. Get in."

She's like the all-seeing eye. She knows where I live. She knows everything about me. I have to find out what she's up to. I take one last agonized glance at the ominous Nyx grounds before slipping into Kat's car.

"Good girl," Kat snaps, her voice both mocking and commanding. "We've got a hell of a ride ahead us. Fasten your seatbelt."

The instant her car roars off the compound, my phone erupts with a volley of texts from Trinity. Weary, I appraise the screen.

> I know you're the killer.
>
> I'm going to prove it.
>
> I made the connection, Morgan.
>
> Hope you know what you're doing.

I do. I turn off my phone and shove it into my purse, refusing to reply. Kat's hand tightens its grip on the steering wheel, her knuckles straining white. I notice her nail polish is chipped.

"Who was texting you? I'm betting it was Trinity Powers."

I raise a brow. "That's not her real name. It's Zuri Williams. And she went to Woodford."

"So that's why she seemed vaguely familiar." She nods. "Don't worry. I'll take care of her. Nobody can find out you're Morgan Rane."

"Why? Because you tried to kill me?" My eyes search her

face for any signs of emotion. There are none. "And now two other people are dead?"

She drums her fingers on the steering wheel, shoots me a side glance. "You know, if I placed a bet on who the killer is, I'd put all my chips on Trinity. That whole drama she had about being locked in the sauna. I'm wagering it was a distraction." She lowers her voice into a whisper. "They—meaning the police—haven't found the murder weapon."

I put my knee on the dashboard, sinking lower into my seat, feeling the blade press into my rib. What she doesn't know won't kill her.

"What did you tell the detective? You didn't tell them that you're Morgan Rane? Or that I'd tried to kill you?"

"Would they even believe me? They don't think she exists."

"Right," says Kat, lips pursed. Then, as if the tension between us is a twisted joke, she laughs. "You're back in my inner circle, baby. I'm glad you didn't die. And now because we've forgiven each other, I'd kill for you." She bursts into a mirthless laugh and taps a few keys on her steering wheel, blaring Prince's song. "I'd even die for you, Liv."

Her words give me pause. I stare straight ahead, responding to her questions about Sienna's actions with stilted responses. Finally, I've had enough. "Kat," I say, "I really don't want to talk anymore."

"I don't understand," she replies, squeezing my hand. "We have our future to think of. It's going to be so bright."

After Kat drops me off, I lug my bag up the steps and walk into my apartment, dreading the worst. And it's just as I'd imagined it—like a nuclear bomb has gone off. Drawers ripped from the dressers, clothes scattered everywhere—things I didn't even know I owned are thrown across the floor. The couch cushions are not on the couch, the mattress on my bed is flipped, and the smell of something chemical-like clings to the air. My kitchen cabinets have been left wide open like they're screaming for help, my cooking utensils on the ground.

This is my home, and now it is wrecked, gutted, exposed. The police have been here, digging through my life—surely looking for my letter openers. And they took them. I know this because when I look in the open drawer where I always keep them, they are not there. Probably at some lab being tested.

Although I feel violated and furious, I mostly feel hollow. It's like the world is ripping out the last sense of security I've had in this city, in this neighborhood, where I used to feel at ease. All I can do is slump onto the floor, taking it all in, trying not to cry, trying not to scream.

My phone rings.

"It's me. I wanted to let you know that your floor at my place is available... if you want to move back and we can work on Nyx..."

I swallow a deep breath. "No, Kat. I need some time away from you. I'll see you at Steven and Mark's funeral."

"Wait, Liv, I'm not finished..."

"I am."

But not with everything.

After I hang up on Kat, I make a call. "Mom, it's me," I say with a shaky voice.

"Are you OK, Liv? I've been watching and reading the news. And I've tried calling countless times..."

"I know. I'm sorry," I say. "Things have been incredibly

crazy." I pause. "What do you think about me coming for a visit in a couple of weeks? I can finally meet my baby brother and—"

"Of course, Liv," she says, cutting me off. "I'll buy your ticket. And I have a surprise for you..."

Does the woman know me? "Mom, I'm really over surprises."

FORTY-SIX

(NOW)

KAT

After I drop Liv off at her run-down apartment above the bookstore, I drive home, my thoughts drifting between Liv and her alter ego, Morgan, getting lost in the spaces between what we were, what we are right now, and what we might never be again. I'd promised her everything—the moon, the stars, the universe. She'd only uttered a few words when she left. Words that hurt. "I need some time away from you, Kat. Time to think. I'll see you at the funeral."

And then she slipped out of the car, vanishing into the night, as if she had never been by my side at all, never heard anything I said or maybe heard it all too well. I thought I saw tears in her eyes, but as I stare into the brights lights of the Manhattan skyline, I start to doubt myself.

I park in my garage and leave my bags in the car. Frank can get them later. When I open the door, the feeling hits me hard—a cold slap of reality. I may have everything in the world, all the money a woman could ever dream of, but what does it matter when there's no one to share it with?

Liv is that person for me. She always has been, even under the guise of her alter ego. I've always believed we were kindred spirits, destined for each other, and I'd do anything to protect her.

As I take off my shoes, I think of her book and the messages conveyed within her words. What did her silence mean? Those looks that seemed to pierce right through me—what were they trying to tell me? That she hates me, but she loves me, too? That I love her, but wish sometimes I didn't?

I crawl into bed with the only thing that feels certain—a book of our unfinished lives. I pick up the iPad to read the rest of 'In Her Shoes.' I'm flipping through the pages, transfixed. It's like a map through our past, a record of our broken hearts, and an autopsy of everything we've been through. I dive into the pages, trying to escape everything else, determined to read our story to the end. Her feelings for me are intense, and so are mine for her. The words pull me under like a riptide, and I feel myself becoming absorbed in the story, seeing our lives unfold like a movie from Liv's perspective.

I can't wait for her to read my memoir. Then she'll finally know and understand the real me.

FORTY-SEVEN

(NOW)

I spend the following day cleaning up the apartment—filling up three garbage bags with pieces of my shattered life, doing laundry, and plotting out next steps in my head. I'm folding my clothes when a loud knock comes at the door. I amble over to it, dragging my feet, surprised to see Detective Shaw and Officer Abrams standing in the hallway. I squeeze my eyes shut and let out a low groan.

"Ms. Montgomery, we're sorry to bother you," says the detective.

No, he's not.

He eyes my suitcase, lifts up a brow. "Going somewhere?"

"I was hoping to." I scratch my cheek, my heart racing.

He eyes the passport on the console, his lips pinching into a smirk. "Where exactly?"

"Italy. Visiting my mother." I grab the confirmation letter off the coffee table with a shaky hand. "I'm supposed to leave in a week."

Detective Shaw frowns as he scans the paper. "I thought we told you not to cross state lines..."

"I haven't seen my mom in years. She sent me a ticket."

"To rule you out as a person of interest, we'd like for you to do a DNA test," says Officer Abrams, holding up a kit. "Unless you have a problem with doing one? Of course, you can always come down to the precinct—"

"I don't have a problem."

"Great." He grins and puts gloves on. "We'll also print you, if you're OK with that, too."

I sigh. "Don't you have my prints from the last time?"

Abrams shrugs. "Just covering all of our tracks."

"Fine," I say, worry coursing through my veins. I step to the side, letting them in. "Let's just get it over and done with."

Detective Shaw nods. "You're being very agreeable."

His tone says 'you're being too agreeable', his eyes locking onto the garbage bags. I know they'll probably have somebody collect them when I'm not here. "I'd offer you a coffee, but, apparently, I've run out."

"No problem," says Abrams.

A half hour later, they finally leave. I sink down onto the couch, my ink-covered fingers cradling my aching head.

FORTY-EIGHT

(NOW)

KAT

I make my way downstairs to the place that has become a monument to Liv or, more precisely, to the ideal of her I still hold so dearly in my mind. Her former room waits, undisturbed, at the end of the long hallway. I turn the handle and step inside, feeling the subtle rush of her presence.

Although I do have my cleaning staff work their magic, it remains unchanged since the day she left me after what I'll call the 'incident.' Her vanilla scented perfume still rests on the dresser, her lipstick at its side. The silver hoop earrings she used to wear. I linger over each item, letting the memories seep into my mind. They are artifacts of Liv, but they mean something more: evidence of our shared history, proof that she was here.

I pick up the strawberry balm, unscrew the cap, and slather it on my lips. Then I spray myself with her perfume and lay down on her bed. Yes, some people may call this an obsession, but for me it's more of a ritual.

I close my eyes, feeling a mix of relief and anxiety. She's probably still questioning why I never admitted that I knew she was Morgan Rane all along. But we both have our reasons for keeping secrets, building walls around our vulnerabilities. The truth is, our individual truths wouldn't have withstood the chaos without each other's support. Now that most of our secrets are out in the open, Liv and I can be friends, a thought that truly excites me.

Liv and Kat take over the world!

It's true that we've both done some terrible things—inexcusable actions that could haunt us. Every action has a reaction. But the fact remains, we've both survived the darkness that could have consumed us. I bring my wrist to my nose, inhaling the scent of her perfume that lingers—her choice in fragrances is something I'll never fully understand, yet I've always respected her for her individuality. And I know she's always respected me in return, as does everyone else, though sometimes I question the logic of that respect. Take Trinity, for example. She's wanted to be me since high school.

I pull out my phone, feeling an urge to connect with Liv, to bridge the silence. I type a message, hoping to convey my optimism.

KIS:

I'm excited for the future. Our future.

I sit there, staring at the screen, waiting for a response. Seconds turn into minutes.

KIS:

Are you ignoring me?

She doesn't reply. I know she has her phone. And, thanks to Frank's surveillance, I know she's home. Why is she doing this to me? The silence on her end frustrates and maddens me, considering everything we've been through together. So I send another text.

KIS:

We still have a lot to talk about.

I slump back onto the pillows, staring at the ceiling, remembering how we'd laugh amongst the stars. Finally, after what feels like an eternity, I hear a ding. I sit up to read the message.

LIV:

I told you that I need some alone time. Just give me some space.

The sting of her pushing me away gnaws at my brain. I don't like being ignored. Perhaps I'll change my approach.

KIS:

That's no fun.

I stare at my phone, waiting for a response that doesn't come. Now, I'm left wondering why she feels the need to distance herself from me. I suppose I'll give her some time. A predator always has to be patient because the real power lies in knowing *when* and *where* the prey runs and, most importantly, *why*.

FORTY-NINE

(NOW)

One week later, Mrs. Shepherd stands rigid beside her son's casket. Across from her, Mr. and Mrs. Knight cling to each other, their grief tangible. The sky is gray. It's raining. The perfect atmosphere for a double funeral.

I stand apart from the others, a solitary figure in a simple black dress that cost more than most people's monthly rent. I know this because Kat purchased it for me when I lived with her—the price tag reading over five thousand dollars. Our toxic "friendship" always came with a price.

"Ashes to ashes, dust to dust," says the minister, dropping a handful of dirt on the casket.

Kat watches from beneath her umbrella, also positioned at the edge of the gathering. She's not watching the service. She's watching me. Her black hair is pulled back severely, emphasizing the sharp angles of her face.

The minister's words fade into the background as snippets of hushed conversations reach my ears.

"I think she did it. Placed the blame on Sienna. She probably murdered Mark, too."

These comments come from Charlotte Shepherd, Steven's mother, whose gaze keeps drifting to me with undisguised suspicion. The elderly woman leans heavily on her husband's arm, though Richard Shepherd seems barely steadier himself. I understand. They've lost their only son, and now can only watch as his fortune passes to a virtual stranger.

The Knight family is more contained in their grief, if not their suspicion. Mark's parents stand close together, the two of them maintaining a careful distance from me. My head lowers and I shake it, sucking in a breath. When I look up, I see Kat whispering in somebody's ear. That person is Trinity Powers and she's smiling.

When the minister finishes his sermon, the mourners begin to move forward to place roses on the caskets. I approach Steven's first, placing my flower with steady hands, my face a perfect mask of respectful grief. But as I step away, I find myself face to face with Charlotte Shepherd.

"You must be pleased with yourself," she says, her voice low but sharp enough to cut.

"Mrs. Shepherd, I—"

"Don't," Charlotte hisses. "Steven was worth more to you dead than alive, wasn't he?"

Richard pulls gently at his wife's elbow. "Charlotte, not here."

"Where, then? At the reading of the will? Oh wait, we've done that already. Surprised us all, didn't it, Olivia?"

Several heads turn, and for a moment, the rain seems to fade away as everyone watches this confrontation. I straighten my spine. "I was as surprised as anyone," I say. "Steven was a generous man, and I think he wanted to set things right—"

"Generous?" Charlotte steps forward, unable to contain herself. "Is that what you call it? He changed his will one week before he was murdered, leaving everything to you."

Richard Shepherd speaks up, his voice surprisingly firm. "My son was not a fool," he says. "If he left everything to Ms. Montgomery, he had his reasons."

"Reasons we don't know," Charlotte retorts.

"Perhaps we should find out those reasons before we condemn the girl," Richard suggests.

The Knight family draws closer, forming an enclosed audience. They haven't said one word to me, and I don't think they will. Rain starts to pelt the ground, growing steadier.

"The police have questioned me extensively," I reply, trying to keep my composure. My hands curl into fists at my sides. "They found no evidence connecting me to what happened. None whatsoever."

"And they won't," mutters Kat, stepping to my side. Her jaw is set, eyes narrowed against the rain.

The crowd around us bursts into shocked whispers, falling silent as a sleek black car pulls up, tires splashing in a puddle. The windows roll down to reveal Detective Shaw.

"I hope I'm not interrupting," he says, though his tone suggests he doesn't particularly care if he is. His gaze sweeps over the group, lingering momentarily on Kat. "There have been some developments in the case."

"What developments?" Charlotte demands, pointing at me. "Is it about her? And the inheritance? How she killed my son?"

"And ours?" says Mrs. Knight with a low growl. "And set up my daughter for it? That girl has always been trouble."

Detective Shaw's expression remains neutral. He simply

blinks. "Ms. Montgomery's inheritance is the least of our concerns. She is no longer a person of interest. The evidence we've procured doesn't lie, neither does DNA." He nods at me. "Have a nice time in Italy. You're free and clear to go."

Kat's gaze whips to mine. She clasps my wrist and whispers, "You are not leaving me. Not after everything I've done for you."

"But I am," I say, releasing my arm from her grip.

As the rain continues to fall, a collective gasp falls over the crowd. I exchange a brief look with Kat, watch her mouth drop open when Detective Shaw asks her to come with him and then I turn on my heel.

If I have my way, the lies she's buried won't stay hidden for long.

FIFTY

(NOW)

KAT

Liv isn't playing by the rules, the ones I've clearly established. She's acting like we don't have a shared history, acting like a brat. I suppose that's my fault; I'd spoiled her rotten and now I can finally see how truly rotten she is. Detective Shaw escorts me into an interrogation room. I sit in an uncomfortable metal chair, my arms crossed over my chest.

"Would you like a water?" he asks.

"No, thank you," I say. "I just want to know what this is about."

He rolls his shoulders, the pudge on his neck making me cringe. "I think you know. Mark Knight has left you a portion of his estate." He thumbs through some papers. "And you were in dire need of money. Spent all of your inheritance—all the designer clothes, the mega yacht, the taxes on your home, buying Nyx."

I let out a harsh laugh. "Think again. Regardless of what

piddly amount Mark has left me, I'm set for life. Maybe you should get in contact with my financial planner? I'd give you his information, but you have absolutely no right to question me like this and the status of my financial situation is private."

He shoots me a grin. I recoil, mostly because of his stained teeth. "We have great reason to believe you killed Mr. Knight." He pauses dramatically. "You had two motives for killing him—his relationship with Ms. Montgomery and the money."

I snort. "Get real."

"I am." He sits up straight. "Your DNA. Your hair was found all over the crime scene."

"I own the resort."

"That doesn't explain the strands under his nails."

My lips curve into a grin. "Like my finances, my sex life is absolutely none of your business."

His eyes go wide and his jaw drops. "You were still having relations with him—even though he was dating Ms. Montgomery?"

"My relationship with Mark has always been complicated —on again, then off again. Somehow, we always end up back together. He and Olivia had broken up." I wasn't planning on outing her, but she's left me no choice, mostly because she's left me. Now is the perfect time to make a power play. "Did you know Olivia is actually Morgan, the daughter of Tobias Rane?"

Shaw nods, slowly. "I do. Trinity Powers made the connection."

I startle. I'd told Trinity everything in confidence, off the record—promising she could have the story when I'm good and ready. I'm going to kill that duplicitous bitch.

"I'm glad that's settled," I say. "Am I under arrest?"

His face crumples for a moment. "You're not."

I stand up, wipe my hands on my skirt. "Then, I'm leaving. And the next time you want to speak with me I will have an attorney by my side."

I'm in a taxi, headed back to my townhouse. When I arrive, I see the lights of cop cars flashing on the street, men and women carrying things out of my place. I shake my head, tell the driver to wait a few minutes. A minute turns into an hour. While waiting, I text Liv.

KIS:

> When do you come back from Italy? You have to read the end of my memoir. You're in it. Everything is.

Three dots. To my surprise, she responds immediately. I can imagine her expression, her hands shaking.

LIV:

> Next Friday. Saturday night OK?

KIS:

> Perfect. Buzz yourself in. You know the code.

LIV:

> It hasn't changed?

KIS:

> Leopards don't change their spots. Do they? Seven o'clock sharp.

LIV:

> See you then. I'll being a bottle of champagne.

KIS:

I'll be waiting.

I grin and set down my phone. If Liv thinks she can escape my grasp, she's wrong. I rub my hands together. So many plans. Not much time.

FIFTY-ONE

(NOW)

I'm sitting on a direct flight from New York to Naples—anxious to finally see my mom and excited to meet her new family. Finally, eight hours later we land and, after nervously going through security, I grab my bags. Mom and Gianni wait in the terminal, Mom racing over and embracing me. Tears stream down her cheeks. I've never seen her so emotional and, once I get over the jolt of seeing her, I realize I'm crying, too.

"I'm so happy you're here, Liv," says Mom, once she pulls herself together. "This is Gianni," she adds, with a nod to her husband, "and this is your baby brother, Carlo."

Shy, Carlo hides behind Gianni's legs, peeking his little head out. With his Mediterranean complexion, he looks nothing like me. Gianni is dressed impeccably, tall with brown eyes and a kind smile. Of course, Mom has aged since the last time I saw her, but everything about her glows—her complexion, her eyes. She looks happy.

I scoot down and try to say hello to Carlo. He tucks his head under the flaps of Gianni's black jacket.

"He'll warm to you," says Gianni, his Italian accent thick. "*Andiamo*." He takes my suitcase and grunts, "You pack rocks?"

I shrug. "No, I brought my journals."

"Why?" asks my mom.

"Because I don't want anybody reading them," I say, cringing, thinking about when I caught Kat in my room.

Mom nods and pinches my cheek. "You look beautiful, Liv. All grown up and so fashionable. I like that hair color on you. Really makes your eyes pop." She squeezes my hand. "You've really changed."

"I guess I have," I say.

"We're so happy you're here. Lots to talk about. But we'll wait until the meal for our discussion. It's better that way."

"The Italian way," says Gianni with a nod of his head.

We head to the car, a red Fiat 500X, Mom insisting I sit up front so I can enjoy the scenery on the hour-long drive, Carlo cuddling up to her in the backseat. We just keep to small talk, me stealing sideways glances at Gianni, the way he bangs his hand on the steering wheel, yelling "*Pazzo*" when a driver cuts him off, the way he smiles at my mom and Carlo in the rearview mirror.

My mom, it seems, is fluent in Italian, and she explains that Carlo doesn't speak English.

"Are you going to send him to school?"

"School! Of course!" blurts out Gianni. "He already start. Have little girlfriends."

I turn my head, glancing at my mom. "He's not being home schooled? I guess *you've* changed, too."

She shoots a look at Carlo. "Liv, we'll talk when we're at the house."

"OK," I say, slumping in my seat, staring out the window.

Soon, after leaving the congestion of the very alive city, we're on the highway, passing by an exit for Pompeii. "I'd like to go there while I'm here," I say.

"We take you," says Gianni with a wide grin. "But I share a story with you now."

As Gianni gives me a history lesson on when Mount Vesuvius erupted, destroying an entire city, I listen, nodding and looking out the window. Our drive has changed from highway to steep roads with hairpin turns. I roll down the window, breathing in the lemon- and olive-scented air, the Mediterranean Sea, my thoughts once again turning to Kat and how stupid I'd been taking her up on the offer to live with her when I re-met her in Greece.

History. The past. I wonder if I'll ever be able to move on.

"This Nocelle village," says Gianni. "We five hundred meter above sea."

I gasp, taking in the sea view, the villages down below, the bright yellow lemons and red peppers hanging from wooden structures or in large wicker baskets, the pink-hued church.

A few minutes later, he pulls over, parking the car on gravel. "This my place. We have ten-minute walk." He points to my shoes. "Might want to change."

"Right." I look down at my kitten heels. "I don't think I brought anything practical."

"That's OK," says Mom. "I have sandals in the back. Are we still the same size?"

"I don't think my feet have grown since I was twenty-two," I say, refraining from saying "when you abandoned me." There's a time and a place for everything.

As I throw Mom's sandals on, Gianni grabs my suitcase with a grunt. "It has wheels," I say, but he carries it anyway.

"Too many steps," he says.

"Come on, Liv," says Mom. "Follow us."

And so I do. We walk up steps, pass stone buildings, and meander down a flagstone path, finally ending up at Gianni's home. "*Benvenuta*, Liv," says Gianni, opening the large carved wooden door.

I stand, stunned, surprised at the truly out-of-this-world view their home has, noting the terrace overlooking the sea, so peaceful away from traffic and noise. No wonder my mother didn't want to leave. I want to stay here, too.

I don't know if it is a rude question, but I have to ask. "Gianni, what do you do for a living?"

"I retired now," he says. "This my grandparents' home left to me when parents..." He stops talking, pointing up. "Family owned limoncello distillery in Sorrento. I sold eight years ago, after first wife..." He points up again and makes the sign of the cross. "Met your mama. Fell in love." He shrugs and pats his belly. "Now we live la dolce vita."

"Don't just stand there, Liv, come inside," says Mom. "Gianni will put your bag in your room."

My jaw slack, I follow her in. She steps outside onto the terrace. My eyes are drawn to the table, the beautiful blue and yellow lemon-patterned tablecloth, the dishes set out with piles of food—antipasti, olives, the drinks chilled and ready to be poured. All I can think—this is paradise.

"Gianni is taking Carlo on a walk," says my mom, "which leaves the two of us to talk. Have a seat."

I nod numbly.

"I'll start," she continues, settling into a chair. "I was very young when I met Tobias... and, well, I was infatuated with him, moved to his property in the Catskills, a compound of sorts, so many people around. When I became pregnant with you, things with Tobias began to shift." She pauses, a tear sliding down her cheek. "At the time, I didn't realize I wasn't living in nature, like he'd said, but in a cult." She pauses, swallowing. "He thought he was a god, above it all, above everything. I knew I needed to escape, get out of there, and then—"

"Kat tried to kill me," I say.

Mom reaches for my hand. "And then he was arrested, and we had a chance to create a new life for ourselves."

I meet her eyes, soft and concerned. "Does Gianni know about our past?"

She lets out a soft laugh. "There's no hiding from the past when"—she latches onto my hand—"the daughter you'd left behind shows up on your doorstep."

I look out at the sea, the azure blue, thinking about the dream I'd shared with Sienna in Greece. Staying. Opening up a bar. I'm not upset with my mom anymore and the peace of forgiveness washes over me. "That's it," I say. "Forget New York. I'm moving here."

Mom's lips curve into the tightest of grins. "We were hoping you would say that."

"You were?"

"It's time for your surprise."

"Ugh. I told you that I hate surprises."

Her smile widens. "And I told you that you'll like this one."

She rises from her chair, ushering me to follow. She opens up shuttered doors and then points. "This is your room. It's yours—nobody else's. And I've been hoping for this day."

Tears form in my eyes. The room is a dream, complete with a canopy bed, draped with Italian linens, and a writing desk in the corner.

A black-white-and-blue-feathered magpie swoops over our heads, landing on the wooden railing. Both Mom and I go stiff, motionless, only our eyes darting to the side. "I take it you're afraid of birds, too," she says, barely moving her lips.

"Petrified," I reply. "Especially seagulls."

"Me? I'm afraid of geese. A flock attacked me at the compound."

No wonder I'm terrified of geese, the memory of Mom running and screaming coming back to me. "I think I remember that."

"You were five." Her shoulders contract and then she waves a napkin. "Is it gone yet?"

I look over my shoulder. "It's gone."

Gianni walks onto the terrace with Carlo on his shoulders. "Are we to celebrate? All truth out?"

"We are," I say, stepping up to embrace my mom in the tightest of hugs.

"Let's eat," says Gianni, hoisting Carlo into a chair. He ruffles his hair and then uncorks a bottle of wine.

Carlo gives me a shy smile and I realize I've always had a family. For the first time in a long while, I feel content, until my phone buzzes with a text. I let out a shocked gasp.

> Liv, we still have loads to discuss. I can't wait to see you on your return. Should I have a car pick you up?

My vision blurs. I can't focus. Mom grabs my phone, looks at the text. "You're not going back to New York. You're staying here."

I meet her eyes. "Mom, this has always been the plan. I mean, I have to tie up all the loose threads."

"I'm not quite sure I understand what you mean by that…"

I lower my gaze so she can't see the lies written in my eyes. "I have to pack. I have to let Brooklyn Bound know I'm leaving. I have to…"

"End things with her once and for all."

I nod and look up. "Exactly."

"I don't like this, Liv."

Neither do I. I know Kat's never been finished with me. No, she's been playing me just like I've been playing her. But this time I'll be getting the last word in.

FIFTY-TWO

(NOW)

KAT

While Liv's been jaunting around Italy eating pasta, drinking Lambrusco, and living la dolce vita, I've been setting my plan into motion. I pull out my phone and text Trinity.

KIS:

> Are we still on for the final interview tonight?

TP:

> If you'll tell me the whole story. And I get an exclusive.

I laugh at her initials—TP, like toilet paper. She'll be cleaning her mess up.

KIS:

> It's definitely an exclusive.

I rub my hands with anticipation. Yes, I know Liv absolutely despises surprises and she'll definitely hate the one I have in store for her. Tobias taught me well. Blackmail. Works like a charm. I have everything I need to put Liv where she belongs—right under my thumb and I'm going to press her down hard.

FIFTY-THREE

(NOW)

Kat won't be happy she has to wait for me. But I will be late for this very important date. There are many preparations to be made.

It's nine at night and I'm standing in front of Kat's door, a bottle of her favorite champagne in my bag, along with a bottle of limoncello, and I buzz myself in.

"Liv, is that you?" she asks, her voice coming over the intercom system. "I thought you were a no-show. I'm in the jacuzzi. On the roof. Join me. It's a beautiful night."

I make my way to the roof deck, thinking, yes, a gorgeous night for getting even.

When I get to the roof, I find Kat splayed out in the water, a champagne flute dangling from her elegant fingers. "I hope you brought more."

"I did," I say. "And something else, too. Limoncello. What's your poison?"

"Both." She laughs. "You know," she says, eyeing me up and down, "I love your dress. The lemon pattern. The blues.

Reminds me of the one you wore the second time we met in Greece. I've missed both of you—Morgan and Liv."

"Cut the crap, Kat." I stand rigid. "What do you want?"

She smiles, that slow, knowing smile that once made my heart race with something between fear and fascination.

"The same thing I've always wanted. Your friendship." She gestures to the jacuzzi. "Let's wash off this tension sparking between us. Join me."

I'm on edge, not quite prepared for kind words. But Kat always likes to throw her prey off guard before she attacks. "You know I'm not a fan of water. And you know the reason why."

She chuckles. "Let's not rehash the past again. We're civilized people, after all."

"Is that what we are?" I ask, the weight of her words pressing down on my chest.

Something flickers across her face—pain, maybe, or recognition. "Darling, there are no heroes in this story. No villains either. Just survivors." Her voice lowers in tone, soft, almost gentle, and then it goes deep. "Because when they dig deeper—and they will—they'll find both of our fingerprints. On everything. Don't you remember your father's lessons about the trees, how we're all connected?"

She's right. There's no clean escape, no way to untangle myself from this web without destroying her completely.

"What's your endgame?" I ask, finally taking a seat, placing my bag to the side. "What do you really want?"

She leans forward, arms on the side of the jacuzzi, her eyes locked on mine. "I told you. I want your friendship. No more secrets, no more lies. I'm offering you a truth for a truth." She motions to a book on the table behind me. "My memoir. The real version. I had it printed expressly for you.

Read a couple of chapters. The ending. I think it's really eye-opening."

I pick it up, hesitantly. The cover of the book is of a woman dressed in black, the background stars in the sky. The title, in silver, is *Goddess of the Night.*

Holding back a disgusted sigh, I flip through the pages, reading quickly, as Kat watches me. Out of spite, I want to suggest a new title: *The Ramblings and Lies of a Diabolical Narcissistic Sociopath*

"You can't publish this," I whisper. "Do you want us both to go to prison?"

"Could be fun." She splashes me and howls out a laugh. "We'd be roommates again."

I sink deeper into my seat, overwhelmed by her absurd theatrics. "You're not funny."

Kat shoots me a conspiratorial wink. "Don't worry. I'm not publishing the version you've just read. Even though it holds the truth."

"Your creativity astounds me," I reply with a brittle laugh.

"Am I making it up? I have surveillance of you sliding underneath the chassis of my car," she declares, chin thrust up defiantly. She gives me a grin when my shoulders go rigid. "Relax—I never turned it over to the police. Had Frank scratch it from the security cameras. You did me a favor." She points to a folder set on the bar. "Take a look at that file. I have photographic proof."

"It seems like you're still playing by my father's rules." I stare straight ahead, my mind reeling. "You were supposed to die in that crash..."

"Your father didn't make the rules. He just exploited them. I make the rules."

My jaw goes slack. It's then I notice the necklace she's wearing, sparkling in the light. "You killed Mark?"

She laughs and then brings a manicured finger to her lips. "Hush now, that's our little secret. I was protecting you. Now we can move on with our lives. We're sisters—alike in so many ways..."

My heart stutters. "I'm nothing like you, Kat. And I didn't kill Steven."

"Right," she guffaws. "Then you should probably explain why Frank has a picture of you wearing a blonde wig and a baseball cap outside Steven's place... I know Steven told you that night he'd warned you that he was leaving everything to you. You saw an opportunity and you took it. What? You thought you could set Sienna up? I really do admire your creative ways of thinking, Talented Mrs. Ripley."

I don't know what freaks me out more. The fact she's just admitted to killing Mark, the fact she's been watching me, or the fact she knows what I've done. Worse. "You've been stalking me?"

"I always keep an eye on my investments, especially when they've paid off." She laughs. "I'm glad to have my little lamb back in the fold."

"I'm not a lamb."

"I know." She grins, her hands flying to her neck. "I do have the necklace. I told you I'd get it back one day. I saw an opportunity and I took it." She raises a brow. "Where's the knife? I don't have it."

I don't respond.

"Look, I'm offering you a way out. I won't tell anybody that you are Morgan Rane and that you're a killer if you come back to me..."

She just doesn't get it.

"I don't care if people know who I *was*. I'm a different person now." I stand, moving to the railing. "It's just a story. One we keep telling ourselves because we're too afraid to write a new one." I turn to face her. "I'm not going back to Nyx. I'm not going to be your partner or your puppet or your 'sister.' And I'll tell the cops you're a killer, too."

For a moment, just a moment, something like respect flashes in her eyes. Then it's gone, replaced by that calculating coldness I know so well. "Then, shall we toast to our story ending?"

"We should." I grab the bottles from my bag and head to the bar. "When life hands you lemons, make limoncello. You always taught me to never show up as a guest empty-handed."

She grins wickedly. "I taught you so well."

My hand trembles slightly as I reach for a crystal decanter and pour. The limoncello glows an unearthly yellow under the lights, almost radioactive in its brightness. Months of planning have led to this moment—this exact, perfect moment. I grab two glasses and pour with practiced precision. "All I need is ice."

"You know where it is."

I nod and turn my back on her. As I place cubes in our drinks, I add an extra ingredient into hers—one I'd used gloves picking when I'd taken them from Nyx's garden. I walk over and give her the limoncello.

"Cheers." I raise my glass, but I don't take a sip from mine.

Kat swirls the glass, studying the liquid with appreciation. "Homemade?"

"My mother's husband," I say, watching her raise the

glass to her lips. "Brought a bottle back for a special occasion."

She pauses, the glass hovering an inch from her mouth. Her eyes narrow almost imperceptibly. Always suspicious, always calculating. That's what makes her such a formidable opponent. Such a dangerous friend.

"You first," she says with a thin smile.

"To new beginnings." I lift my glass, maintaining eye contact. I drink from my glass and raise a brow. "Here, we can switch glasses if you're so paranoid."

She finally takes a small, cautious sip. "Delicious," she pronounces, setting the glass down. "Though I detect something... unfamiliar."

"A hint of bitterness," I say. "Unavoidable with this particular recipe."

Kat smiles, but it doesn't reach her eyes. "Are you trying to scare me, Liv? Because we both know you don't have the stomach for what you're implying."

I lean against the railing, overlooking Central Park. "You know what your problem is, Kat? You still think you can always win every game."

She smiles. "Don't I? Then why are you still playing it?"

"Because I'm rewriting the rules," I say with a low growl. "Who do you think you are?"

"I know who I am. I'm a goddess."

I turn my back to her and put on a pair of nylon gloves. "You aren't and you will never be a goddess. If you survive, have fun in prison. I'm sure the inmates are going to worship you."

It's then I lunge toward her, wrapping my hands around her neck, plunging her into the water just like she'd done with me. Her mouth goes wide with fear. I force her body deeper into the jacuzzi, watching her eyes lose their luster, watching the bubbles until they no longer pop to the surface. In addition to 'drowning,' it won't be long before the hemlock works its magic and her entire system shuts down.

Before I leave, I have to act quickly. Breathless, I grab the glasses, the bottle of limoncello, the file of photos, and the book, making sure not to leave any of my DNA behind. If they find any, I can easily explain that I used to live here. I leave a typed-out note on the table, also to be found in the files of her computer.

I'm sorry for everything I've done. I didn't mean to hurt so many people. Forgive me.

I forgive you now, Kat. I guess we're even, now that I'm finally done with you.

Katherine Isabelle Sterling has just committed suicide with the murder weapon. KiS. Or should I say the kiss of death and the bane of my existence? For Kat, this thing between us has always been about power. And I've taken her power away. I look at her still form one last time, throwing the letter opener in the jacuzzi. Kat's DNA will be found on it, not mine.

Kat has what she's always wanted; she's now truly a goddess of the night.

I erase all security footage. I erase everything—including her manuscript. Once a hacker, always a hacker. Finally, I change out of my wet dress in 'our' closet, adding it to my bag. I look at my watch. I've accomplished all of this in less than twenty-five minutes. Which leaves me five minutes to wipe everything down.

After leaving Kat's, I walk two miles before hailing a cab

back to my apartment, shaking. Back home, I light the fireplace, and I burn the book and the incriminating photos. Then, for the next week, I move forward on auto-pilot—tell Brooklyn Bound I'm moving to Italy, pack up my things. During this time, not one person comes to question me, and there's not one word about Kat's death, which has me looking over my shoulder every few minutes.

FIFTY-FOUR

(NOW)

I've been back in Italy for a few months now.

There has been no news of Kat's 'suicide,' not one word about her confession. I'm wondering if everything that happened actually happened. I think of Trinity's statement, how powerful people can brush things under the rug, thinking they are untouchable. Come to think of it, it's been a while since I've received text threats from Trinity. Like Kat, she's disappeared into thin air.

"Any news?" Mom asks casually as she refills my water glass, but I catch the worry in her eyes. "About her?"

"Nope," I say.

"What about Nyx?" she asks, her expression unreadable.

"Mimi's taking it over. I've signed my shares to her. As the primary shareholder, she'll be turning Nyx into a foundation for abused women." I smile. "Selene's Light."

"You got Kat. And you got her good."

I gulp and walk to the edge of the terrace. Below, the village of Positano glitters like fallen stars, the Path of Gods winding away into darkness. The darkness has never frightened me. I've learned to see in it, to find my way.

That night, I open my laptop and begin to write, not about Kat, not about Sienna, not about the past. I write about the Path of Gods, about the way light changes on the Mediterranean Sea. I write about becoming someone new. There are stories we tell others, and stories we tell ourselves. The truth lives somewhere in between.

By the following afternoon, pages from a new manuscript sit on the terrace table, gleaming bright white in the afternoon sun. I decide to walk down the 1,750 steps from Nocelle to the village, leading me to the beach. One step at a time, I make my way onto the sand, breathless. The tide is coming in and I wade in up to my knees, feeling the cold water chilling me to the bone. I think back to the day when Kat tried to kill me, the way my lungs froze. To the night I'd killed her.

Behind me, something moves in the water—a sleek shadow beneath the surface, there and gone. But when I turn to look, there's nothing but the endless, empty sea. Just my imagination. Just a ghost story I tell myself. I could write another book. I could tell the whole ugly truth about us. Could finish what Kat had started. What I'd started.

Just another ending I choose not to write.

For a moment, I hesitate. I'm not afraid of water anymore, of drowning. It's in the water I'd found the strength to live, to fight for my life. And I know what to do now. I'm going to swim like my life depends on it.

FIFTY-FIVE

(ONE YEAR LATER)

It's been one year since I walked away from Kat's offer, from the townhouse, from Nyx. One year of silence between us. It's been one year since I killed Kat and haven't heard a word about her death. Sienna, still in the psychiatric facility, sends emails sometimes. She knows the truth—or a version of it. My eyes dart to the balcony when a magpie lands on the railing, its blue, black, and white feathers iridescent in the sun. This time, I don't flinch.

Sadly, or not sadly, Kat's fake memoir, *Under the Influence*, has been pulled from publication, considering she never turned in her edits or the final draft. A scandal that SilverGate has to deal with—thanks to me.

With everything that has been going on, Rebecca has pushed up my publication date. My book, *In Her Shoes,* hits the New York Times Best Seller list before it even launches —and it's been on there for four weeks so far. Mimi and Rebecca, well, they're the talk of the town, so they're both thrilled.

Mom and I arrive at my book launch together. After we enter the packed space, Mom latches onto my hand as the questions roll in.

"Is the character of Emily based on Katherine Sterling?"

Everything always circles back to Kat. "I'll leave that up to the readers to decide."

I force a smile and make my way to the podium to read a chapter, the event ending to resounding applause.

Right after the book launch, Mom and I head back to Nocelle. I'm sitting on the terrace, drinking wine and eating olives while looking at the sparkle of the Mediterranean Sea.

As usual, the breeze carries the scent of lemon and salt, my laptop open to Word with the best of distractions—Mom serving us course after course and kissing us on the cheeks, Carlo playing with trucks making 'vroom vroom' sounds, as Gianni plays Italian/American songs on his guitar. I look up to see my mother leaning against the frame in the doorway, the breeze blowing the curtains. I wonder how long she's been staring at me. I catch her doing it a lot these days.

She walks over to me and I grab her hand, and we sway to the tune. "I could never ask for a better family."

She blurts out a laugh, shielding the sun from her beautiful blue eyes. "Just wait until you really get to know me."

"I already do," I say.

She grins, holding up her glass, and we toast.

"Should we turn on the news?" She points at my laptop and wiggles her brows. "Maybe there's more news about your book. The film rights?"

"I can't wait."

I pull up the site we've been watching entertainment segments on, and a reporter comes onto the screen. "The trial nobody knew about until today has us shocked, the attempted murder of heiress Katherine Sterling of Sterling Spirits."

My mom's eyes bug out wide, as do mine.

"She's... Hold that thought. She's here now."

My stomach drops.

"Ms. Sterling," he says as she sashays down the steps, dressed to the nines in a sleek Chanel skirt suit. "You're looking well."

"I'm feeling well," she says with a smile. "A cat always lands on their feet and, well, has nine lives." She laughs, her green eyes blazing into the camera. "I believe I've already gone through two of them. Right now, I'm ready for anything and everything, especially since the person who harmed me will be taken down."

I suck in a breath. She's threatening me.

"Why are we only getting wind of this trial today?" the reporter continues.

"I had to take supreme measures to protect myself until this trial was over. She'd killed Steven Shepherd and Mark Knight, and then she came after me." She lets out a shaky breath. "I did die for three minutes, but thankfully my bodyguard, Frank, found me in time. What she'd assumed to be hemlock was not—it was simply a special variety of parsley that's often confused with the poisonous plant." She lowers her gaze. "She did manage, however, to leave a deep scar on my heart. It's going to take a while for it to heal."

Kat's eyes focus on the camera and it's almost as if she's looking directly at me. My spine goes rigid. My fingers go numb.

"Are you able to tell us who is being charged with these heinous crimes?" continues the reporter.

I clench my teeth together, holding my breath.

"Trinity Powers. She'd been obsessed with all of us, but mostly me. She wanted me to go down for crimes I didn't commit. It didn't help she'd kept so many files on all of us— especially the board with all of our photos on it, connected by red threads. Made her look deranged, like a stalker. Like the killer she is." She raises her chin high, looking down on the reporters. "Her fingerprints were found on the murder weapon, a letter opener she'd stolen from me during an inter- view. The evidence against her has sealed her fate—life in prison with no chance of parole."

Stunned, I watch as Kat saunters to a waiting limousine. She's turned Trinity into a sacrifice. An offering. And she's gotten away with it. I nearly choke on my tongue.

"I can't believe this," says my mom with a gasp.

Neither can I.

Mom squeezes my shoulder, her eyes sparking with worry. "Do you think she's going to try and come after you again?"

"Kat doesn't take rejection well." I pick up my glass of water, chugging it to get the bad taste out of my mouth. "Never has."

"You made the right choice turning down her offer." She pops an olive into her mouth. "But while we're on the subject of Kat, the story that's making you a success is hers instead of your own."

The truth of her words lands like a physical blow. My book—the one that earned me this luxury of writing in paradise—is still orbiting Kat's world. And Kat's still alive.

"Your father thought he was a god," Mom says quietly. "Kat thinks she's a goddess. What do you think you are, Liv?"

The question hangs between us as Carlo races onto the terrace, toy airplane in hand, Gianni following with a guitar.

"Volare!" Gianni sings, strumming playfully. "Oh, oh! Cantare, oh, oh, oh, oh!"

Carlo tugs at my hand, wanting me to fly with him. I stand, letting him pull me into a clumsy dance. Over his head, I catch Mom's eye.

"I'm happy," I answer her. "I'm just me. Well, the new me."

Mom laughs. "There was nothing wrong with the old you."

But there is. She doesn't know the truth.

Mom walks across the terrace, placing a bottle of one of my favorite sparkling and effervescent Italian wines—Lambrusco—on the table. I stare at the red liquid, thinking of blood.

"Liv, honey, are you OK?"

I rub my eyes. "I'm fine."

"I have a question I've been meaning to ask you." Mom pours us glasses. She clears her throat. "Do you ever want to visit your father?"

There it is—the question that's been haunting the periphery of our conversations. We've been dancing around the topic of Tobias for months now, both of us more invested in rebuilding our fractured connection.

I can't deny the truth: he raised me with dedication, perhaps even love. Beyond manipulating me, he was a father figure—teaching me to ride my first bike, sitting in the orthodontist's waiting room while I got braces, indulging my teenage whims. More than the material things, he instilled confidence in me, encouraged me to embrace my abilities.

But the good memories are contaminated by what he's done to other people, by what I've done.

"Maybe," I finally whisper. I squeeze her hand. "I don't know. I need time to untangle everything."

She shoots me a melancholy grin. "He may have been a lot of things, but some of what he did was good."

I blink. "What's that?"

"He gave me you."

Later, as the sun sets in glorious hues of hot pinks and oranges, I sit on the terrace where my new story waits to be written. As I breathe out, ready to start, a text chimes in. I stop mid-thought and pull out my phone, glaring at the screen.

KIS:

Bang! Hunting season? It's started.

There are so many questions I want to ask—like why Trinity? Why didn't she tell the police about me? But I really don't want the answers. Before I reply, my eyes shoot toward the sea, and I find myself turning to the words of famed Sufi mystic and poet Rumi: "Listen to the sound of the waves within you." I know what I want to say.

ME:

It's never been over for you, but it's over for me.

KIS:

We're connected.

ME:

And now we're not.

I block her number. I know who I am now. And what I am is enough—without Kat's approval, without her gaze. And I'm glad I've never truly fit into her world and, well, she's never going to push me out of mine. She can try to come after me. She can watch me, spy on me. But she'll be all alone in her narcissistic misery.

It's time for me to turn the page and write my own story. It's time for me to live my best life.

A LETTER FROM THE AUTHOR

Thank you for reading *The Writers' Retreat*. I hope Liv and Kat's story opens up some very lively discussions. If you'd like to keep up to date with all my Storm Publishing releases, you can sign up here:

www.stormpublishing.co/samantha-verant

And if you'd like to hear about all my upcoming releases and bonus content, including the occasional French recipe, please feel free to sign up for my author newsletter.

www.eepurl.com/UH8cP

If you enjoyed this book and could spare a few moments to leave a review, that would be hugely appreciated. Even a short review can make all the difference in encouraging a reader to discover my books for the first time. Thank you so much! Merci beaucoup!

Inspired by my own writing journey, the concept of this book started off with plagiarism, landing on what would happen if somebody stole a manuscript with the malicious intent of destroying a writer's career and, well, it moved on from there. Like Liv, I'm a plantster and the plot twists—from cliques to cults to a story within a story—grew and evolved as the manuscript took shape.

With that said, I love hearing from readers and I hope you'll get in touch!

All my best wishes,

Samantha Vérant

www.samanthaverant.com

facebook.com/AuthorSamanthaVerant

instagram.com/samantha_verant

tiktok.com/@authorsamanthaverant

bookbub.com/profile/samantha-verant

ACKNOWLEDGMENTS

A huge merci goes to my fabulous editor, Kate Smith. Thank you for cutting the fat, killing all of the extraneous darlings, and, once again, pushing this book to become its very best version.

I'm thrilled and proud to be a member of the Storm Publishing family.

Hearty thanks goes out to our trailblazer founder Oliver Storm, editorial operations director Alexandra Begley, copy-editor Laurence Cole, proofreader Amanda Rutter, page designer Naomi Knox, brilliant cover designer James Macey, and supremely talented voiceover artist Laurel Lefkow. There were a couple of Bees in this book and I can't wait to create some buzz with the fabulous marketing and publicity team of Elke Desanghere and Anna McKerrow.

Thank you!

Finally, thank you to the readers I've connected with and those I've yet to connect with—thank you for joining me on this wild publishing journey. Happy reading! Cheers!

www.ingramcontent.com/pod-product-compliance
Lightning Source LLC
Chambersburg PA
CBHW010429170726
48283CB00011B/3128